The Last
Collection

Books by Seymour Blicker

Blues Chased a Rabbit
Shmucks
The Last Collection

The Last Collection

Seymour Blicker

William Morrow and Company, Inc.

New York   1977

For my brother Stanley

Published in the United States in 1977.

Copyright © 1976 by Seymour Blicker

Published in Canada in 1976.

This book is not to be sold in Canada.

Printed in the United States of America.

1   2   3   4   5   6   7   8   9   10

Library of Congress Cataloging in Publication Data

Blicker, Seymour (date)
     The last collection.

     I. Title.
PZ4.B6486Las3   [PR9199.3.B5]   813'.5'4   76-54309
ISBN 0-688-03156-0

Chapter One

Morrie Hankleman sipped at his drink and gazed slowly around the large boardroom in the offices of Shenkler and Bregman. On a long credenza he observed several dozen potted plants and various assorted floral arrangements each with its own card congratulating Marty Shenkler and Earl Bregman on the opening of their new office in Place Centrale.

He spotted his own plant dwarfed by a gigantic cactus next to it and regretted that he had not gotten something larger.

He sipped at his drink and let his eyes drift from person to person, trying to guess their line of work.

A large part of Shenkler and Bregman's practice was devoted to criminal law and so Morrie Hankleman knew that of the hundred-odd people who were in the room, more than a few had some links with the Montreal underworld.

He spotted a large, heavy-set man dressed in a flashy checkered suit which seemed several sizes too large for him. To Hankleman he definitely looked like a criminal. He had the face of a killer, Hankleman thought. Ruthless, cruel.

A few minutes later the man was introduced to him, and he recognized the name as that of the leading real estate lawyer in the country.

He made a few more attempts at categorization, but was proved to be wrong on every count.

The man he thought to be a judge turned out to be a disbarred lawyer, the woman he thought to be a high-priced prostitute was in fact a movie producer, the young man with the long hair whom he judged to be a drug pusher was Marty Shenkler's eldest son.

Morrie Hankleman walked over to the credenza. Humming nervously to himself he deftly removed the name card from his flowers and slipped it onto the large cactus. Then he removed the original card from the cactus, glanced at the name and shoved it in his pocket.

He laughed to himself. Lawrence Wellish. He could picture the scene between Shenkler and Bregman tomorrow. *How come Wellish didn't send a plant? I don't know. We'll have to raise our fee for him.* Morrie Hankleman laughed to himself again, but he wasn't happy.

He wasn't even having a good time. It was actually a nice party. A lot of people; a lot of action; the kind of party where a person could make some good contacts. He should have been really enjoying himself, but he wasn't and he knew he wouldn't be able to until he had done something about Artie Kerner. For the last month he'd been unable to think of anything else but Artie Kerner, who had become a 24-hour-a-day obsession with him.

Morrie Hankleman's thoughts were suddenly interrupted by Earl Bregman's voice. "You enjoying yourself, Morrie?" Bregman said, putting an arm around Morrie Hankleman's shoulder.

"Great party, Earl. Just wonderful. Great mix of people."

"Yeah, yeah. Everyone seems to be having a good time. I'm pleased. I'm very pleased with it."

"You should be, Earl."

Earl Bregman nodded appreciatively. "Did you try to identify any more people?" he asked with a devilish smile.

"A few."

"Were you wrong or right?"

Hankleman shrugged. "Umh ... half and half."

"Looks are deceiving, eh, Morrie?"

"Sometimes."

"Look over there," Bregman said, pointing towards a corner of the room.

Hankleman turned to look at a group of five men who were standing around in a small circle.

"You see those guys there?"

"Yes, I see them," Hankleman replied.

"What line of work do you think they're in?" Bregman asked, smiling wryly.

Hankleman studied the men in the group for a moment. "They're lawyers."

Bregman shook his head with self-satisfied authority. "No. Uh, uh. That's the boys," he said, proudly.

Hankleman looked again. All of the five men appeared to be in their late forties or early fifties. All were dressed in well-fitting and obviously expensively tailored suits. Four were heavy set, paunchy men. One was slight in build and seemed no more than about five-foot-seven or -eight. The bigger men were crowded around him, listening as he spoke.

"If you had to choose one to lay on some muscle, which one would you pick?"

Without hesitation, Hankleman pointed at the largest of the five men. "The big guy with the pushed-in face."

Bregman laughed knowingly. "C'mon over. I'll introduce you."

They walked over towards the group. As they approached, Hankleman could see that the slight man was still talking and everyone was listening intently. Bregman didn't intrude on the group. He nudged Hankleman. "Listen to this guy," he whispered.

Hankleman nodded and pressed slightly forward.

"Anyway, so Moishie here lends em de dough. ... What was it, eight big ones, Moishie?" the thin man asked, looking at the large man with the pushed-in face.

"Yeah," the big man replied. "Eight hundred."

13

"Right," the thin man continued, "so he gives em de eight hunnert an he waits. De guy is supposed to repay in turdy days. I mean it was like peanuts, right? Buptkas."

Everyone nodded.

Hankleman was now interested. He pushed up against the thin man who gave him a quick, hard look and continued talking.

"Anyway, a munt goes by... nutting happens. Moishie calls em. 'Tomorrow,' de guy says. Tomorrow comes ... no dough. Moishie sends em out a letter from de office, right?"

Everyone nodded, Hankleman included.

"Again nutting. ... Moishie calls em an tells em in plain talk to come up wid de scratch fast. De guy says, 'gimme an extension till nex munt.' Moishie's a nice guy, right?"

Everyone nodded. Hankleman followed suit.

"So Moishie says, 'Okay, ya got till de end of nex munt.' De end of de nex munt comes, Moishie don hear from dis chaim putz. ... Moishie gives em a call. 'I ain't got de dough,' de mooch says to Moishie, 'gimme till tomorrow.' Moishie gives em till tomorrow. Tomorrow comes, no mooch, no money. Moishie gives em a call. 'Where's de dough?' Moishie asks. 'I ain't got it,' de guy tells Moishie, 'and furdermore,' he says, 'you ain't getting it. You want it, sue me!' Dats what he says, jus ly dat."

A series of deprecations were now loosed by the men listening.

"What did you do, Moishie? What did you do to the shmuck?"

"Listen to the Hawk. The Hawk is telling the story," Moishie said.

"So what happened, Solly?"

Hankleman pressed closer to the thin man, now tentatively identified as Solly the Hawk.

"Anyway, so I'm at de shvitz when Moishie calls ta gimme de word," the Hawk continued in his laconic manner. "'I got a liddle problem wid a mooch,' he tells me. 'Don worry, Moishie, jus leave it wid me, I'll handle it.' Moishie gives me de

14

address of de mooch. I ged dressed an I go up ta see em. He's a big zhlob. Like even bigger den Issie Shissel." The Hawk raised his hand a good foot over his own head and then spread both his hands to show the breadth of the man. "An wide ly dis. ... He's dere wid some breezod; a real meece bear dat looks like he jus lugged her from de lower main street. Someting dat you wouldn't fuck even wid a flag over her face."

Everyone laughed appreciatively at the Hawk's vivid description.

"Like wid no teet so she'd be perfect for a blow job."

Again everyone laughed.

"So go on, Solly," someone urged.

Solly the Hawk continued in his slow, easy-going manner.

"So anyway I tell him who I am, why I'm dere, an I tell him dat like Moishie needs de dough and he wants it right away. Of course, I tell him in a nice way because I don wanna offend like his magismo, you know his manliness, especially in front of his ugly breezod. He looks me up an down like he's going to measure me for a suit, an me, like I know what he's tinking, because you know, I been trew dis many times before already. So he's tinking, 'Dis liddle jerk wants money? I'll trow em out on his head.' Finally, after he gives me de once over, he says wid like a smirk on his face, 'I can't pay. I ain't got de dough,' he says, 'and I'm not paying!' Me, like I'm ready to try an reason wid de mooch, but before I can open my mout, he says, 'An you can tell dat Jew dat he ain't never gonna get paid.'"

The Hawk paused as his audience reacted with a volley of curses.

"Dat burns me up for tree reasons. Number one because he's insulting Moishie in front of me; number two because he's like trying to make points on me like as if he don't know I'm a Heber too – as if anybody couldn't tell from one look at my face; and number tree because he's trying to look like a hero in front of his ugly broad at de expense of me, especially after I was careful not to offend his magismo in front of de breezod.

Anyway, so I figger it's enough. I'm not going to waste my time putzing around trying to reason wid dis mooch. So I tell em, 'Look, mooch, whadda ya jerking me off here? Tomorrow I'm coming back. Eidder you have Moishie's dough or I break boat yer arms an put you in de hospital for a couple of munts.' De broad looks at me like she's gonna drop a shit hemorrhage. De mooch sits dere like he don believe what he jus heard. I walk out. A minute later, I'm on de street walking up to my Lac which is parked near de corner, when like I suddenly hear a noise behine me. So I turn around an I see de mooch is running for me like he wants to cut my nuts off. He rushes up to me and I can see dat he's out for blood. What do I know? I don't know from nutting. Right away I give em a shot in de batesem. He goes down. I give em anudder shee-zot; dis time in de hee-zaid. It's good because I'm wearing my heavy shoes. Right away he starts ta bleed, but he's, you know, like rolling to get away. So I give him anudder shot in the kishkas. De mooch makes like an 'oofhh!', you know like a big balloon wid all de air coming out. Den fer good luck I lay a few more inta him; like one in de balls, anudder one in de haid, an so on and so fort. Next ting I know, somebody grabs me from behine, like around de neck."

Hankleman watched intently as the slight, hawk-faced man demonstrated how he had been grabbed.

"What do I know. ... If someone grabs me from behine, I hit, right?"

There was a chorus of affirmation and a series of nods.

"So I turn fast, an I hit. I give em like what my mudder used to call a 'frosk in pisk.'"

Everyone laughed appreciatively.

"A zetz wid de back of my hand ... he goes down fast like a skittle and twice as stiff."

Solly the Hawk paused and looked around slowly.

"So go on, Solly," someone said. "What happened?"

Solly the Hawk raised a hand as though simultaneously demanding patience and promising satisfaction. He took a drag on his cigarette and slowly exhaled. Hankleman watched the smoke drift away.

16

"So it was a fuzzer," Solly said nonchalantly.

"A cop?"

"Fuck me!"

"Oh shit, no."

"Tabernac!"

"Yeah," Solly said. "I laid him out flat on his kisser. He was out like a light. Before I know it, his partner comes up to me like wid his piece out. He tells me to get against de car. He's nervous so he's like talking loud. ... You know me, I don like loud talk, so I say, 'Ask me nicely, officer.' He says, 'Please get against de car.' He says, 'What happened?' I say, 'Dis mooch assaulted me.' De mooch meanwhile is still yelling from de shots I gave em, an de udder fuzzer is like trying ta pick himself up from de street but everytime he tries ta stand up, he falls down. 'I dunno from nutting,' I say. 'I was just pertecting myself from dis mooch.' Meanwhile, de udder fuzzer gets up, walking like funny, like he's drunk."

Solly stopped, waiting for the laughter to subside.

"He comes over to me like he wants to hit. I say, 'I'm sorry, officer, I tot it was a friend of de mooch what jumped on me.' He's a sensible kid, de fuzzer, so he don't do nutting, but dey tell me dey gotta take me down to de station. 'Okay,' I say, 'but de mooch gotta come too.' Dey agree. Meanwhile de mooch gets up an tries to walk away, but de fuzzers grab em. Dey tell em he's gotta come down to de station. He looks at me an he starts to yell, 'I ain't going wid him. He's crazy. He's gonna kill me!' He's yelling. He's like afraid to get inta de fuzzers' car wid me. Finally dey tell em dat he can sit in de back wid one fuzzer an I'll sit in de front wid de udder fuzzer. Finally he agrees. So dey take me to de station wid de mooch.

"We get to de station an dey take me alone to see de Chief, who by de way knows me by name. But he pretends like he don know me from a hole in de head. He says, 'What's your name?' I say, 'Gimmie a cigarette.' He says, 'What's your name, estsi?' I say, 'Gimmie a cigarette, tabernac.'"

Hankleman began to laugh with all the others.

"Finally he gives me de cigarette an den I say my name. Den he says, 'Where d'you live?' I say, 'Gimmie a light.' He says,

'Where d'you live, estsi?' I say, 'Gimmie a light, tabernac.' He gives me a light an I tell em where I live. Den he says, 'What happened?' I don say nutting. ... I just cut de cheese and let go wid a real breezer. Loud like."

The group was now in hysterics and Hankleman was laughing as heartily as everyone. Perhaps even harder for he realized that he might have found a solution to his problem with Artie Kerner.

"De chief pretends like nutting happened, like he ain't got ears or a nose. ... He says, 'What happened?' I say, 'I jus farted.' He says, 'I mean before, not now.' I don say nutting. I jus let anudder one go right away."

The men were still convulsed with laughter. Solly the Hawk waited calmly for it to die down.

"Anyway, finally he stops asking questions an den I explain him how de mooch tried to jump on me and so on an so fort. Anyway, to make a long story short, de fuzzers lemme go an de nex day de mooch shows up at Moishie's office wid de money."

"Beautiful, Solly," one of the men offered.

"Dat was de only trouble dat I bin in wid de cops in over ten years' time," Solly the Hawk said.

There was a round of compliments from the listeners and Hankleman couldn't resist offering his own. It was obvious that everyone liked and respected Solly the Hawk.

Bregman grabbed Hankleman by the arm and pushed him forward. "Solly, I want you to meet a friend of mine," Bregman said.

Solly the Hawk turned. 'Sure ting, Earl," he said smiling.

"Solly Weisskopf, this is Morrie Hankleman." Hankleman extended his hand.

The Hawk shook it gently. Hankleman had expected a bone-crushing grip and was surprised by the gentle, unaggressive shake. "Pleased to meet you," Solly the Hawk said, staring directly into Hankleman's eyes.

"Same here," said Hankleman, returning the gaze. "I enjoyed your story. It's a classic."

Solly the Hawk nodded politely.

18

Hankleman was thinking of something else to say when the big man called Moishe pulled Solly away to the side. Solly excused himself and walked away. Bregman pulled Hankleman by the sleeve. "That guy is the toughest human being in the city of Montreal. He's almost fifty now, but he could tear this room apart with everyone in it."

Hankleman shook his head. "It's amazing. He doesn't look it."

Bregman laughed and nodded knowingly.

"That's a mistake a lot of people made," Bregman said. "He's an incredible guy. Him and Big Moishe Mandelberg have been partners for over twenty years. They're almost like brothers."

"They're shylocks?"

"Yeah, that's right. The Hawk does the collecting. It's like an ego thing or something with him. He likes to collect. The fact is he's got a better mind than almost anyone in this room and they all know it. Aside from collecting, he thinks up ideas. Cons. You know?"

Hankleman nodded.

"I could never figure the guy out. Basically he wouldn't hurt a fly and he's probably the least violent person I know, but he always collects ... one way or the other."

Hankleman nodded.

"He does free-lance work too," Bregman continued. "Or at least he used to up until about a year ago."

Hankleman had a feeling that Bregman was trying to tell him something.

"You know, Morrie, regarding your little problem with this guy Kerner. ... Well, it's just possible that Solly might be able to ... you know ... help you out."

Hankleman nodded again.

"He might help you out ... just to sort of keep in shape."

Hankleman kept on nodding his head.

"Why don't you talk to him, Morrie?" Bregman said, smiling.

Hankleman kept on nodding.

Chapter Two

Artie Kerner walked down the corridor until he came to the door marked 'Harold Lehman, M.D.' He looked around quickly and, seeing no one, darted inside shutting the door behind him. He was nervous. He didn't want anyone to see him going into a psychiatrist's office. He looked around the waiting room and saw it was empty.

He could hear the murmur of voices coming from behind a door marked private. He pressed closer to the door trying to hear what was being said. He could hear a woman's voice.

"Thank you very much, Doctor," she said.

"It's all right," a male voice said. "I'll see you back here the same time tomorrow."

Kerner could hear the sound of footsteps. He moved quickly away from the door towards the far corner of the waiting room.

The door marked private was suddenly opened. Kerner pretended to scratch the side of his face, attempting to hide it. With his hand in that position he stole a glance towards the doorway as a pretty, thirtyish-looking woman came out, followed by a gaunt-faced, bespectacled man.

"Oh hello there," the doctor said. "You must be Mr. Kerner?"

Kerner tried to acknowledge the greeting and, at the same time, still keep his face hidden. He half-turned and forced a distorted smile, feeling his stomach churning.

"I'll be with you in a minute, Mr. Kerner, as soon as I say goodbye to Mrs. Griff," the doctor said.

Kerner turned so he was looking directly at the wall.

"Anyway," the doctor said in a loud voice, "don't worry too much about your husband, Mrs. Griff. Maybe he'll come around soon. Don't forget, there are some women whose husbands haven't serviced them in ten years. Yours has only been holding off for a year."

Kerner heard the sudden slamming of the office door, followed by the sound of a woman's heels clacking quickly away down the outside hallway.

"Now then, Mr. Kerner, step in here, please," the doctor said.

Kerner turned and followed him into the office. For a moment he felt dazed. He couldn't believe the sight. It was the biggest private office he had ever seen. He estimated its dimensions to be at least 30' by 40'. In one corner was the doctor's desk; a huge walnut monstrosity shaped like a fat boomerang. It was easily four or five times the size of a normal executive-type desk. It was so large that Kerner estimated a dozen people could have lain on it without any trouble.

The entire left side of the room was given over to a setting that reminded Kerner of the play *South Pacific*. There beside him he observed a reproduction of a South Sea lagoon, complete with real palm trees, a thatched-roof hut and a waterfall with real water coursing down into a pond. Soft lights played on the water.

"I like to have a pleasant atmosphere where I work," said the doctor, walking towards his desk.

Kerner nodded, still slightly stunned.

The doctor sat himself behind the gigantic desk which at that moment seemed like a piece of lethal war machinery to Kerner.

The doctor reclined his huge leather chair by pressing a button on the desk. Not only did the chair go back, but it went

21

down as well, so that in a moment only the doctor's head and shoulders were visible. To Kerner he looked like a commander in the turret of some strange wooden tank.

"Sit down, please, Mr. Kerner," the doctor said, pointing at an area about twenty feet in front of his desk.

Kerner observed a small cot and a tiny wooden chair.

"Or lie down if it'll make you more comfortable."

Kerner had a sudden urge to turn and bolt for the door, but he remained. So far everything seemed a little crazy, but who was he to judge what was crazy, given the problem that he himself was plagued with.

Kerner sat down on the little chair, which wasn't much bigger than the kind he had when he was four or five years old. His knees came up almost to his chin. Maybe he should have chosen the couch, he thought. It might have been a little more dignified.

Suddenly the doctor pushed another button and a spotlight came on directly over Kerner's head. A circle of light surrounded the little chair. Kerner again felt an urge to get up and leave, but again he restrained himself. He had heard about this Dr. Lehman. Many of his ideas were extremely avant-garde, but he had a high reputation and apparently there were people who claimed he had cured them of the most bizarre ills.

Kerner looked up at the doctor nervously, feeling like a fool, exposed, out in the open on his little chair, while the doctor sat half-hidden and protected by his massive fort-like desk. Kerner didn't know what to expect. He had never been to a psychiatrist before and felt embarrassed, even ashamed, about being there.

It was hard having to admit that he had a problem that he couldn't solve by himself. For the first time in his adult life, he needed help and he didn't like the idea at all.

Kerner sat waiting for the psychiatrist to say something, but the doctor just sat quietly in his enormous chair with his head back and his eyes closed as though he were sleeping.

After a few minutes of silence, Kerner said, "Aren't you going to ask me anything?"

The doctor looked up as though he had just been rudely awakened. "Um? What?" he grunted.

"Aren't you going to ask me anything?" Kerner repeated.

"Me ask you? Who's the patient, me or you?"

"Me ... I mean, I'm not actually a patient," Kerner said hesitantly.

"So if you're not a patient, Mr. Kerner, do you mind telling me what you're doing here wasting my valuable time?" the doctor said, a note of controlled anger in his voice.

"Uh ... well, there are a few things ... no, actually it's just one thing that's bothering me, which I thought I should discuss with a competent person."

"Like what, for instance?" the doctor said, pressing a button so that his chair suddenly rose a foot higher.

"Like ... well ... it's sort of ..."

"What? What! Get it out already," the doctor shouted, moving his chair even higher.

Kerner felt very unprotected. "It's this problem I have ... you see it ..."

"What? What is it already! Don't be selfish, Mr. Kerner. Share it with me."

Kerner hesitated. He was finding it very difficult to begin. He was finding it much more difficult than he had thought it would be – in fact, he was finding it almost impossible.

"Well," said the doctor.

"Well ... I have this problem," Kerner said.

"Yes, we've established that. Now just what is this problem, Mr. Kerner?"

"Well, it's nothing much really ..."

"So if it's nothing much, is it really necessary to pay me $50.00 an hour?"

"I thought you said it was $35.00 an hour," Kerner said, caught by surprise.

"Before, yes, but now that you've aggravated me, I'm raising it to $50.00 an hour. You got me angry just now, Mr. Kerner, and I believe in giving expression to my anger; ventilating it, as it were. It's a lot healthier than keeping it in."

"But you told me $35.00!"

"So I lied. Big deal. Sue me."

Kerner stared at the doctor in disbelief. He could feel a tightness in his chest. He prayed that he wouldn't get an attack of nausea until he could get out of there.

"Lying is good now and then," the doctor continued. "A little deception on occasion never hurt anyone, right?"

Kerner shrugged noncommittally. "Well, I don't know, but I just don't think it's fair to charge me $50.00 when you told me on the phone it would be $35.00."

"How do you know it was me on the phone, Mr. Kerner, eh, eh, eh? Answer that one." The doctor shouted, half-standing on his chair.

Kerner's nervousness increased. Was this typical? he wondered. Perhaps this was some type of avant-garde technique employed by the doctor to provoke some childhood memory.

"You can't prove it was me on the phone, can you, Mr. Kerner?"

"No," Kerner said meekly. "But..."

The doctor cut him off. "Okay. ... Now if you keep arguing, Mr. Kerner, in another minute I'll raise my fee to $55.00 an hour, and every minute of arguing after that, it will go up another $5.00 an hour."

"I'm not arguing anymore," Kerner replied.

"Good."

"Maybe..."

"Yes? Yes?" said the psychiatrist.

"Maybe you could make it $40.00 an hour instead of $50.00."

"Look, what do you take me for?" the doctor asked angrily, pressing a button so that his chair was suddenly pushed forward. "You think this is the old Rachel Market on Main Street or something?" he asked, propping himself against the desk top. "I don't bargain." He pressed a button and the chair went back. "If I say $50.00, it's $50.00. I'm a man of my word," the doctor said and gazed up at the ceiling.

"Maybe we could saw it off at $45.00?" Kerner asked quietly.

The doctor's seat jerked forward. "I said $50.00, and it's $50.00." He slammed the top of the gargantuan desk and then, pressing his button, was carried down and almost out of sight behind his battlements.

"Okay, how about $47.50?" Kerner suggested, knowing that with his problem every penny counted.

"It's $50.00 or nothing," the doctor said, suddenly coming back into view. "It's a matter of principle!"

"Well, okay, but I just don't think it's fair."

"Look, Mr. Kerner, in life one has to pay for one's mistakes. You got me angry. You have to pay for that. Now enough talking about money. Let's hear about your problem."

Kerner's nervousness increased. Now he suddenly felt the first suggestion of nausea and that made him determined to try and discuss his problem. He fought down a slight panic which the sick feeling provoked in him.

"I want to discuss my problem with you, Dr. Lehman, but I'm finding it very difficult to start. … Maybe you could ask me certain questions about what you think it might be, and then if you hit on it, I'll just answer yes, and maybe then I'll be able to discuss it."

"All right, Kerner, if you want to act like a two-year-old child, we'll accommodate you and do it that way."

Kerner was about to protest the insult as well as the fact that the doctor had dropped the Mr. from his name, but he held himself back.

"Now let's see," the doctor said, rubbing his head. "You're in love with another woman."

"No, I'm not married and I'm not in love with anyone."

"All right, you're in love with another man!"

"No," Kerner replied. "I'm not queer."

"Are you sure about that, Mr. Kerner?" the doctor asked, fixing Kerner with a hard stare.

"I'm definitely not in love with any man."

The psychiatrist looked at Kerner suspiciously, squinting his eyes. "Are you trying to tell me you're not a fag, Mr. Kerner?"

"Look! I'm definitely not! What is this? I mean, come off it. What kind of therapy is this?" Kerner half-shouted, raising himself out of the little chair.

The doctor appeared unperturbed. "I'm hardly ever wrong. The minute I saw you in my waiting room, I thought, Oh, oh, possible latent homo … of course, I could be wrong."

"Well, you are wrong, as a matter of fact," Kerner said angrily. "I'm no queer."

"Well, I'll take your word for it for the time being. Now let's go on and see if I can hit on your particular perversion, shall we?"

"It's not a perversion," Kerner said, reacting with defensive quickness.

"Let me decide that when I hear about it, okay?" the doctor snapped.

What am I doing here? Kerner wondered. Not only was the doctor making him nervous, but he was starting to feel the sickness coming over him. This man could never help him, he thought; but still, if there was the slightest chance that he could be aided in this strange office with its South Sea setting, he must take it, no matter what.

The doctor suddenly pushed another button and water began to fall from the ceiling into the pond like a sudden rainburst. "Could your problem be that you can't get it up?" the doctor asked, hunching forward across his desk.

"Get what up?"

"Your cock!" the doctor said.

"Are you serious? I'm very potent."

"Very potent, huh? Can you make it hard at will, like I can? … Eh? … Well?"

"I don't know," Kerner replied, flabbergasted.

"You don't know!" There was an incredulous sound in the doctor's voice.

"No, I don't know. Is that a crime or something?"

The doctor ignored Kerner's counter. "If I said to you, 'Raise me a hard-on in sixty seconds,' could you do it?"

"I'm not sure. ... I've never tried it. ... Well, maybe I could. ... Yes! I think I could."

"You *think* you could?"

"Yes, I could. I definitely could."

"Are you absolutely positive?"

"Yes, I said I could. Don't you believe me?"

"Believe you? Why should I believe you? You've already lied to me once."

"What? I haven't lied about anything!" Kerner shouted.

"Yes, you have," the doctor said calmly with a light tone in his voice.

"About what?"

"You lied to me about being a fag."

"I'm not a fag, goddamn it! I have no reason to lie to you," Kerner said angrily. He stood up and grabbed the little chair. "And what the hell do I have to sit in this crazy little thing for?" Kerner threw the chair aside. "It's for a midget!"

"If you don't like the chair, you can always lie down on the cot."

"I'll sit on it," Kerner said.

"As you wish," the doctor replied. "Just, please, no more lies, Mr. Kerner."

"I didn't lie. I'm not queer or impotent. Those are not problems of mine. Mine is ..."

"Yes? Yes, what? Tell me! Get it out already. Let's hear it! Yours is ...?

"I don't know what's the matter with me. I just can't seem to start talking about it ... it's sort of ... humiliating. Maybe you could ask me something else?"

The doctor pressed a button and sank almost out of sight again. "You're getting me very angry, Mr. Kerner."

"I'm sorry. Believe me, I'm trying. I can't help it."

"You'd better help it because it doesn't pay to get me angry. Now I'm going to ask you a few more pointed scientific questions relating to what your problem may be. If we fail to get anywhere with these, we'll have to take another approach."

Kerner shivered, afraid to think what that other approach might be.

Why? Why? Kerner wondered, why did he come here? Why did he have to be so unfortunate to have a sickness so unique and so bizarre that it seemed beyond cure? He felt all alone, helpless. He wanted to cry.

The doctor was now pressing a series of switches. The sound of thunder suddenly burst out of hidden speakers, and a strong wind coursed through the room as though a large fan had been turned on somewhere. The rain continued to fall on the lagoon and Kerner was now rapidly getting drenched from the sheets of rain that were being swept across the room by the hidden wind-making machine.

Kerner got up and, dragging the couch with him, moved several feet to the side and sat down.

The doctor came into view again. Kerner fixed him with an angry look.

"You know," the doctor said, "I think I know what's bothering you."

"You do?"

"Yes," said the doctor. "One of the most common problems that my male patients seem to have is penis anxiety."

Kerner waited.

"In effect, they feel that the size of their tool is inadequate. ... Now is that it?"

"No," Kerner said. "No, I don't want to talk about anything like that. That's not a problem of mine."

"Good. I'm actually sick and tired of hearing about the problems guys think they have with their petzels. Every second guy starts off like, 'Uh, Doctor ... it's about my organ', or, 'Doctor, it concerns my genital member', or, 'Doctor, it sort of has to do with my whatchamacallit.' Then they all proceed to tell me that it used to be a lot bigger but that somehow when they weren't looking it shrank."

"No, I don't have a problem with my thing," Kerner said, self-satisfied.

"With your what!" the doctor shouted incredulously.

"With my thing."

"What thing? C'mon out with it. Say it!"

"Say what?" Kerner asked, confused.

"You know what I mean. Give your thing a name. Don't be ashamed to call it what it is. It's not dirty. We're in the midst of a sexual revolution, man! Don't be embarrassed. Now call it something appropriate."

"You mean, like prick?" Kerner asked.

"Right. Very good. Now we're getting somewhere. What else?"

"Cock?"

"Good, good. What else?"

"Rod?"

"Yes, yes. Very good."

"I know a lot more," Kerner said, feeling a sudden surge of enthusiasm.

"It's enough, it's enough," the doctor grunted. "Don't you feel better now?"

"No. I didn't feel bad to begin with, at least not about that. I told you. Besides, you said you were tired of hearing about guys with that type of problem."

"That's true, I am tired of it. But my professional responsibilities compel me to deal with this problem, if and where it exists, no matter how aggravating and distasteful I find it. So then, Mr. Kerner, what is the length of your prick?"

"Pardon me?" Kerner's jaw dropped.

"You heard me!"

"You're not serious, Doctor, are you?"

"Come on now, don't play games, Mr. Kerner. This is serious business. I'm sure you've measured it several thousand times. Everyone has, you know."

"Really?" Kerner replied. "Have you?"

"Yes, once or twice," the doctor replied matter-of-factly.

"Only once or twice? I thought you said everyone did it thousands of times?"

"That's true, but I don't include psychiatrists in the general statement. We tend to be less anxious about such things due to our deeper insight into ourselves. ... In any case, when I said once or twice, I meant once or twice today."

Kerner squinted with disbelief and wiped the side of his face where the rain had wet him. He pressed his hand against his cheek for reassurance. He seemed to be losing touch with reality. The doctor's talk and the strange room with its lagoon and rain and thunderclaps were making him dizzy. Again he felt an urge to weep but he forced it down.

Maybe, just maybe, he thought, something good would come out of all this craziness. Or perhaps he was only grasping at straws. It seemed hopeless, utterly futile. This strange doctor was definitely making him frightened but his sickness made him even more afraid. Why couldn't he verbalize it? Why was he so ashamed? He had kept it all to himself for six months. If he'd had one close friend, perhaps he would have been able to discuss it with him, but he had no close friends and no one that he trusted. Once again he tried to force himself to talk, but he couldn't.

Meanwhile, the doctor had gotten out of his chair and was walking towards the lagoon. He walked into the thatched hut and continued speaking from inside.

"Yes, everyone does it," the doctor said. "It's just that certain categories of professionals do it less than others. Some do it more. For instance, from my experience, architects do it by far the most of any group. From my experience, they measure on the average about every fifteen to twenty minutes."

The doctor came out of the hut still talking as though he were making a speech. "For example, I have one patient who, irrespective of where he might be at the time, whips out his pisser like clockwork every fifteen minutes just to see if it's still there and to ascertain that it hasn't shrunk during the preceding period of time. In the building where he lives, he's known as the mad flasher. Many a time someone waiting for the elevator has been surprised when the elevator doors open to find him bent over his tool with a tape measure. But he's not the exception. He's more the rule. Another one cut out all his pants pockets so he could shove in a caliper every thirty seconds or so to see if the circumference was holding steady." The doctor climbed back into his seat.

Suddenly, almost as though he had no control over the words, Kerner shouted, "I'm addicted!"

The doctor's chair shot high into the air. "I knew it! I knew it!" he yelled, peering down at Kerner. "I knew there was something wrong with you the moment I saw you. 'Here comes a real sicko,' I said to myself. Cock measuring isn't good enough for you. You have to be a lousy junkie, eh? I could tell you were arrogant the minute you walked in the door."

Kerner tried to protest, but the doctor rolled right over him.

"Don't worry, Mr. Kerner, we'll effect a cure, even if I have to rip this ugly sickness out of you with my bare hands. ..."

"I don't think you understand. It's not ..."

"Don't worry, my friend, I understand. What are you on? Coke? Shmeck? Nembutal? Mandrax?"

"No, you don't understand ..."

"Stop playing around with me, Kerner," the doctor yelled. "You're making me paranoid and in one minute my fee will soar to $75.00 an hour."

"You're not letting me talk. I thought the patient was supposed to do the talking while the psychiatrist listened."

"I don't believe in that bullshit. In my office we both talk. You talk until I get sick and tired of hearing your voice. Then I talk so I can pay you back for making me sick and tired. In other words, you talk when I want you to."

Kerner was getting angry. "Well, chacun à son goût," he said sarcastically.

"Okay, okay, Kerner. You're not impressing me. I can speak French too. I also speak Yiddish, so, 'Gay cocken offen yam.' You know what that means? ... It means, go shit in the ocean."

Kerner started to get up. It was no use; the man was obviously crazed. He had to get out of there. His chest was beginning to constrict and his stomach was knotted. He felt like throwing up. He got off the couch and turned towards the door.

"Where are you going, Mr. Kerner?"

"I'm leaving," Kerner said and walked quickly to the door.

"You're a shlepper, Kerner!"

"You're crazy," Kerner replied angrily and went outside. He opened the waiting-room door and went out into the hallway. Behind him he could hear the doctor yelling.

"Kerner, you're a shlepper. You have no faith. That's your sickness. You have no faith!"

Kerner started to run. He ran all the way to the stores on Sherbrooke Street.

Chapter Three

Morrie Hankleman sat at his desk unable to work. No matter what he tried to think about, his mind kept coming back to Artie Kerner. He had never thought it possible to hate someone as much as he hated that man. Kerner was going to pay his dues. One way or the other, he was going to pay. No one was going to take Morrie Hankleman for a ride; not after what he had been through.

For six years he had worked his ass off as a department manager for the Blue Star chain of food stores. Then they had promoted him to store manager. He had worked in that capacity for another two years. All the while he was thinking of ways to get into something on his own. He had a lot of ideas but no money to implement them.

The time was passing. He had hoped to be at least well-off if not wealthy by the time he was thirty, but things weren't turning out that way. He was getting desperate. He wanted to make some big money, to relax, to play the big shot, to come and go as he pleased. He couldn't see himself working for the Blue Star chain for the rest of his life but he could see no other alternatives.

He felt he had to break out or die. He was ready to go for broke if only something would fall his way. And then it did. He was promoted to vegetable buyer for all the Blue Star stores on the island of Montreal – thirty-four of them. The increase in his salary wasn't insignificant but he couldn't have cared less about that. He would have gladly taken the promotion with a decrease in his salary because, from the very moment he was told about his new function, Morrie Hankleman knew exactly what he would do.

He didn't do it immediately. First he familiarized himself with the job and the people with whom he had to deal. It wasn't long before he was ready to make his first move.

Some of the salesmen sounded him out the very first time they met him. They all had their own style. Some were subtle, and some were less subtle, but it didn't take Morrie Hankleman long to know which men he could deal with. He took his first payoff one month after he had assumed his new job. He never looked back.

By the end of the first year, he had put $50,000.00 in a Swiss bank.

It was shortly after the end of that first lucrative year that Morrie Hankleman began thinking seriously about what he was going to do. He knew eventually the word would get around that he was on the take and he wanted to get out clean. If he was lucky, he could go on taking indefinitely; if he wasn't, he might have another year or two.

He began investing cautiously in the stock market and got to know some of the inside people. Then one day he got wind of a major promotion job. He was advised with absolute certainty that a mining stock on the Montreal exchange, then selling at $1.00 per share, would soon begin a steady rise to a minimum of around $10.00 a share. Hankleman thought about it for a full day. His source of information was a man well connected with the big promoters. Moreover, he and this individual had whored around together and for him to con Hankleman would be a dangerous thing on his part, given that Hankleman knew enough about his private life to completely destroy his marriage and his reputation.

Hankleman decided to move. He took $20,000.00 and, using margin, purchased $40,000.00 worth of the stock. Then he waited. He waited under the most extreme pressure of his life. He slowly withdrew into a shell so that, by the third day, he was communicating with people in monosyllables. On the fourth day after he had bought the stock, it began to rise. At first it made its ascent slowly and Hankleman was having his doubts. He contemplated pulling out with a slight profit, but held on, withdrawing further into himself. On the tenth day, his wife took their child and left. Morrie Hankleman was too involved with his stock to give this more than a moment's thought.

Then suddenly at the end of the second week, the stock began to skyrocket, going up a dollar per day per share.

By the end of the third week, it hit $5.00 a share. At that point, unable to stand the pressure and feeling as though he might have a nervous breakdown, Morrie Hankleman sold, and collected close to $200,000.00.

The next day he gave his notice to the Blue Star chain and became a changed man. He felt magnanimous; he called his wife back and she came. Now he had money and he was a free man. But at the same time he realized what people meant when they spoke about the heavy responsibility of having money. He had to be careful. If he was cautious he could make his money grow; if he wasn't he could piss it all away.

He began to think about reasonable investments. He consulted with people whose expertise he respected, and finally he bought several small apartment buildings with good revenues.

But he wasn't satisfied. He couldn't help but compare the return on any investment with the profit he had made on the one stock-market deal.

He decided to go into the business of lending money. He would go into second mortgages for which there was a great demand by serious people. At the same time, he made up his mind to try his hand at pure short-term money-lending where he knew the profits were unbelievably high. He passed the word around that he had money available for any kind of loan.

Now as he sat at his desk thinking about all this, Morrie Hankleman realized that he had made a few mistakes. Perhaps his first mistake had been to go into the business of shylocking without thoroughly understanding all of its intricacies. Perhaps his second mistake had been to place too much trust in credit reports. His third mistake had been to lend money to Artie Kerner.

Morrie Hankleman stood up and walked out of his office. His first two mistakes he would take care of himself. In another fifteen minutes he'd be meeting with the man they called Solly the Hawk. That would be the first step towards rectifying his third mistake.

Chapter Four

Solly the Hawk sat at his desk in the office that he shared with his partner, Big Moishie Mandelberg. He glanced over at the big man who was busy haranguing someone on the telephone. The Hawk looked at his watch. The man, Morrie Hankleman, would be there soon, probably to discuss a collection, the Hawk thought. Why else would he want to see him?

He thought back to the party at Bregman's office the night before. It had been nice seeing some of his friends and acquaintances from the old days, and they had been happy to see him as well, he thought, or at least some of them had. A few had looked at him somewhat nervously. Of course, he could understand it. A kind of myth had grown up around him over the years and often when he was introduced to people for the first time, they would look at him with what Solly knew was fear in their eyes. Then they would just mumble or stammer a few unintelligible words as though afraid to say anything that might offend him and incur his wrath which, to their minds, could be unleashed violently and unpredictably. Some would simply keep a respectful distance; others would hang around and ass kiss.

The ass kissers, he disliked. They wanted something from him. It was as though they were trying to insure themselves for the future – just in case. No, he didn't like the ass kissers. As for the others – if they were afraid of him, that was their problem.

The truth was that he hated violence. In all the hundreds of times that he had gone out on a collection, he had actually resorted to physical violence only seven times. He remembered each incident in clear detail. He had never on any of these occasions initiated the action, but in each case had merely defended himself against violent men who, for one reason or another, had reacted crazily to his request for payments owed. In fact, in all those instances where he had fought, he would gladly have walked away to avoid a confrontation had he been able to. In many cases that was exactly what he had done; simply walked away. But on those seven occasions, he'd had nowhere to walk away to.

Of course, he had to admit that in a way he had helped promote his image. He enjoyed collecting and he loved talking about his various jobs. He enjoyed telling a story to the boys. He liked to make them laugh and he felt good when he was talking and saw how they hung on his every word.

Since they always seemed to want to hear about those jobs where violence was used, the Hawk accommodated them, but he never lied. Sometimes he added certain embellishments to make the stories more appealing but the kernel of each story was the truth.

Since he had only seven stories involving violence and since he was continually being called upon to relate them, Solly the Hawk was able to perfect each one to the point where it was a perfect masterpiece. Every story combined a basic conflict between good and evil. Elements of greed, envy, lust, were always involved. He was always able to inject a large dose of humour into each one.

The Hawk knew these stories were repeated to others by his audience, so when he sometimes wondered why such a myth had grown up around him, he knew that, to some degree, he had no one to blame but himself. Now, as he sat at his desk, he couldn't help smiling at his own little weakness. If that would be his worst weakness, he would be happy.

His thoughts turned to Morrie Hankleman again and he looked at his watch. Hankleman's appointment was for ten o'clock. It was now a quarter to ten.

The Hawk was anxious to find out what kind of proposition Hankleman would have. He had already made up his mind that if the job was straightforward, he would take it on.

The Hawk's thoughts were suddenly interrupted by Big Moishie's voice. "So you're really going to do something for this Hankleman?"

The Hawk shrugged. "I dunno. Maybe. I'll see first what kine of deal he's got. If it's good, I'll probly take it on."

"I didn't like this putz when I met him last night at the party, Solly. He's a sniffer. You know?"

Solly the Hawk shrugged again. "Whaddo I care. So long as he has a legit deal I'll consider it. I could use a liddle action, Moishie."

Moishie Mandelberg gave a half-shrug and scowled to indicate his displeasure. "I didn't like the way he was talking to you. Like he was talking down to you. Like he was talking to a gorilla. Like maybe you had trouble understanding plain English."

"Whaddo I care," the Hawk replied with a smile.

"On the one hand he was sucking your ass and on the other he was talking down."

"Whaddo I care," the Hawk replied. "It's nutting new. Like dey say, I'm laughing all de way to de bank. ... Besides, I gotta keep busy. I can't sit in de office all day stroking. Right?"

"Right," Big Moishie said, nodding. "I just didn't like the way he was talking to you."

"Who gives a shit, Moishie. It doesn bodder me. Besides, we don even know what he's got ta offer. Let's hear first what his story is. Right?"

"Right."

The Hawk glanced at his watch. "He should be here any minute now," he said.

"Did you feel his hand when he shook hands with you?" Big Moishie asked.

"Yeah."

"It was like shaking hands with a sticky washcloth. I never felt such a wet hand in my life. It was like dripping water."

The Hawk nodded. It was quite true. Hankleman did have a very wet hand.

"Not only was it wet, but it was sticky like a leech. I had to go wash my hands after I shook with him. It was like wet glue. I don't trust people with wet, sticky hands."

The Hawk shrugged but he knew what the big man meant.

Suddenly the secretary's voice came over the intercom. "There's a Mr. Hankleman here to see you."

"Tell em ta come in," the Hawk said.

Big Moishie caught Solly's eye and scowled again. The Hawk ignored his partner's look as Morrie Hankleman came barrelling into the office and headed right for Solly's desk, his right hand extended.

The Hawk winced inwardly as he took the wet hand in his own.

"Nice to see you again so soon, Mr. Weisskopf," Hankleman said, smiling magnanimously.

The Hawk shook his head in acknowledgement and waited for Hankleman to greet his partner, but he didn't.

"I tink you remember my partner, Mr. Mandelberg," the Hawk said.

"Oh, yes. Nice to see you," Hankleman said and winked at Big Moishie.

Solly twitched as Hankleman did this. No one winked at Big Moishie. Moishie Mandelberg gave the slightest nod of acknowledgement and shot a quick glance at Solly.

"Have a seat, Mr. Hankleman," the Hawk said, motioning at the chair opposite his desk.

Hankleman sat down.

"So you said las night dat you tot dat I could maybe help you wid a liddle problem dat you got," the Hawk said.

"That's right," Hankleman said, nodding vigorously.

"So what's de problem?"

"There's a guy that owes me some money."

"Yeah ... so?"

"Well, he won't pay up."

"Yeah ... so?"

"Well, I want what he owes me."

"Yeah ... so?"

Hankleman looked nervously at the Hawk. "Well, so I need someone to collect it."

"How come?" Solly asked, his face showing no expression.

"How come? Because he won't pay up."

"So why dontcha sue em?"

"Sue him?"

"Yeah, sue em. If somebody owes you money, you sue em. Right?"

"Well ... normally yes; but in this case I can't."

"Why not?"

"Well ... you see ..."

"Look, what's de story? Are you a shylock?"

"Well, sort of."

"What sort of? Eidder you're a shylock or you're not a shylock. So whad is it?"

"Yes, I guess you could call me that. Yes. Yes, I am. I mean, I just started off in the business."

"Okay, so you lent a mooch money an he don wanna pay up. Is dat right?"

"That's right. Artie Kerner. That's his name."

"How much does he owe?"

"Approximately thirteen thousand dollars."

The Hawk smiled inwardly. It was a nice amount.

"So how come he won't pay?"

"I don't know. He says he's good for the money but he needs more time. He was supposed to pay me back a month ago."

"How much interest are you charging dis guy?"

"Well ... that's sort of personal ... I mean."

"Throw him out," Big Moishie grunted suddenly without bothering to look up.

Solly raised his hand as though to calm his partner. "Mr.

Mandelberg is very sensitive about being trusted by everyone who we take on a job for," the Hawk said quietly.

"So Mr. Weisskopf asked you a question. What rate of interest did you charge this Kerner?" Big Moishie said gruffly.

"Twenty percent a month," Hankleman said grudgingly.

"Five points a week. So he was paying you like aroun five hunnert a week vigorish?"

"No. It was a closed-end type of deal. I loaned him $9,000.00. After thirty days he was supposed to pay me back $11,000.00. But he said he didn't have it. Now it's almost two months, so he owes me about $13,000.00."

"He didn't offer ta give you nutting?"

"No. He's trying to burn me. I know it. When he first came to me, he told me that he had just made a big loan from the bank and that they wouldn't extend him any more credit. He has a small chemical business that he started a few years ago. He told me he made the bank loan to enlarge his warehouse but he needed a little extra which the banks wouldn't give him. I believed him. I checked him out. On paper he looked good. I got a credit report on him from Canada Investors. They said he was solvent; that he had a going concern. It looks like he paid someone off there to give him a good rating because, a little later, I found out he was in big trouble. Right now I hear he's on the verge of bankruptcy. For all I know, he's getting ready to blow town. I wouldn't put it past him."

"If you were smart, you would have had him pay you interest each week," Big Moishie said matter-of-factly.

"Yes. Yes. I know," Hankleman replied.

"So why dontcha do dat now?" the Hawk asked. "Let em start paying you five, six hunnert a week."

"No, I just want the whole thing right away."

"Maybe take a piece of his business," the Hawk suggested.

"No, he wouldn't go for that. And besides, like I said, it's not worth anything anyway. He's probably going to fail. I just want all that he owes me right away. I know he can come up with it."

"How do you know?" Big Moishie asked.

"I know the type of person he is. He's got money stashed somewhere. He's just trying to burn me."

"You tink he was planning ta bail out even when he made de loan from you?"

"To bail out?" Hankleman said.

"To go bankrupt."

"Oh, I don't know. Probably. I heard that at one time he had a good business. Now all of a sudden it's supposed to be worth nothing. So he must have been pulling a lot of money out."

"In my experience, Mr. Hankleman, de kine of person what goes to a shylock does not go to him wid de idea of shafting him."

"I'm not saying he initially planned to rip me off. I'm just saying that he's trying to do that now."

"Does he gamble, dis Kerner?"

"I don't know. I hear he's something of a playboy."

"He goes for de broads, eh?"

"That's what I heard but I don't know for certain."

"Has he got a family or someting here?" the Hawk asked.

"Not as far as I know. You can be sure if he had any family I would have gone to them and put the pressure on them. I would have threatened the ass off this Kerner through his family if he had one."

The Hawk shrugged. He knew if he glanced over at Big Moishie he would find that he was steaming. It was an unwritten but well-understood rule that they never involved a debtor's family in any of their collections. They would never try and get to a man through his family even if he was the most vicious bastard.

"You know dat we usually only do our own collecting, Mr. Hankleman," the Hawk said.

"Well, I heard that you sometimes did some free-lance work."

"Yeah, I used t'do a liddle but lately nutting much. I'm not so young like I used to be. Anyway, whadda ya need somebody like me. You could get a couple of boys ta do what you need."

"No, I need someone who knows what he's doing. I can't afford any flack, if you know what I mean."

"What do you mean?" Big Moishie asked gruffly.

"Just what I said. I need someone who can collect my money efficiently," Hankleman said, turning towards Moishie Mandelberg.

"Just for the record, Mr. Hankleman, I want you to know beforehand that, in spite of anything you may have heard, we don't lay a finger on anyone."

"Of course. Of course. I understand," Hankleman said quickly to Big Moishie.

Solly could see the slightest suggestion of a knowing smirk at a corner of Morrie Hankleman's mouth.

"That's why I wanted Mr. Weisskopf to do this job." Hankleman turned back to face the Hawk. "I heard that if anyone could collect without causing any waves, it was you."

Solly the Hawk just stared at Morrie Hankleman.

"Look, I just started in this business," Hankleman said, a slight whine in his voice. "I've got to collect this fast, otherwise the word might get around that I was taken. Then I'll be finished before I even started. I can kiss my ass goodbye in this business."

For a long moment the Hawk just stared at Hankleman who fidgeted slightly in his seat. The Hawk glanced over at his partner who looked away, picked up the phone and began dialing.

Solly looked back at Hankleman. "Okay, I'll take dis ting on. My fee is turdy-five percent of whatever I collec from de mooch."

"Thirty-five percent!" Hankleman gasped. "That's almost $5,000.00!"

"Throw him out," Big Moishie suddenly muttered, slamming the receiver down.

44

"Wait ... wait. Take it easy," Morrie Hankleman said loudly, raising a conciliatory hand. "Look, I'm new to this game. All right, I accept those terms. It's a deal. It's better than nothing, I guess."

"Better than nothing!" Big Moishie shouted, jumping out of his seat. "Don't do us any favours, my friend. I don't need you here to insult us."

"Who's insulting? Look, all I meant was ..."

Big Moishie cut him off. "You go after this Kerner yourself and you'll end up with a pile of dreck in your hand." He sat down slowly.

"Look. Look, I'm sorry. I didn't intend to insult anyone here. It's just that it's a lot of money," Hankleman said, attempting to sound contrite.

"It's a lot of money, but $13,000.00 is even more, so if you think thirty-five percent is too much, the door is over there" Big Moishie said, pointing behind Hankleman.

"Look, I apologize. It's a deal," Hankleman said.

"Outside you'll find lots of hooligans," Big Moishie continued. "For fifty bucks apiece they'll do whatever you tell them. You want a head broken, they'll break you a head; you want an arm broken, they'll break you an arm; you want two, they'll break you two. But I don't have to tell you what will happen to your money. If you're lucky and they don't kill him, maybe, just maybe, you'll get something back. But the chances are you'll end up talking with the police and you'll be up shits creek without a paddle. Solly Weisskopf is an artist, my friend. The Picasso of this business, for your information. You should be thankful it's only costing you thirty-five percent."

The Hawk raised a hand as though to pacify his partner whose face was now puffed to twice its normal size. Big Moishie calmed down and continued talking in a more tempered voice.

"To collect money in this business takes brains, not brawn, Mr. Hankleman. This is what separates the men from the boys, the artist from the journeyman, the Hawk from the shleppers." The big man sank back in his seat.

"Look, I apologize. I didn't mean to offend anyone. I understand what you're saying. That's why I came to you. I know you're the best. That's why I'm here. Thirty-five percent is great. I'm sorry if I..."

"Don't worry about it," the Hawk said with a wave. "We'll take it on. But deres like a few conditions dat we have."

"Sure. Sure. You name it," Hankleman said eagerly.

"Number one. We got turdy days to deliver de goods. Of course, dats wid de unnerstanning dat if it should take dat long den we get dis guy Kerner ta come up wid an extra amount equal to de twenny percent interest."

"That's fine with me," Hankleman said, nodding.

"I mean, who knows. Maybe I'll be able ta deliver like in a week, but in any case I need turdy days maximum. Okay?"

"Sure. Sure. That's fine."

"Number two. From dis minute on you gotta have nutting ta do wid dis guy. You jus like lay off. Don call em; don talk to em. Don send em no letters. Okay?"

"Sure," Hankleman replied. "I'll leave it entirely in your hands."

"Dats good," the Hawk said. "So we got a deal here. We don't need no papers. Our word is our agreement."

"We don't even have to shake hands on it," Big Moishie said.

"Right," the Hawk added, remembering Hankleman's hands. "We don even gotta shake hands."

"That's all fine with me," Hankleman said, smiling.

"Now have you got anyting like a file on dis Kerner guy?"

"Yes, I have a file on him. It's nothing much."

"Send it over to me. It could give me a liddle edge to make tings easier. Ya never know."

"Sure, I'll send it over."

"Once I know a liddle bit more about dis guy, I'll like pay em a liddle visit an have like a liddle talk wid em. I can't promise you nutting but usually I deliver."

"That's great, Mr. Weisskopf. Thank you. Thank you very much."

Morrie Hankleman stood up and extended his hand to Solly. The Hawk winced as he took the wet, sticky hand in his own. Hankleman released Solly's hand and started towards Moishie Mandelberg's desk with the same sticky, wet hand extended, but Big Moishie had already pretended to have dropped something on the floor and was now hunched below the desk as though searching for it.

"We'll be speaking to you, Mr. Hankleman," Big Moishie said, showing no inclination to come out of hiding.

"Yes. Well, thank you, and I'll wait for your call."

Hankleman turned and went out. Solly wiped his hand on his pants' leg.

"He got you, eh?" Big Moishie said with a laugh as he lifted himself back into his seat.

"I couldn't get away," the Hawk said with a chuckle.

"We should each keep a fake hand in the office for when he comes around. Every time he comes we slip the fake hand up our sleeve and let him grab it."

Big Moishie began to laugh and the Hawk joined him. After a moment the big man grew serious.

"I don't like that guy and I don't trust him."

"Nutting to worry," Solly the Hawk said.

"He's a mooch. I smelled him out the minute I saw him at the party last night."

"Nutting to worry," the Hawk replied. "It could be like a very easy five gees."

"Just be careful when you talk with him again, and make sure to find out the whole story about this Kerner."

"Don worry. I'll check him out careful like."

"Yes. Be careful."

"You know I'm always careful."

"This time be extra careful. I just don't like this deal. I don't know why. I just don't."

"Nutting to worry," the Hawk said laconically. "Nutting to worry."

Chapter Five

When Solly the Hawk said there was nothing to worry about, he meant it, and the one person who knew to take him at his word was Big Moishie Mandelberg.

They had been partners for twenty-two years. Moishie had started things off when he had parlayed a fifty-dollar bet at the track into a fifteen-hundred-dollar stake. He decided to put the money out on the streets. Within a few months, he had a going concern dealing mostly with compulsive gamblers, small-time hoods and frappers. A few years later, he hired Solly as a collector on a commission basis. The Hawk was so effective in carrying out his responsibilities that they soon formed a partnership. However, it was not only the Hawk's abilities as a collector that appealed to Big Moishie, it was also his talents as a thinker. In fact, Moishie knew that Solly's success was due more to his intelligence than his muscle.

To the people who knew about Solly the Hawk, he was simply a tough, ruthless man who didn't take no for an answer; but to Big Moishie who really knew him, he was anything but that. Tough? Yes. Physically there was no one tougher. Even as a boy on City Hall Street there was no one who could beat him. Ruthless? Yes, but only if he was up against a ruthless person. The real truth about Solly and the key to his success as a collector was that he was a master psychologist. The thought had occurred to Big Moishie more than once that had Solly come from a different background, he could have – would have, without a doubt – become a famous man.

The Hawk had *saichel* – insight, judgement and common sense. Along with this he had imagination and courage.

And he applied these qualities when it came time to go out in the streets and collect.

In the early days when they were first getting the business off the ground and when their clients were of questionable character, the Hawk had to rely more on his toughness and his courage than on his intellect. As the business grew, however, they were able to become more selective in their choice of clients to a point where they were dealing in most cases with businessmen, bookies and people of some means. They were people who, for one reason or another, had gotten over-extended and needed cash in a hurry.

There were very few problems and, where difficulties did arise, they were resolved in most cases by Solly going and, as he put it, 'having a liddle talk wid dem.' A little talk by the Hawk usually cleared things up in a hurry.

The thing that Big Moishie could never quite understand was why the Hawk enjoyed collecting so much. There were times when he felt that Solly was actually hoping he would have to go out and have a little talk with someone. Big Moishie liked nothing better than to sit in his office and not move a muscle. People would come, people would go. Deals would be made. Big Moishie would sit. They came to him. There was no reason for him to move. If they didn't come to him, there was always the telephone. Why should he have to get up and run around?

Solly, on the other hand, was always on pins and needles. He couldn't stand the office. He had to be on the move. He was always ready to pay someone a little visit; always prepared at the drop of a hat to go have a little talk with someone who was in arrears on a payment.

As their own venture became more successful, Solly had

more and more time on his hands. With his partner's approval, he began to take on free-lance jobs. At the same time, he began concentrating more on various ways to beat the system, which to him was basically corrupt, full of loopholes and run mostly by wolves with voracious appetites. Next to collecting he most enjoyed thinking up gaffs, and over the years he and Moishie had come up with some ingenious schemes for ripping off the system or the players in it. There was a point where they had so many good ideas that they opened a consulting service to sell them for a sizeable fee, but soon stopped when they saw their ideas were often wasted by incompetents.

Sometimes one of them would come up with a plan that could keep them busy for weeks or even months. The record gaff was one such deal.

Solly had discovered from a friend who owned a music store that a major record company had a very interesting sales incentive policy. In order to encourage the retailers to carry their label, they offered a plan whereby at the end of the year the retailers could return any unsold records and receive a rebate of $3.00 per disc. The company would then sell these returned records to discount stores or jobbers for $1.00 apiece.

The Hawk quickly made contact with half a dozen acquaintances in the retail record business to set things up. Then, acting as a jobber, he began buying huge lots of records at $1.00 apiece from the manufacturer. He brought them to those stores with whom he had made arrangements. The store owners then returned them to the manufacturer for $3.00. For his trouble, the store owner kept a dollar; Solly and Big Moishie took two.

It took almost three months before the record company wised up and that was due only to the greed of one of the retailers who tried to go into this on his own and inadvertently tipped the manufacturer.

Before it all came to an end, however, Solly and Big Moishie had made something in the vicinity of $28,000.00. This particular scheme was one of their all-time favourites in terms of the amount of satisfaction it had given them. It was a scheme which had taken advantage of a loophole in the system. They had found the loophole and exploited it. And it was all legal.

It was clean. True, someone had to lose somewhere along the line. Better it be a gigantic record company with a hundred subsidiaries worth a half-billion dollars than some poor shmuck who would get sucked into a deal through his own greed and lose his pants.

He had never had the slightest compunction about pulling off that kind of deal where the big machers were ripped off. In fact, he'd never had any reservations about conning anyone who was stupid and greedy enough, nor had Solly; that is, until now.

Big Moishie had noticed him changing over the last year. It had come slowly. It was nothing he could put his finger on but there had been a change. He couldn't define it, and if someone were to have asked him to explain himself, he would have been at a loss for words. Quieter, more subdued? Yes and no. He still talked as much as ever; was still forever telling stories. But … He couldn't put his finger on it.

If not for the telephone gaff, Big Moishie probably wouldn't have given it much thought. It was Solly's indecision about concluding the telephone gaff which convinced him that the Hawk had changed.

Two years before, they had bought a large tract of land some seventy miles north of Montreal, after it had been brought to their attention by a very knowledgeable individual that the provincial government was seriously considering that particular site for a new university which would eventually accommodate forty to fifty thousand students and would be spread over as much as five hundred acres.

They moved fast to buy up as much of the area as possible. Most of the land was barren and off the beaten track and was worth at most about $200.00 an acre. However, because the land was owned by many individuals, it took them a while to put it all together in a block and, as they went from one prospective seller to another, the word got around that some-one was buying up land and the price rose so that, by the time they had made their final purchase, their cost averaged out to around $250.00 an acre. But they weren't unhappy, knowing that in the not-too-distant future they would easily turn the land over for at least three or four times what they had paid for it. A cousin of Claude Lemay's acted as front man to buy the land.

There was an old farmhouse on the site and Lemay's cousin moved in there rent-free and did a bit of truck farming. A back-to-back deed locked away in the safe in Solly and Big Moishie's office showed that Lemay's cousin had sold the land to them and that they were in fact the real owners.

Unfortunately, things didn't work out as they had ex-pected. After a year had passed, the government announced that they had been planning a great university in the Lauren-tians but that this project was now postponed indefinitely. The Hawk and Big Moishie decided to unload their land. They weren't interested in holding onto it now, especially when they could be putting their money into something with a fast return. The problem was that when they put the land up for sale, they not only couldn't get their price but they couldn't even make back their original investment.

This, coupled with the fact that they had originally been hoping to make a substantial profit, disturbed them. It bothered them so much that, after receiving a few ridiculously low offers for the land, they decided to take Draconian meas-ures to resolve their situation. They discussed it as they did all of their ventures, trying to come up with an idea, an approach, a solution.

Then Solly decided to take a week off and go down to the Concord in the Catskills. It was there that the Hawk found what was to be the answer to their land problem in the person of Marvin Saltpeter.

Marvin Saltpeter was a man looking to make a fast buck. He had money. Black-market money that he had made from his motel just outside of New York City. He was looking to get into something, preferably in land and preferably in Canada. He heard there were some big deals to be made in Canada. Americans were buying up land like crazy in Quebec. Solly let him talk. Occasionally he would drop a word here and there about land dealings. Saltpeter kept talking.

Solly continued to drop the odd hint here and there, suggesting that he was more than knowledgeable about the real estate situation in Quebec; that he had access to sources which, if properly used, could make a man wealthy overnight. Saltpeter kept talking. Yes, he heard you could shmear in Quebec. That was a big thing in Quebec. Just like in South America. A little greasing in the right place and you could be a made man. Saltpeter's eyes were bulging as he began to question Solly about everything. "He looked like he was going to shit in his pants," was the way Solly had described Saltpeter's excitement to Big Moishie.

The Hawk hadn't really planned to con Saltpeter, but the more Saltpeter talked, the more his greed became apparent. He seemed like a gigantic leech ready to suck up anything and everything that he could latch onto. Who did Solly know? Who could be reached? How? He'd show Solly his appreciation. He'd look after him. He loved land deals. He wanted a land deal. He needed a land deal. He had lots of money. Money was no object. Who did he have to talk to? Who did he have to shmear? When Solly finally made the decision to take Marvin Saltpeter, he felt a warm glow spread through him.

Every man was greedy about something at one time or another, and most men, given the opportunity for unlimited gain, would take it without serious question, but the Hawk was a snob. Men could be greedy but they should at least have the class to keep it under control a little, to disguise it. He always felt that those who could not were potentially capable of the most evil acts and deeds.

He set Marvin Saltpeter up for the kill. "Yes," Solly told him. He knew the head of the Quebec Roads Planning Department. With the proper introduction, he could be reached. They were now planning a major extension of the Laurentian

Autoroute. Solly had already bought up several sites over which the new road would pass. He'd see what he could do for Saltpeter. He would call him if he could set things up. That was the basic groundwork.

Back home in Montreal, the Hawk and Big Moishie began to think how they would handle their fish now that they had him hooked. Finally, after many days of talking it over, they decided on a plan. The Quebec Roads Planning Department was located in the Confederation Building on Bleury Street. This government agency occupied the entire second floor of the structure. They inquired and found that there were a few small vacant offices on the third floor. Using a shell company, they rented one of these spaces on a month-to-month basis.

Then they brought in an ex-Bell Telephone technician by the name of John Sanky. Sanky's first job was to locate the main telephone conduit for the building. Once done, he found the cable leading to the main switchboard of the Roads Planning Department. He cut into this line and linked it up to a master console in the office on the third floor. This meant that any call destined for the offices of the Roads Planning Department would ring first on the master console in the office on the third floor.

The idea then was that Solly would call Marvin Saltpeter in New York and tell him that he had set up a deal whereby Saltpeter would get certain inside information for a fee. Solly would say that he wanted to stay out of it and that Saltpeter could do the deal himself; that he had already spoken with the Chief of the Roads Planning Department who was expecting a telephone call from Saltpeter. Saltpeter would come up to Montreal. The clincher would be the telephone call. If Saltpeter had any doubts, he would look up the address and telephone number of the Roads Planning Department. He would see that they checked with the address and phone number given to him by the Hawk. Solly and Big Moishie were certain that this simple fact would erase any doubts in Saltpeter's mind.

He would call the number and ask for Mr. Guy Gervais,

the head of the Department, identifying himself as Mr. Marvin Saltzman from New York. Waiting in the office on the third floor would be a woman usually used by Claude Lemay as part of his call-back system in his bookie operation. On the day when Marvin Saltpeter was to phone the offices of the Roads Planning Department, she would take all incoming calls. She would then pass all those calls, except Marvin Saltpeter's, through to the main switchboard downstairs where the receptionist would deal with them in her normal manner.

When Saltpeter called, Lemay's woman would pass it off to a second phone next to her which would be answered by another female employee of Lemay's. After all, someone in Guy Gervais' position had to have his own private secretary. It wouldn't appear good if the call went directly to Lemay-Gervais. During the brief time that the receptionist and the secretary were on the phone with Saltpeter, a tape recorder would be playing, giving off background noises of a large bustling office – typewriters clacking, people, voices, etc.

After the secretary answered the second phone, she would pass the call to a third phone, simultaneously shutting off the tape so that Saltpeter would get the effect of sudden quiet such as one would unconsciously expect in the office of a high government official.

To carry the effect all the way through, Lemay would answer in French and carry on for a bit in that language even after Saltpeter had identified himself. After the preliminary introductions, Lemay would arrange a meeting at a rented house in the country. The house would be properly set up to suggest that it was the home of an important planner. One room would be set up as a work area, with drafting tables, large wall maps, graphs, aerial photographs and other relevant items.

Lemay-Gervais would demand a relatively small payment up front of $4,000.00, and a document signed by Saltpeter stating that once he had sold off the land which he would purchase through Gervais' tip, he would deposit ten percent of his profit on the transaction to an offshore company in Grenada. The idea was that the relatively small up-front payment would not get Saltpeter's back up and give him any doubts about being ripped off immediately. However, if the small size of the initial payment gave him any doubts, these would be dissipated by the knowledge that he would have to make a substantial payoff after the land was sold.

All in all it was a good plan and both Solly and Big Moishie had no doubts that it would work.

Everything was set up and it remained only for the Hawk to call Marvin Saltpeter and get the ball rolling.

And then suddenly Solly decided to hold off on the plan. He came into the office and said that he was having his doubts. He didn't think it was a good plan. He didn't think it would work and it was too risky.

Big Moishie suspected – no, knew – that these were not the real reasons that were suddenly causing Solly to have second thoughts. Not only was it a good plan, it was an excellent plan. Any gaff of that general type was as good as the degree to which it hooked a sucker, and Marvin Saltpeter was hooked and hooked good. Before Solly had left Saltpeter at the Concord, he had given him an unlisted phone number in the event that Saltpeter wished to make contact. This phone was situated in another room, five floors above their business office in a space which had been rented for them by a front man so that it could never be traced to Solly or Big Moishie. A telephone answering device received all messages automatically, and it was checked daily.

Saltpeter had been calling every day. He had the money; he was ready to shmear. Did Solly set it up yet? When could he come up to Montreal and meet Solly? Just give him an hour's notice and he'd be up in a flash. Just give him the word.

Then Solly would call back and tell him that Mr. Gervais, the head of the Roads Planning Department, was either out of town or sick or he wasn't ready to deal as yet, or some other excuse.

The more Solly delayed, the more eager Saltpeter became. Big Moishie had listened to all of Saltpeter's messages. Those that had come in during the last few days were semihysterical pleadings of a man who sounded like he was at the end of his rope. By the very tone of his voice, let alone his actual words, Big Moishie knew they had a classic mooch on the hook. They had a man who was certain that he was about to grab the pot of gold at the end of the rainbow. Their plan would work all right. It would work all by itself; and as far as the risk was concerned, it was minimal. In any event, they didn't argue about Solly's temporary reluctance to proceed. Big Moishie figured that Solly had his own reasons and eventually would make them known to him. He had decided not to force the issue, and if not for the fact that Solly had suddenly taken on the collection for Morrie Hankleman, Big Moishie would have let things lie. But now he was bothered to the point of distraction. He couldn't figure it but he knew there was something wrong somewhere.

Chapter Six

It took Morrie Hankleman only about ten minutes after leaving the office of Solly Weisskopf and Moishie Mandelberg to begin regretting that he had hired them. He had become over-anxious. He should have persisted in his efforts on his own for a little longer and it would have paid off. He just knew it.

Suddenly he was no longer impressed with Solly Weisskopf. He didn't seem particularly clever. There were probably a thousand hoods in town who were just as smart and just as tough.

Now he was going to be out almost five thousand dollars. The more he thought about it, the more upset he became. Why had he been so afraid of hiring a few hoods for a hundred dollars? That was what he had originally thought of doing. That was what he now knew with certainty he should have done. Why should this unimpressive little man be more effective than a couple of six-foot musclemen?

Morrie Hankleman could feel his ulcer acting up. Five thousand down the drain, he thought. But maybe it wasn't too late. If he could get to Kerner right away and threaten him with the name of a real person, Kerner might cough up all the money immediately and no one would be the wiser.

There was a good possibility that Kerner might recognize

the name of Solly Weisskopf or, if he didn't, he would probably check it out and be informed of his reputation.

Weisskopf had said it would be a day or two before he contacted Kerner. He would be waiting for Hankleman's file on him before moving in. Well, he would send the file but, at the same time, he would go and see Kerner immediately. If he was successful and Kerner came up with the money, he would simply call the Hawk and tell him the deal was off. If he was unsuccessful, he would just have to let things ride.

Morrie Hankleman felt his ulcer biting at him. It was as though he had Artie Kerner inside him, gnawing at his guts. Hankleman accelerated the car. One way or another, he was going to shit him out.

Chapter Seven

Artie Kerner sat alone in his office, feeling that there was no hope left for him.

He looked wearily around and felt the silence of the office weighing him down. Not too long ago there had been activity in those surroundings. He'd had a secretary, a bookkeeper, a general manager and a crew of six in the shipping department. Now there was no one. They were all gone and soon he would be completely finished.

He felt tired, tired enough to put his head down on the desk and fall asleep. But he knew that would solve nothing and eventually when he awoke, everything would still be there and he would still be faced with all his problems.

Maybe it would be better if he went to sleep and never woke up, he thought. He was overwhelmed by a panic so great that he was instantly drenched by a cold sweat. He found himself gripping the edge of the desk.

He had an urge to leap from his seat and run but he didn't know where he would run to. He got out of his chair and went quickly outside, drawing in large breaths of air. Cold sweat was still forming on his forehead and he could hear his heart pounding in his rib cage. Kerner put both hands to his head and squeezed them against his temples, trying to control himself. He wanted someone to talk to; someone who would understand and care; a friend; but he had no friends.

Why had he never made any friends? Was it by choice or by chance? ... Or neither. Maybe it was because he had never trusted anyone. Someone had once said that it was better to trust and take the chance of being deceived by one's friends than to shame oneself by not trusting them. Maybe that was why he had no friend to comfort him now.

As he thought this, he suddenly heard the words of Dr. Lehman, the psychiatrist, sounding in his head.

"You're a shlepper, Kerner! You have no faith!"

Artie Kerner went back into his office and dialed the number of Dr. Lehman.

Chapter Eight

An hour after Morrie Hankleman had left the office, Big Moishie was still aggravated. He disliked everything about Hankleman. For some reason, the fact that Solly had agreed to take on the collection job for him infuriated Big Moishie – particularly since he was still undecided on finishing their deal with Marvin Saltpeter. The more he thought about it, the more angry he became. He glanced over at the Hawk who was busy scanning the morning newspaper. The air had to be cleared, Big Moishie thought to himself, and the time to do it was now.

"Solly," Big Moishie said.

The Hawk looked up from his desk. "Yeah?"

"We got to talk."

"About what?"

"About you."

"So let's talk," the Hawk said.

The big man began to nod his head. "Okay…"

The Hawk waited expectantly. He was quite certain he knew what his partner was about to discuss and he was glad.

"For twenty-two years there's been no bullshit between us. Right?"

"Right," the Hawk said, giving a short emphatic nod.

"As a matter of fact, even when we were kids there was no bullshit."

"Dats true, Moishe."

"But now I don't feel right. ..."

"You mean, because of de Saltpeter deal?" the Hawk asked.

"Yes, that's it. I can't figure it out. You tell me it's no good, it can't work, he's not hooked."

Solly nodded slightly and didn't interrupt.

"I have too much respect for you and too much faith in you to believe that you really mean that. ... I know he's hooked and because I know it, then I know that you know it too. Which is why I can't figure it out."

Solly lit up a cigarette as Big Moishie went on.

"You heard the last call he made. The man was hysterical. He was begging you to set the deal up. He sounded like he was ready to crack up. We could do anything we want with him. We could take him for every cent he's got. You know it and I know it. Am I right, Solly?"

Solly the Hawk gave several almost imperceptible nods and said nothing. He kept his eyes fixed on Big Moishie who continued to talk.

"So what I'd like to know is, why don't you want to do this piece of business?"

The Hawk leaned his head in his hand for a moment. He wanted to answer his partner honestly and in such a way that he wouldn't hurt him or insult him. He knew exactly what he wanted to say. He had thought about it long enough.

The Hawk lifted his head and turned towards Big Moishie. "A few munts ago ... I dunno, maybe four, five, six munts ago ... maybe even longer, I started tinking about tings. Like fer twenny years I could never talk about my work wid Helen. For twenny years my own wife doesn really know exactly what I'm doing. As far as she knew, I was in de finance business. Mind you, she knew. She knew I wasn't legit, but she never said nutting; but I could never talk to her ... or my daughter eidder. If dey asked me, 'How did it go t'day at de office?' what could I tell dem? It was fine. T'day I put a mooch in de hospital fer two weeks. He paid up right away. It was a good day! You know whad I mean, Moishie?"

Moishie Mandelberg nodded slowly.

"A whole part of my life I could never talk ta dem about. An also when de kid was growing up I was always worried dat she would like hear somewhere. You know, like from a school friend or somebody, about whad her fadder did. ... Mind you, today I'm sure she knows dat what I do isn't exactly kosher. I mean, de kid's not dumb. She's a smart kid ... an a good kid. ... Anyway, like I say, I started tinking about alla dese tings. Dey boddered me ... a lot. I mean, de kid's twenny already. Any day she could come home an tell me she's getting married. I mean, I don even know why I started tinking dese tings. I jus did. Like I was tinking, I'm getting old. Okay, I could live ta be a hunnert an ten, but I could also pop off like next week. You know? Look at de guys we know. Dere popping off like flies. Right?"

Big Moishie nodded.

"So whad did I do wid my life so far? I asked myself. I mean, I was tinking dat I wanna do someting different. Someting good. Ta give, not ta take. You know what I mean, Moishie?

"Yeah, I know," Big Moishie replied.

"I mean, money I don need. I got enough so I don hafta worry. I could sit on my ass for de nex fifty years jus on de intrest. I'm not a big spender. I was tinking I'd like ta have time ta travel wid de family, ta be closer wid dem. Ta do someting good. De more I tot about it, de more depressed I got. It was making me crazy. Dats why I wen away to de Concord. ... Maybe you noticed I didn look so hot at de time."

"I noticed," Big Moishie replied with a wry smile on his face.

"I had ta tink it out. Ta look at it like from all sides. Ta figger out what ta do. Anyway, I knew I wanted ta get out. I figgered I would come back an discuss it wid you an maybe we could get inta someting legit ... tagedder like. Anyway, I was tinking, tinking, tinking. It was like driving me crazy because I didn know what else I could do if I got out. Also maybe I figgered you weren't gonna give up dis business so after twenny-two years I would be on my own. I was mixed up. But, anyways, after a few days I decided for sure dat I was gonna get out. Like I felt I jus couldn cut it no more wid gaffing and wid shylocking. I jus couldn.

"So den jus when it looks like I made up my mind, I meet Saltpeter in de bar. I tell you, Moishe, like I didn have even de slightest notion ta ace dis yotz; but de minute he opened his mout, it was like I saw red. I wanted ta take him. I wanted ta squeeze him like a liddle bug. I didn even care about de scratch we would make. I jus wanted ta break him because he was a mooch. De more he talked, de more I hated him. I couldn figger it out. I started ta wonder why I hated dis guy so much. After all, what'd he want? Money. De same as everybody. Dats what I wanted too. Anyway... I set em up in spite of de fact dat I kept tinking dis is not what I should be doing.

"Den when I got back ta town, I started tinking it over again. I decided dat if I really wanted ta get out, ta make a new start, den I shouldn do dis ting. Den he calls me an de minute I heard his voice again, I wanted ta break him. Dats when I filled you in on him an we started ta set up de office wid Lemay."

Big Moishie nodded and dragged on his cigar.

"Den I started tinking about when I was coming up. I wanted ta make it. I woulda done anyting. Even t'day I would do anyting if I was broke. If I was broke, I wouldn have such fancy tots about going legit. If I needed de scratch, if I was choked, I wouldn give it a seccun tot. His money would already be in our bank. Dats when it hit me. I like saw someting in him dat made me realize dat in my own way, I was a mooch too; dat maybe everybody was a mooch in dere own way. De only difference between me an him was maybe dat I could control myself a liddle better.

"Den I tot, but maybe I'm really even more of a mooch den him because look what I did ta make it. I went into a business dat was dangerous. I was ready ta risk my life ta make it. Anyway, I knew dat inside me dere was dat same mooch like in Saltpeter, an I didn like it. An whatever I didn like in me, I saw written all over his face."

Big Moishie nodded understandingly.

"Anyway, I was struggling wid myself. I couldn't make up my mind what ta do. Dats why I kept saying we should hold off.... It was a struggle, believe me. Anyway, finally last week I tole myself: It's enough already. Leave em go. You don need dis. Dats what I finally decided. I was jus waiting for de right time ta tell you. I was actually tinking about telling you like today or tomorrow but now I told you."

For a few seconds Big Moishie said nothing. With his lips pursed he simply nodded his head slowly. Finally he said, "I understand, Solly. I understand what you're saying. But what I don't understand is if this is the way you feel, then why did you take on this collection job for this Hankleman putz?"

"Why? ... I know it's crazy, Moishie, but I got it in my head ta do one last collection. I have ta prove it to myself dat I'm not going out because I lost my nerve. Like in de deal wid Salt-peter, like we boat know, dere was no risk an when I decided not ta do it I knew why. But wid de collecting dere is a risk. I mean, we boat know anyting can happen. I just gotta prove ta myself, ta make sure dat I still have it, dat I'm not going out fer de wrong reasons. Ya know whad I mean, Moishie?"

"Yes, I know," the big man said. "Maybe after we finish with Hankleman we can sit down and discuss what we're going to do – that is, if you want to do something together."

"Are ya serious, Moishie?" the Hawk asked excitedly.

"Sure. Why not? I've been doing some thinking too, you know. I have enough money too. But what do I do with it? Sweet fuck all. I have no kids, so who am I going to leave it to? My wife? Even she couldn't spend it all in a hundred years. Maybe I'm tired of it all too. Eh? Why shouldn't I want to get out? Am I so different?"

"I'm sorry, Moishie."

"What for? You didn't do anything. I'm the one who should be sorry because I've been thinking for years and I never said a thing to you. If I had, then maybe it would have saved us both a lot of tsouras."

The Hawk shrugged. "It's all wadder under de dam, Moishie."

"I know, I know."

For a few seconds neither man spoke. Big Moishie flicked his cigar and stared off across the room. Finally he turned to the Hawk. "Anyways, Solly, I feel good. I feel very good," he said, grinning.

"Me too, Moishie. I feel very good also."

"We'll talk after we finish with this Hankleman putz. Meanwhile, like I said, be careful on this job."

"Nutting ta worry," the Hawk replied with a grin.

Chapter Nine

Morrie Hankleman arrived at Artie Kerner's office shortly before noon. The office was a one-storey plant consisting mainly of warehouse space with offices in the front. Finding the reception area deserted, Morrie Hankleman walked towards the nearest office, the door of which was ajar, and looked in. Artie Kerner was sitting at his desk with a faraway look in his eye. At first he wasn't aware of Hankleman standing there. Hankleman made a scraping noise against the door and Kerner looked up suddenly.

"Oh hello," Kerner said unconcernedly.

Hankleman became angry. For some reason, he was expecting Kerner to look shocked, perhaps even afraid, at seeing him there.

"For the last time, I need my money."

"I'm going to pay you, Mr. Hankleman, but it's going to take just a little while longer."

"That's what you told me a month ago and two weeks ago and last week. Do you take me for some kind of idiot?"

"No, no, I don't. Believe me. I'm just in a bind. I'm being choked." Kerner put both hands to his throat.

"You're being choked. What about me? Eh! What about

me? I lent you $9,000.00 on good faith. You were supposed to pay me back in thirty days. Now it's going on two months."

"You said I could get an extension if I paid you the interest. I told you I'd pay it."

"I never said that!" Hankleman snarled.

"You did. I remember it very clearly. I can pay you the interest. I'll give you a cheque now," Kerner said.

"I never said that. I just know one thing. I want what you owe me now. All of it."

"I can't give it to you now. I'm really sorry. Please believe me. I'm in big trouble but I'm good for the money. I'll pay you every cent I owe you. I promise you. You won't lose on me."

"I won't lose on you! No? No? I've already lost, my friend. What you did to me I'll never make up."

"I'll make it up, I promise."

"Don't promise me nothing, you cheap piker. You made me look like shit. D'you understand?"

"Why do you say that?" Artie Kerner asked innocently.

"Why? Because the word is already out that on my first loan I got burned."

"I didn't say a word to anybody. I don't talk about my financial problems to anyone."

"Look. I paid my dues, Kerner. D'you understand? I don't ever intend to go back. You heard you can't go home again, eh?"

Kerner nodded.

"You know that, eh?"

Kerner nodded again.

"So I'm not going back again. I'm not going to allow you, my first mistake, to fuck everything up."

"I'm not going to fuck anything up. Believe me, I'll be good for the money. I swear to you, by the end of the month you'll have the whole bundle."

"You just don't understand," Hankleman said. "Or maybe you just don't want to understand."

"I understand, I understand…"

"Look, just let me finish, okay?" Hankleman shouted, cutting Kerner off. "Don't fucking patronize me. I don't need it from anyone, least of all a piker like you."

"There's no need to insult me," Kerner protested.

"Don't tell me who I can and who I can't insult. If I want to insult you, boy, I'll insult you. If you don't want insults, pay up the money and you won't get insults. Okay? So just shut up and listen," Hankleman shouted, burning now with self-righteous anger. "I was saying that maybe you just don't want to understand, because if you did, you would realize that I cannot function properly till you're all paid up. My credibility is gone. You understand? Every mooch in town will be after a loan from me with the idea that they don't have to pay it back. You've made me a philanthropic organization overnight. You understand what I mean?"

"I understand what you're saying but I don't think I agree with you. I swear to you, I didn't tell a soul."

"You swear? You swear!" Hankleman rasped. "What good is your word? I have your lousy marker with your name on it. It's not worth a piece of shit. And you swear," Hankleman said scornfully.

"Look, I ..." Kerner began to protest again but Hankleman cut him off with a wave of his hand.

"But it's not only that. It's more than just the money. The money alone is enough but it's more ..." He paused for a moment as though to catch his breath.

Kerner waited without saying a word.

"It's also a matter of principle. Nobody is going to beat me, not even for a dime!" he said viciously and slammed a fist into his open palm. He walked up to Kerner's desk and leaned over it. "Not for a fucking dime. You understand?" He stared hard into Kerner's eyes, trying to see something there.

"I'm not trying to beat you. I'm an honest man. Just give me half a chance and I'll prove it to you. I'm going to make it good!"

Morrie Hankleman shook his head slowly and deliberately. "No ... No ... You're not going to make nothing good. For me

70

you're going to make everything bad. I know it. You think I'm a shmuck or something?"

Kerner started to reply. "No ... I don't ..."

Hankleman cut him off in mid-sentence. "I don't need an answer from you on that. What you think or what you say has no validity. D'you understand?"

"Of course ..."

"Don't talk! I don't need an answer from you, friend. I'm not asking, I'm telling."

"Look, Mr. Hankleman ..."

"And don't fucking Mr. Hankleman me. I know what I am to you, you lousy psychopath. You don't give a shit about anything or anyone. You're a mooch. You're a nothing. You're garbage. You don't deserve to exist in this fucking society. You're a parasite. You live on other people. You suck their blood. You just know how to take. I know your type. Everything is take, take, take! Take what you can get and fuck em. So don't fucking Mr. Hankleman me because I don't want to know about it."

Morrie Hankleman was on the verge of violence and he knew it. The more he yelled, the calmer Kerner seemed to become. He would have liked nothing better than to grab Artie Kerner by the hair and beat his face to a pulp against the top of his genuine rosewood desk. He tried to calm himself, a little frightened by his own fury.

He was well aware that he hated Artie Kerner's guts. For the last four weeks he had fantasized regularly about hurting him in every conceivable way. He had felt great anger, but nothing to compare with the unmitigated hatred that consumed him now.

Hankleman tried to calm himself. He wanted to lead up to his threat about Solly the Hawk on a note of coolness. That would create a greater effect. He made an extreme effort to relax but he found it difficult because as long as he looked at the face before him, he could think of nothing else but smashing it. He stood there at the edge of Kerner's desk and tried to catch his breath.

Kerner was reluctant to make any attempt at discourse. He felt that Morrie Hankleman could attack him at any moment.

"I want to ask you something," Hankleman said finally in an overly calm voice.

"Yes, sure. What is it?"

"I know you live in a three-bedroom apartment at the McGregor House, right?"

"Yes, that's right, I do."

"So how come you can afford a $500.00-a-month pad if you're so choked?"

"I got a special deal," Kerner replied quickly.

"How special? So you're paying $400.00 a month, $350.00 let's say..."

"No. no, I'm paying less. I got a fantastic deal. I know the owners."

"Okay, so you're paying $300.00 a month..."

"No, much less. I'm telling you. It's incredible the rent I'm paying."

"Okay, $200.00 a month," Hankleman said.

"A tiny bit less," Kerner said, gesturing with his fingers.

Hankleman threw up his arms. "Ah! What am I doing here? You're a lunatic. I can't reason with you so there's no use trying..."

Hankleman was suddenly interrupted by a knock on the office door. A delivery man poked his head through the doorway. "I have a C.O.D. package here from Ogilvy's," he said.

Kerner stood up quickly and approached the delivery man. He started to push him out the doorway. "Oh, I think you must have the wrong place. It's probably for next door."

The delivery man held his ground. "No, it's the right address. It's for a Mr. A. Kerner. C.O.D. $400.00."

"Oh, right, it must be the new calculator for the office," Kerner said, grabbing the package from the man and forcing a nervous smile.

"No, sir, it says..."

Kerner cut him off abruptly. "Okay, okay. Never mind. It's my calculator. I'll pay you for it."

Kerner put the package down, pulled out his wallet and paid the man.

Hankleman watched as Kerner peeled off a series of bills from a large fold and felt his teeth clenching uncontrollably. It was no use. He was trying to beat him for thirteen thousand dollars but that would never be.

The delivery man went out. Artie Kerner carried the package back to his desk and placed it down out of sight near his chair. "I've got to keep my business going. This new machine is an absolute necess..."

Hankleman cut him off with a brusque move of his hand. "I don't want to know about your lousy calculator or about your business. All I know is you're trying to beat me for thirteen gees. You'll never do it, I promise you that. Yesterday I had a talk with a man. His name is Solly Weisskopf." Hankleman paused, waiting for a reaction from Kerner. "Does that name ring a bell?"

"No," Kerner replied, shaking his head.

"He's also known as Solly the Hawk. *Now* does it ring a bell?" Hankleman asked, smiling broadly.

"No," Artie Kerner replied. "Should it?"

Hankleman forced himself to remain calm. He was sure Kerner was playing games. He was certain he knew the name and knew it well.

"I think it should ring a bell," Hankleman said quietly. "He's very well known in the finance business."

Hankleman stopped and waited for Kerner to say something, but he didn't bite and that made Hankleman lose some of his self-control, and the fact that he lost some of his self-control made him then lose almost all of his self-control.

"You never heard of him? Eh! You're full of shit. You heard of him plenty! You probably heard of him so much that he's coming out of your ears. Right?!"

"I don't know who he is," Artie Kerner said mournfully.

"Well, if you don't know, believe me you're going to know. ... He's a collector, you know? You know what I mean? A strong-arm man. A goon. He's a killer. A ruthless psychopath who would just as soon kill you as say hello to you. For fifty bucks he'll put you in the hospital for a year. And I'll tell you, I'm paying him a lot more than fifty bucks. He's going to come and see you. He's going to come and have a little talk with you. And, believe me, if you don't come across, you can kiss your ass goodbye. That's all I want to tell you. I give you twenty-four hours more and after that, goodbye!"

Artie Kerner felt his heart quicken. He wanted to say something further to Morrie Hankleman, to make him believe that he wasn't a dishonest man, that he would repay him in full if given a chance; but in an instant, Morrie Hankleman was gone.

Artie Kerner felt a wave of depression and nausea sweep over him. He was frightened. Then suddenly his foot knocked against the package on the floor. He reached down and picked it up. He quickly began to unwrap it. He removed all the paper and lifted the cover of the exposed box. He looked inside and a smile broke across his face.

Chapter Ten

Morrie Hankleman spied a pay phone just around the corner from Artie Kerner's office. He stopped his car, got out and went into the booth. He dialed the number of Ogilvy's. Identifying himself as Mr. Arthur Kerner, he explained that he had recently ordered an item for $400.00 which was to have been delivered to his office that day but hadn't come as yet. Would they be kind enough to tell him when it would arrive. He waited as the sales clerk went to check. A moment later he was informed that the crystal statuette which he had ordered had gone out that morning. It should be arriving momentarily. Morrie Hankleman hung up the phone and walked back to his car. He smiled viciously to himself. Artie Kerner's new calculator for the office turns out to be a crystal statuette.

Morrie Hankleman felt much better. Artie Kerner was trying to burn him. There was no longer any doubt about that. When a man who owed close to $13,000.00 claimed he was broke and then went out and spent $400.00 on a crystal statuette, there was no doubt he was a cheat.

Morrie Hankleman gritted his teeth and depressed the accelerator of his big Mercedes. He peeled around the corner of Park Avenue, heading for the Mountain Road. Ahead of him an old man was hobbling across the street against the red light.

Hankleman accelerated and veered the car towards the man, blasting on the horn. The old man made a stumbling, panicky dash for the curb.

Hankleman slowed the car and stuck his head out the window. "Get off the road, you fucking old arsehole!" he cursed.

The old man reached the safety of the sidewalk, turned and shook a feeble fist at Hankleman. "Netzi!" he shouted.

"Up your ass, you alte cocker!" Hankleman screamed. He floored the car and roared up the Mountain Road, laughing.

Fucking old people, he thought. They should all be kept out of sight or put to sleep. He couldn't stand the sight of them. They were all ugly, weak, senile. He could feel his ulcer pain beginning to gnaw at him again.

A sneer formed on his face as his thoughts went back to Kerner. That fucking Kerner! He was probably laughing at him at that very moment. Laughing at how he was shafting Morrie Hankleman. Solly Weisskopf and his fat partner were probably laughing at him too. Laughing at how they were going to collect almost five thousand dollars because Morrie Hankleman was a stupid shmuck who couldn't control his own business affairs. Why had he gone to those hoodlums? he cursed himself. He knew why he had gone to them. He had first thought of simply hiring a goon off the streets for a hundred dollars but he had been afraid. He had been afraid because of the very reasons mentioned by Moishie Mandelberg. An amateur couldn't be trusted. He had known that before Mandelberg had mentioned it to him. There was always the chance that an amateur could run into trouble and under a little pressure from the police he would spill his guts about who had hired him. Then he, Morrie Hankleman, would be in big trouble.

But now he realized that had he not made a deal for collection with Solly Weisskopf, he would hire a couple of goons and take his chances. Now that the collection had been arranged and he knew that he would only get back sixty-five percent of what was owed, he knew what he should have done and what he would do if he could do it over again. Unfortunately, he couldn't. He had made a deal and for the next month he was bound by it. There was always the chance that his talk with Kerner would yield some positive results but it was highly unlikely. He knew for certain that Kerner was trying to burn him. He had the feeling that Kerner was doing it just for the sake of doing it – because it probably gave him pleasure.

The sneer stayed on Morrie Hankleman's face. He ripped the big Mercedes up the Mountain Road, his hands clenched on the wheel.

He pictured Solly Weisskopf and Moishie Mandelberg convulsed with laughter as they talked about him. He was sure from the ache in his gut that his ulcers were now bleeding. He didn't like the way Mandelberg had spoken to him. Who did he think he was? He was a hood, a criminal, a con man.

Hankleman suddenly became aware of a hitchhiker standing up ahead on the roadside. He smiled grimly to himself as he noticed that the hiker was a fat girl with a big camper's knapsack strapped on her back. Hankleman began to chuckle as he drove by the girl.

When he was about a hundred feet or so past her, Hankleman jammed on his brakes and let out a sharp blast on the car horn, then turned to watch the girl who was now looking up the road towards him. Hankleman opened his car door and got out. He began motioning for the hiker to hurry along. As the girl began to run up the slope, Hankleman got back into the car and watched as she trundled towards him, panting under the load of her knapsack.

Hankleman watched as she approached, wheezing with exhaustion but smiling. When she was within fifty feet of the car, Hankleman began to drive away very slowly, watching the girl through his rear-view mirror. She continued to follow the car, which Hankleman kept just twenty feet or so ahead of her.

Maybe he would be able to break his record with this girl, he thought. He had once kept a fat girl hitchhiker, fully loaded with camping gear, chasing his car over hilly terrain for three-quarters of a mile before she collapsed from exhaustion. He was sure at that time that if she hadn't run out of steam he could have kept her going for two or three miles.

For Hankleman that incident had proved that people will go to incredible lengths to deny that they have been fooled. He would never allow himself to be so stupid. Now he grinned as he watched the girl struggling up the hill after his car. He looked at his mileage indicator. So far he had kept her running only about one-tenth of a mile. Suddenly the girl drew up and began waving a heavy fist in the air. Hankleman turned to watch as she collapsed wearily in a heap by the road's shoulder and rolled over on her side.

Hankleman accelerated and drove quickly away, laughing crazily. After a minute his laughter subsided and his thoughts went back to Solly Weisskopf and Moishie Mandelberg. They were probably still laughing at him, he thought. Five thousand dollars down the drain! There was nothing he could do about it. Unless of course, for some reason, they were unable to collect within the thirty days. That thought gave Hankleman a sudden lift, but it lasted only for a moment because he immediately realized that if a pro like Solly the Hawk failed to collect in thirty days, then certainly no one else would succeed, especially not an amateur goon off the streets.

In any case, there was no sense in even thinking about it because the man they called Solly the Hawk would collect and Hankleman was sure he would manage it long before the end of the thirty-day period. He was a professional strong-arm man and he would use every trick in the book, including violence, to get what he was after. No matter that Mandelberg had said that they never resorted to violence. He didn't expect them to admit to laying on muscle but he knew they would and with very little urging. No, they would collect all right, unless Artie Kerner died or went into hiding. ...

What if he, Morrie Hankleman, forced Kerner into hiding or into leaving town until the expiry of the thirty days!

For another instant, Hankleman's spirits were raised, but again they quickly fell as he realized the implications of this idea. Since he had already threatened Kerner without success, threats would obviously not be sufficient to make him leave town; and even if the threats were successful and Kerner did leave town, who was to say he would return in thirty days, if he returned at all. The only way he could be assured of keeping Kerner out of Solly Weisskopf's reach for the thirty-day period and still retain some control over the situation would be if he were to have Kerner abducted and kept on ice somewhere. No! That would leave him open to a charge of kidnapping. That could mean life in prison if anything went wrong and, besides, the price of such an operation would probably cost him just as much as Solly Weisskopf's commission. It was all getting too involved and Hankleman put a hand to his stomach to ease the pain.

What if Kerner decided to blow town on his own? Hankleman thought suddenly. A chill passed through his body. Kerner obviously had other creditors after him. He had no family ties in Montreal. The chances were he was already planning to get out. It would be his luck that Kerner would blow town just before Solly Weisskopf came calling. Then he'd spend the next twenty-five years in some other country laughing and talking about how he had burned this dumb shmuck Morrie Hankleman back in Montreal.

Hankleman could feel his teeth grinding again. He had to make sure that Kerner didn't leave town. Somehow he had to keep tabs on him. Yes, he had to know where he was at any given moment.

Hankleman slammed his palm down hard on the steering wheel. He knew exactly what he was going to do.

Chapter Eleven

Teddy Regan was staring up at the T.V. set on the far wall of the Ace Tavern. He tilted his glass of draught beer and downed the contents in one long swallow. He placed the empty glass down with the two dozen others that filled the entire centre of the table. He shifted his two-hundred-pound bulk in his chair.

"That's twenty-five candles, Jerry," he said to the smaller man seated opposite him.

Jerry Shmytxcyk just scowled.

"What the fuck's buggin' you?" Teddy Regan asked.

"Nothin'."

"Nothin', eh? You've been pissed off all night."

Jerry Shmytxcyk hunched forward over the table. "Yeah, okay," he said, nodding his head. "I'm pissed off. Yeah. You know why?"

"No, why?"

"I'm gettin' pissed off because I been gettin' us all the work. I got us the last three jobs."

"So what?"

"So I oughta get more than half of what we get paid."

"Hey, fuck off, eh!" Regan snarled. "You're just fucking

lucky you got me ta do these guys with you. You couldn't handle any of em by yourself."

"Oh yeah?"

"Yeah, prickface. What happened last week with that frog that we did in Pointe-aux-Trembles? Eh? ... He would have fucking killed you if I hadn't been there."

"I was handling him pretty good."

"Fuck you, ya were. ... He was kickin' the shit outa you."

Shmytxcyk grimaced and made no reply.

"You couldn't even break his arm like you were supposed to," Regan continued, pointing a thick finger in his friend's face. "I had ta bust it for you. Christ! Three fucking whacks with the big bat and you didn't even make a dent in him."

"I was tired that day. Fuck! I'd been up drinkin' all night. I had a bad hangover."

"So did I. I was tired as shit but I bust his arm without even tryin'. We wouldn'ta got paid if I hadn't bust it. Okay? So don't gimmie that shit about gettin' more money."

Teddy Regan turned away from his friend and signalled for the waiter. "Six more draught over here!"he shouted, holding up five fingers.

"Why don't you get us a fucking job, eh?" Jerry Shmytxcyk asked.

"Don't worry about it. I got the word out we're available. I got the word out with the big boys. Not those small-time fuckers that you know. Fifty bucks for bustin' up a guy," Regan said, spitting disgustedly on the floor. "That's bird shit! ... Don't you worry about it. I got the word out to the right people and when they start callin' we'll be gettin' big bucks. ... Maybe two, three hundred for a job. ... You fucking wait and see."

"Well, I ain't fucking seen nothin' yet," Shmytxcyk countered glumly.

The waiter appeared and put the six draughts on the table. He then began removing some of the empty glasses.

"Leave the fucking candles alone, eh," Regan said.

"Sorry," the waiter replied and put the glasses back.

"Pay em for the beer, Jerry."

"Hey, fuck! I paid for the last round," Shmytxcyk complained.

"I don't give a shit. Just pay em."

"I'm always payin'."

"Will ya just fucking pay em."

"Okay, okay," Shmytxcyk said. He pulled some change out of his pocket, counted it and threw it on the waiter's tray. The waiter walked away.

"That's six fucking rounds I paid for. ... You only took two."

Teddy Regan ignored his friend's remark. He turned away and looked around the tavern.

"I'm always payin' double," Shmytxcyk said.

Regan turned back towards Shmytxcyk. "Look at that prick there."

"Where?" Shmytxcyk asked, looking around.

"There," he said, pointing at a young man seated a few tables away.

"Oh yeah ... I see him. So what?"

"He looks like a fucking queer," Regan said.

"Yeah, he does," Shmytxcyk replied.

"What the fuck's he doin' in here? Why don't they stay in their own bars."

"Yeah."

"They're all over the place."

"Yeah."

Teddy Regan drained another glass of beer and slammed it down on the table. "They oughta stay in their own fucking bars."

"Yeah."

"I'd like ta punch him out."

"Yeah, me too."

"Let's punch the fucking shit out of em."

"Okay."

Teddy Regan turned his chair to the side. "Don't make it too fucking obvious. Let's try and make it look like he started it."

82

Shmytxcyk nodded in agreement.

Regan turned in the direction of the man. "Hey, queer!" he shouted.

The young man looked up.

Teddy Regan and Jerry Shmytxcyk began throwing glasses at him.

Chapter Twelve

"I hope you realize how lucky you are that I'm seeing you after your rude behaviour last time, Mr. Kerner," Dr. Lehman said, lying back on his big leather chair.

"Yes, I'm really grateful to you, Doctor," Artie Kerner replied from where he sat on his little chair in the centre of Dr. Lehman's gigantic office.

"You should be grateful," Dr. Lehman said matter-of-factly as he put his legs up on the desk top and crossed them. "I have people breaking my door down to see me. Serious people who want help."

"I realize that and I'm really sorry about the way I left the other day."

"I'll accept your apology and now, just before we begin, let's establish that my new rate for you is $60.00 an hour. Is that agreed?"

"Yes. All right," Kerner replied. He wasn't going to argue. He had to put his faith in the doctor and hope for the best.

"Now," said the doctor, "we were able to establish in our last session that you were a pervert..."

"Wait a minute. I'm not a pervert. I said I was addicted."

"Look, Mr. Kerner, don't start with me, okay? If I want to think that you're a pervert, then I'm entitled to think that you're a pervert. I'm the doctor, not you!"

Kerner nodded and made a conscious effort to say nothing.

"So, as I was saying before you opened your big mouth, I was able to establish, despite all your attempts at concealment, that you had a strange perversion which had to do with some form of addiction. I was also able to establish, if you remember, through some sharp Socratic questioning, that your addiction did not involve drug abuse. Am I right so far, Mr. Kerner?"

"Yes," Kerner said.

The doctor suddenly began spinning himself in his chair like a top. After several seconds he stopped and jumped out of his seat. He walked over to the pond area and seated himself at a table located next to the little thatched-roof hut. Motioning to Kerner, he said, "Perhaps you'd like to join me over here, Mr. Kerner."

Kerner got up and went over to the table. He stretched his legs and looked up at the large, coloured sun umbrella mounted above the table.

"Sit down, please."

Kerner sat.

"Now then, let's begin, shall we?"

Kerner started to relate his problem. "Well, you see ... at one time I had quite a bit of money and I didn't ..."

"You had money?" the doctor snapped. "So big deal, you had money," he said with a sarcastic sneer. "I don't need you to tell me about money. Do you know how much I make in a year?"

"No," Kerner said, beginning to feel strange again and trying to keep calm.

"No, I didn't think you would know. You wouldn't believe it. So I'll tell you. I made three hundred thousand this year. Three hundred biggees; and that's from working only ten months. I take off two months to travel each year. Okay? So don't talk to me about money because I can probably buy and sell you. I'm in everything – real estate, oil, stocks, gold. You name it, I'm into it. I have a finger in every pie. I'm like a bloody financial wizard. I'm like a money-making machine. I'm

85

some kind of genius! Okay, now go on with your problem, Mr. Kerner."

Kerner sat there gape mouthed for a minute, trying to regain his composure. Finally he started again. "I was trying to say that I no longer have any money, which makes it so much harder for me. ..." He paused, hoping the doctor would say something, but he had put his head down on the table top and was now making snoring sounds. "You see," said Kerner, "I'm addicted to buying!"

The doctor shot up in his chair. "To what?" he asked, a sharp ring in his voice.

"To buying. I have to be constantly making a buy," Kerner replied suddenly, feeling as though a weight had been lifted from him. "I know it sounds crazy ..."

The doctor cut him off with a wave of his hand. With his eyes narrowed to razor-thin slits, he hissed, "Are you playing games with me, Kerner?"

"No, I swear, Doctor, I'm not."

"I think you might be making me a bit paranoid again so I'll just tell you now, so as to avoid confusion later, that each incident of paranoia provoked by you will mean a jump in my fee of ten dollars per incident."

"Believe me, Doctor, I'm desperate," Kerner pleaded. "This is no joke. I know it's very unusual but it's ruining me. It's ruining my life. Unless I can make a buy every half hour, or hour, or few hours, depending on how effective my previous buy has been, I begin to go through a very painful withdrawal situation."

Dr. Lehman said nothing and Kerner thought back to how it had all begun. It had started six months before. It just happened one day that he began to feel sick. He was overwhelmed by a prolonged wave of nausea of such force that he felt he was about to die and, at that moment, would have preferred death to a continuation of the sickness. He threw up non-stop for close to fifteen minutes. After that, he began to feel somewhat better, but because of the uncertainty of the original attack, he decided to see his general practitioner, Dr. Bender.

It was while he was sitting in Dr. Bender's waiting room that he began to think about a certain attaché case that he had seen a few days before in Carlisle's Men's Store. Burnished alligator skin with a thick brown cut velvet lining and ten-karat gold clasps. He couldn't get the image of this case out of his mind. He pictured himself driving down to Carlisle's and purchasing it, taking it in his hands and caressing the cold hard skin of the alligator. Suddenly he found himself on his feet.

He could see the case looming in his mind, its dark colour gleaming with richness. At that moment he could even smell it. He had to buy it. He had to buy it immediately. He didn't know why, nor did he care to know. All he knew was that he wanted it and wanted it badly. The more he thought about the purchasing of this item, the better he felt.

He sat down and tried to push the picture of the case out of his mind, but as he suppressed the image, he began to feel tense and nervous. A moment later the nauseous sensation which had originally brought him to that waiting room returned with a vengeance. He doubled over in his chair, then dropped to his knees, praying for relief and hoping he would not vomit on Dr. Bender's carpet.

Again he began to think of the attaché case. It filled his mind as though it was projected on a gigantic Cinemascope screen. He had to buy it. The feeling of nausea was lessening in intensity now. He stood up and walked quickly out of Dr. Bender's office. He would call later and apologize, but now he could think only of getting downtown as fast as he could and making a buy.

He sped down to Sherbrooke Street and, leaving his car in a no-parking zone, ran into Carlisle's. He burst through the door and rushed to the area where he had last seen the case. His eyes scanned the high shelf, passing quickly over the other items stocked there.

The case was gone. Again he was overpowered by a terrible feeling of nausea which threatened to come barrelling up into his throat. Kerner caught the eye of a sales clerk.

"Where's that alligator attaché case I saw in here the other day?" Kerner said to the young man.

"Oh, yes, that was a nice one, wasn't it?" the clerk replied, smiling enthusiastically.

"Yes, it's very nice. Now where is it?" Kerner snapped.

The clerk's face fell sharply. "You mean the one with the gold latches, don't you?"

"Yes," Kerner half-shouted, trying to keep himself erect in spite of the cramps which were contracting his belly.

"That's the one that had the plush brown interior, if I'm guessing right."

"You're guessing right," Kerner said, wanting to bash the sales clerk in the face.

"The one imported from Italy?" the clerk asked, smiling.

Kerner was sure the sales clerk knew what he was going through now and was trying, for some sadistic reason, to prolong his agony. He wanted, at the very least, to insult the clerk but he knew that wouldn't be wise. The clerk would then tell him it had been sold. He tried to force a pleasant smile now.

"I don't know where it's imported from but we're talking about the same case."

"I believe we might still have one," the clerk said.

Kerner felt the pains in his stomach dissipate. He gave the clerk an overly appreciative smile.

The sales clerk looked up at the shelf that Kerner had already scanned. He turned back to Kerner. "I'm afraid we've sold the last one."

Kerner felt the sickness return faster than it had left him a moment before. Again he had the urge to drive a fist into the clerk's face.

"Are you sure you've sold your last one?" he snarled.

"Yes. Yes, I'm sure, sir." The clerk now had a frightened look on his face.

"How do you know you have?"

"I just know, sir. I sold the last one," the young man said nervously, taking a half-step backwards.

"You! You sold it?" Kerner said, advancing towards the frightened clerk.

"I don't know. I'm not sure. Maybe it was someone else. . . .

Yes. Yes, it was another one of the staff. Yes, I remember now. I was out to lunch at the time it was sold and when I came back everyone was talking about how the alligator attaché case had been sold. It was all over the store. I'm trying to remember now who it was that sold it. ... Yes, now it's coming back. Everyone was saying that Larry sold it. Larry Johnston. He's not here now. He sold it. You can ask anyone. I wouldn't have sold it. I liked keeping it around the store. A lot of people wanted to buy it from me but I wouldn't sell it. I kept telling them it's not for sale and they went away. There's no way I could have sold that case. If we get another one, I'll never sell that either except to you."

Kerner was gripping the edge of the showcase. The clerk's voice was an unintelligible drone in his head. The clerk backed away slowly. "Maybe we have another one in the storeroom," he said, now a good twenty-five feet away from Kerner.

Kerner's head snapped up. "You think you do?" he asked, feeling the nausea ease up slightly.

"We might, unless the boss took that one home for himself. He really liked that item," the clerk said, still backing away.

"What the hell is he doing buying from his own store?" Kerner shouted, feeling a tightness spreading throughout his body. "Who the hell does he think he is! The merchandise is for the customers, not for him. What kind of a lousy store is this anyway?" As he finished, Kerner was aware of customers staring at him from all parts of the store. They all seemed to be looking at him strangely but he didn't care. He could see the clerk now sprinting away towards the back of the store, throwing quick frightened glances as he ran.

Suddenly a man whom he recognized to be the store manager approached. "Yes, hello there. Is there some problem, sir?" the manager asked.

"They sold the lousy attaché case," Kerner said, his voice cracking.

"Which one was that?" the manager asked sympathetically, bending over towards Kerner.

"The nice one. The alligator-skin one."

"Oh, yes. Well, just let me check and see if we don't have one in the back."

"Don't waste your time," Kerner said in a choked voice. "Your stupid boss took it home."

The manager blinked almost imperceptibly. "We just might have one left. I'll go and check."

Kerner nodded sullenly as the manager turned and walked off.

He looked around, his eyes wandering from shelf to shelf. He walked over to the section where the men's sweaters were displayed. At the far end of the shelf he spied a beige cashmere one. He moved quickly over to it and picked it up. He ran his hand along the soft material and began to smile. He held the sweater up in front of him to better observe its colouration. He had never seen such a subtle tone of beige, he thought. It was truly beautiful. He looked at the label. *Made in Italy especially for Carlisle's,* it read.

He picked up the price tag. One hundred and ten dollars. He nodded slowly to himself. It wasn't unreasonable. He slung it across his arm and suddenly realized that his symptoms were gone. He felt all better. ...

One hundred and ten dollars. Very reasonable, he thought. Eminently reasonable. He felt great. His face was now one huge grin of pleasure. He was still smiling when the manager returned to tell him that the last attaché case had been sold.

Kerner's stream-of-consciousness recounting of his story was suddenly interrupted by Dr. Lehman.

"Mr. Kerner," he said quietly.

Kerner looked up at the doctor who was now slowly rising above the desk in his chair.

"You're completely bananas."

"I know there is something wrong with me," Kerner said, blushing now with embarrassment.

"Wrong with you!" the doctor half-screamed, giving himself three quick turns in his chair. "You are so fucked up, my friend, that I cannot even begin to comprehend the scope of it all."

90

Kerner was about to protest but, before he could say a word, the doctor continued.

"But don't worry about it. Like I said the other day, we will effect a cure."

"Do you really think there's some hope?"

"Look, my friend, if I could cure the Wasp who was speaking Yiddish, I can cure you."

"The who?"

"The Wasp. Don't you know what a Wasp is?"

"Yes, I do."

"Well, so I had one as a patient. He woke up one morning and went to a board meeting of his company – one of the biggest in Canada. He was about to sign a deal with a multi-million-dollar mining concern from Germany. When it came time for him to speak, he began addressing the Germans in Yiddish. No matter how hard he tried to speak English, he could only talk Yiddish and I mean fluent Yiddish. He spent the entire meeting questioning them about their activities during the war. Then he wanted to know if they gave money to Israel, if they ever did any canvassing for the Combined Jewish Appeal, and so on and so forth.

"Later that same week, he was due to address the Rotary Club, which he did, again speaking entirely in Yiddish.

"A while later he issued a memo in Yiddish to all his company personnel, forty-five hundred people, making Yiddish the official working language of his company in the future.

"He finally, of course, alienated his entire family and all his friends. They forced him, against his will, to come and see me, and I cured him."

Kerner felt a surge of elation. If the crazy doctor could cure that man, then he might have a hope of regaining his senses.

"How did you cure him?" Kerner asked, trying to sound calm.

"That's for me to know and for you to find out or, to put it more plainly, it's none of your fucking business," the doctor snapped back.

"But I just ..." Kerner began.

"What? What?"

"Nothing," Kerner said.

"Right. We're getting off the subject. Let's get back to you and your messhugas, okay? Because from the sound it it, my friend, you're in deep trouble."

"You're right, I am. This damn buying sickness is ruining my life. You can't believe what it's done to me. It just keeps getting worse and worse. If I try to fight it I go through sheer agony. Nausea, cramps, diarrhea, vomiting, nervous tension, splitting headaches, terrible anxiety."

"My heart bleeds for you," the doctor said and pressed a button so that his chair reclined all the way back like a bed.

"Why are you so insulting with me?" Kerner asked, feeling angry.

"Look, don't start with me, okay? You wanted to talk, so talk while you have your chance. If I want to make comments, that's my prerogative. This is my office and I can do whatever I want in here. Okay? So just talk and shut up."

The doctor lay back on his chair and closed his eyes.

Oh God, Kerner said to himself, help me.

"So c'mon. I'm waiting," the doctor said.

"I was saying that I go through agonizing withdrawal whenever I try to control myself from making a buy. ..."

"And I said, 'My heart bleeds for you.' Now go on already," Dr. Lehman mumbled.

"Okay, okay. Don't rush me. I have to think this out."

"*Now* you have to think this out?" Dr. Lehman grunted with his eyes closed.

"Yes, well, I want you to know exactly how this thing is affecting me."

"All right, go on."

"Okay. Let's see ... Right. I've been pulling money out of my business for six months now. I got over-extended. My company has grown quite fast."

"I'm not impressed, Kerner. I finished medical school when I was twenty. Just stick to the facts," the doctor said.

"I'm not trying to impress you. It's part of the story."

The doctor began snoring.

"Anyway, I figured the way the business had been growing I would eventually catch up. I just had to keep buying things. At first it was costing me a hundred to a hundred and fifty dollars a day. Then it went up gradually so I was spending as much as five thousand dollars a week. Even though the business was growing, I couldn't expand fast enough to compensate for the money I was pulling out. I started losing customers. I started paying late to my suppliers so some of them became leery of selling to me in the quantities that I needed, so I lost more customers. It was a vicious circle. I started borrowing from the banks to meet my commitments. Finally, they wouldn't extend me any more credit. Now I'm on the verge of bankruptcy. Any day, any one of three major creditors could force me into bankruptcy. About two months ago I borrowed money from a loan shark. Now he's sending an enforcer after me to put me in the hospital."

"You borrowed money from a shylock?" the doctor said.

"I was buying time. I had to. I began to realize I was sick but I had to have time to figure out what to do about it. I needed time. I also needed money to keep my main creditors off my back for a few months. I was counting on digging up some new business but it didn't work out that way. I still have a few thousand dollars in the bank and a worthless piece of land that I own up North, but this loan shark wants everything I owe him right away. I haven't got it. I'm telling you, Doctor, what I'm going through is a real horror. The thought of being without money to buy terrifies me. I couldn't take it. Thank God I still have my credit cards. If my cash runs out, I'll be able to use them for a while before they cancel them. After that I don't know. I just don't know."

Kerner lowered his head and stared disconsolately at the floor.

"Did you really make an effort to control yourself?" the psychiatrist asked.

"Are you kidding? I tried everything. I tried putting myself to sleep for days using heavy sedation. One time I slept for two and a half days. You wouldn't believe the nightmares I had, and after I finally woke up, I made up for it with a three-thousand-dollar spree. Believe me, I've tried. I've tried everything."

The doctor's chair began to rise slowly. "So let's see," he said as he stopped the chair in an upright position. "To recapitulate, you're a buying addict. It's brought you to the brink of bankruptcy. You've borrowed money from a loan shark and now he's sending a goon after you. Yes, my friend, it sounds like you're in a real jackpot. A real jackpot. ... How do you feel about being chased by a hoodlum who might put you in the hospital, as you put it?"

"It doesn't make me happy!" Kerner replied.

"Is there anything that makes you happy, Mr. Kerner?" the doctor asked sarcastically.

"Just buying."

The doctor nodded slowly. "Something must have brought this all on, Mr. Kerner, wouldn't you say?"

Kerner shrugged.

"Something must have happened around the time that you started acting crazy, wouldn't you say?"

Kerner shrugged again. "I don't recall anything special," he replied.

"What were you doing six months ago, just before all this began?"

"Same as always."

"Which is?"

"I don't know. Like ... you know, working and so on."

"And so on? What does that mean? Do you have a family? Are you married?"

"No."

"How come?" the doctor asked.

"How come I'm not married?"

The doctor nodded.

"I'm not the type. I like to play the field. I can't see settling down with one woman. Not yet anyways."

"Why not?"

"Because I like action."

94

"You mean, pussy?" the doctor said.

"Yes," Kerner nodded.

"You like that old beaver, eh?"

"Yes."

"The old quim, eh, Kerner?"

Kerner nodded.

"And tits. You like tits, Mr. Kerner?"

"Yes, I like tits a lot," Kerner replied. "I just like variety, Doctor. That's why I'm not married."

"Did you ever think about it?"

"About what?" Kerner asked, suddenly feeling tense.

"Don't play games, Kerner. Just remember the fee."

"You mean, did I ever think about getting married?"

"Yes," the doctor replied.

"Not really," Kerner said.

"Mr. Kerner, why are you holding your balls in your hand?" Dr. Lehman asked.

Kerner quickly withdrew his right hand from where it was resting in his lap.

"That's a sign of nervousness, Mr. Kerner. When a man holds his nuts, it's a sign that he's nervous about something," the doctor said, smiling.

"It could also be a sign that his nuts hurt," Kerner replied quickly with a pleased smirk.

"Yes, and if a man's balls are hurting, that's a sign that he's nervous," Dr. Lehman countered with a wicked leer.

"Or a sign that he's been kicked in the balls?" Kerner replied, wishing almost before the words were out that he had not said them.

"Oh, did someone kick you in the balls?" the doctor asked snidely.

"No," Kerner muttered, feeling suddenly angry.

"To tell you the truth, Mr. Kerner, I'd like to kick you there, but I didn't, did I?"

"No," Kerner replied sullenly.

"So why are you holding them?"

"I'm not holding them," Kerner said, raising his hands.

"So why *were* you holding them?"

"I wasn't."

"Kerner, I'm not blind. I know a ball-holder when I see one."

"Okay, so maybe I had my hand there. So what does that mean?"

"Like I said, it showed nervousness on your part. Your hand went to your nuts just as I asked you if you ever considered getting married. Your answer was, 'Not really.' That's not a very definite answer and makes me think you perhaps did at one time consider marriage."

"No, I never did. Like I said, I was enjoying myself too much fucking a different girl every other night."

"I'm not impressed with your cockmanship, Mr. Kerner. Just for the record, I want you to know that I could personally make it with almost every one of my women patients if I was so inclined. Okay? That means I could be scoring as much as ten times a day if I wanted to. Okay? They all want to fuck me, Mr. Kerner. I just want you to know that." The doctor ran his fingers through his hair. "So don't try and impress me."

"I wasn't trying to impress you. I was just telling you why I never considered marriage."

"Okay, okay," Dr. Lehman said, sighing with exasperation.

Suddenly the phone rang.

"Excuse me," Dr. Lehman said and picked up the receiver.

"Hello.... Oh yes, how are you, Mrs. Glintz... uh huh... yes ... yes ... I see ... He does, eh? ... Well, no Mrs. Glintz. I wouldn't say that it means he's a homosexual, maybe a pervert but not necessarily a homo; after all, he wants to do it with you not with a man, right? ... Uh huh ... uh huh ... yes ... Hurt? I can't really say ... no, I don't think I can make that decision for you. It's strictly up to you and your husband ... He wants to use butter? ... You're allergic to butter? ... That's a problem ... I understand. Well, what about cream cheese? ... He wants it only with butter. ... I see, you're allergic to cream cheese as well. ... Hmm. Will he accept any substitute? ... Well, like margarine, for instance? ... Well, explain to him that margarine is healthier than butter. It's much less harmful. ... Sure. ... Of course. ... Sure, I think he'll go for that. ..."

As the doctor continued to speak on the phone, Kerner suddenly thought of Estelle Bercowitz. The memory which he recalled almost in spite of himself was of the day she had said goodbye to him. He saw her in his mind as she stood framed in the doorway of his apartment. He could see the tears in her eyes. He could hear the inflection in her voice. "Goodbye, Arthur," she had said, then turned and went away.

Kerner's thought came back to the present. He glanced up at Dr. Lehman who was still on the phone. As he did so, he suddenly realized that he had lied to the doctor when he said he'd never thought about marriage. He hadn't lied intentionally. For some reason, he had blocked the idea out of his mind.

It had been a while ago. Over six months. At that moment it hit him. He heard Dr. Lehman's question in his mind. *Something must have happened around that time to make you act crazy, wouldn't you say?* Kerner could feel his legs suddenly grow cold. He felt angry. He looked at his watch. He had twenty minutes left. Why was Dr. Lehman wasting his time talking on the phone? He tried to catch the doctor's eye, but he ignored Kerner and continued talking.

"Well, anyways, Mrs. Glintz, those are your options. ... Right. ... Sure, no problem. ... Any time. Just remember to send me a cheque for $25.00 for this consultation. Very good. Goodbye."

Dr. Lehman hung up. "Sorry, Mr. Kerner, it was urgent business."

"It's okay, I didn't mind."

"Don't lie, Mr. Kerner. Of course you minded. You probably felt like telling me to get off the fucking phone, didn't you?"

Kerner shrugged to let the doctor know that he was right.

"Okay. Now let's get back. You were saying?"

Kerner hesitated. He knew exactly what he wanted to talk about but he again felt reluctant to speak.

"You're holding your balls again, Mr. Kerner," the doctor said in a light, lilting voice.

"I was just thinking..."

"Yes?"

"You asked me before if I'd ever thought about getting married."

"Yes?"

"Well, actually, I did once think about it ... very briefly. I mean, there was a girl I liked. ... I met her about a year ago. I remember it very clearly because it was just the day after I'd landed a big contract and I was out celebrating. Anyway, I took her out a few times and I liked her, so I started seeing her quite regularly. But, as I said, I liked variety so even though I was seeing her, I was also seeing several other girls. You know ... three, four, sometimes five others at the same time. But for some reason, I really liked her. There was something about her that appealed to me."

Kerner glanced up at the doctor whose eyes were now closed.

"Anyway, after a few weeks, she told me she wanted me to spend more time with her. I agreed and so instead of sharing my time with her and the other four or five girls, I cut down to seeing her and only two other girls. I mean, the two others varied. They weren't the same all the time. I changed these two others almost every week. Well, this went on for a while, maybe a month or so. Then Estelle, the girl I liked, told me that she wasn't prepared to share my time with any other woman. She told me I would have to concentrate entirely on my relationship with her or she wouldn't see me anymore.

"Well, I thought about it and I said okay. I really liked her. She was the first woman I ever missed if I didn't see her for a few days. But I wasn't really honest with her because I kept seeing at least one other girl at the same time. I couldn't help it. Everything went all right for a while, until I began to feel sort of confined. Trapped. Pretty soon I was seeing two other girls on the side and then three and sometimes four. Estelle started giving me flack again, so I cut down again. I guess I didn't want to lose her, but after a while I started getting angry at her. I started playing around again.

"Estelle told me she wanted to get married. She figured that's what I needed to straighten me out. She said she couldn't take the kind of relationship I was offering her. Either I loved her or I didn't. If I did, I would stop fucking around and marry her. Anyway, I thought about it and finally I said no. I wasn't ready to get married. She said goodbye. I remember when she left I was sure she'd be back, ready to accept me on my terms. But she never came back."

Kerner stopped talking. The doctor was making soft snoring sounds as though he were in a deep sleep.

Kerner now recalled the depression into which he had fallen. A few months after their parting he heard that she had married an accountant from New Jersey. Now, as he sat thinking in Dr. Lehman's office, he realized with startling clarity that it was not long after Estelle left him, perhaps only weeks, that his sickness started.

The doctor stirred in his seat. "Are you leading up to something, Mr. Kerner?"

"Yes. I don't know how important it is, but I just realized that it was right after our break-up that I started this crazy buying thing."

"Ah ha!" the doctor said exultantly. "So you see the connection?"

"Yes, I think I do," Kerner replied.

"You think you do? Either you do or you don't. Now which is it?"

"Yes, I do. Yes, there is a connection."

"Are you saying that just to appease me? I don't like suckholes, Kerner."

"I'm not a suckhole. I really believe there must be a connection."

"Why? Why do you believe that? ... Because I said so?"

"No, I just sort of feel it!"

"Are you sure?"

"Yes."

"How sure?"

"Very sure."

"How sure is very sure?"

"As sure as I can be."

"How sure is that?"

"That's very sure," Kerner replied, taking a deep breath.

"I'm not so sure. How do you know that's very, very sure?"

"I just know."

"How do you know?"

"I just know!"

"But I don't know."

"I know you don't know, but I know."

"So what if you know. I have to know too, Mr. Kerner."

"Why?" Kerner asked.

"No, no," the doctor said, smirking sardonically, "I ask the questions, not you."

"That's fine with me. I'm just trying to make you believe me."

"Okay, okay, I believe you. Yes, I really do, Mr. Kerner. We've made some good progress here today. There's just one other thing I'd like to know before we finish."

"Yes?"

"It's about this great pussy addiction of yours."

"Pussy addiction?" Kerner asked, confused.

"Your great sex drive which you were bragging about a minute ago."

"I wasn't bragging," Kerner protested.

"Just answer the question," Dr. Lehman snapped. "Has your present buying addiction affected your craze for cunt?"

"Well, to tell you the truth, I haven't thought about it very much. I am ... well ... I haven't really been very interested in it lately. But, you know, until now I didn't even give it a second thought. I just haven't been very interested."

"Don't you think that's strange, hm?"

"Yes, I do," Kerner said. It was very strange.

The doctor looked at his watch, then turning towards the door, he cupped his hands to his mouth and shouted, "I'll be with you in two minutes, Mrs. Griff!"

Then, turning back to Kerner, he said, "Well, why don't we end on that note for today, huh?"

Kerner nodded and stood up. The doctor got up as well and walked over to Kerner. He patted him on the back. "Don't worry, Mr. Kerner. You're completely fucked up but I'll cure you."

"Do you really think so?"

"I said so, didn't I?" Dr. Lehman said angrily. "So why are you questioning me?"

"I wasn't questioning you. I just wanted some assurance. I just wanted to hear you say it again."

"Okay, okay. Don't start," Dr. Lehman said with a sullen look on his face. He opened the door to the waiting room and walked out, followed by Kerner. "Hello, Mrs. Griff," the doctor said.

She returned the doctor's greetings as Kerner slipped out into the corridor. Inside he could hear the doctor saying in an angry voice, "That shmuck Kerner. He always argues!"

Kerner walked quickly away.

Chapter Thirteen

It was after eight in the morning when the Hawk left his home, got into his car and began heading for Artie Kerner's apartment. As he drove he tried to draw a mental picture of the man he would soon be confronting but he was unsuccessful.

The file which Morrie Hankleman had sent over the previous evening had listed only the essential facts about the debt itself and nothing about Kerner. It contained nothing about his appearance, his habits, or anything that might have given Solly even a slight insight into Artie Kerner's personality.

In the very early days of his career, when the Hawk was still a novice in the field, everything had been done on sheer nerve. Solly would be given a name. He would immediately go and visit the person and do what had to be done. It was only later that he had begun to be more sophisticated in his operations in an attempt to make things easier and safer for himself.

He realized that it was often useful to find out something concrete about the person he was going to see, and he always tried to do so, even if it meant putting a tail on the individual for a day or two.

One never knew what might turn up through a little prior investigation. Sometimes it was a piece of information which would provide the Hawk with an extra edge and give him the necessary leverage to turn a job over quickly and painlessly.

Along with this procedure of prior investigation, Solly had also begun to use various other methods to help him in his work. The idea of using visual aids to facilitate collections had come to the Hawk after watching an audio-visual demonstration given by a cousin who was in the real estate business. This cousin used a film strip to help sell orange grove acreage in Florida.

"A picture is sometimes worth a thousand words," the cousin had said and Solly had agreed with him.

It was then that he had decided to have his own visual demonstration made up. This consisted of five 8" x 12" photographs which Solly carried around in a leather-bound folder. The photo on the first page showed a man sitting behind a desk with a smile on his face. The caption below the photo read *Before*.

The photo on the second page showed the same man standing beside his desk. It could be clearly observed that the man had only one ear, whereas in the *Before* picture he'd had two. If there were any doubts in the mind of the observer, these were quickly eliminated by picture three which showed Solly and Big Moishie standing next to the desk. Both were grinning and Big Moishie was pointing down at the desk top. A solitary ear on the desk surface was the object of their attention.

On the fourth page was a picture of the same man as seen on page one. This time he was shown to have no ears. The caption below the picture read *After second visit*.

On page five was a photo in which the earless man was seen handing a fistful of currency to Solly the Hawk, who at the same time could be seen handing the man back two ears. The caption below the picture read *Final visit*.

The Hawk smiled to himself as he recalled the effectiveness of these photographs. They had certainly saved him a lot of unnecessary words over the last few years, but, in the final analysis, if the dice were rolling against him, nothing would help him. Neither prior investigation nor pictures nor anything else. A person could never have all the angles figured and an element of uncertainty always existed in the collection business, as it did in life in general.

The Russel Royt collection was a case in point. The Hawk had done a great deal of research prior to making contact. He had found out all about Russel Royt's habits and idiosyncracies. His likes, his dislikes. However, what the Hawk did not know at the time was that Russel Royt owned a trained orang-utan.

During their discussion Royt had suddenly shouted a command which brought the ape bounding out of the kitchen to attack Solly who had then been forced to knock the creature out and to beat up Russel Royt as well.

Yes, the potential for unexpected danger always existed no matter how careful a person was.

Once he had gone to collect from a man who, upon seeing Solly for the first time, immediately began accusing him of having seduced his wife and attacked the Hawk with a two-foot-long electric vibrator. There again, as in the case with the orang-utan, Solly had been forced to knock the man out. All his prior checking had been useless. No matter what a person did, the possibility of violence always existed.

The fact that he had been attacked only seven times in twenty years in the business was sheer luck, Solly thought. What was even more amazing was that in all these years he had never had to initiate the laying on of muscle.

He often wondered what he would have done had he met up with someone who refused to meet his commitment in spite of all threats. Would he have been able to really injure that person without being attacked in advance? Maybe or maybe not. It didn't really matter. The Hawk did not pride himself on being callous or ruthless. The one thing he had always prided himself on was his nerve. He had never been afraid to go up against anyone or anything. That's why he had succeeded in this business.

Now as he pulled his car into the parking area beside the

McGregor House, the Hawk realized that he was looking forward to meeting with Artie Kerner, and the fact that he was going in cold like in the early days made it even more exciting.

He could feel the nervousness in his stomach as he got out of the car. He turned and headed for the front entrance of the McGregor House. He could feel the old excitement rising in his belly. He hadn't felt it that strongly in years and he enjoyed it. It was better this way. It had to be done this way. Just a name and an address. Like in the old days.

The job would be done on sheer nerve. That's the way he had done the first collection and that's the way he would do the last collection.

He pulled open the door and walked into the foyer of the McGregor House.

Chapter Fourteen

Kerner had slept fitfully. Some time around eight in the morning he awoke. He tried to doze off but was unable to. A great feeling of emptiness was threatening to overwhelm him. He sat up in bed and threw a few switches on the console next to him. The room was illuminated.

He let his eyes travel slowly around the room. He got out of bed, aware that his body was rigid. He took a deep breath but he couldn't fill his lungs. He walked over to the wall where he had hung the new lithograph and stared at it. He could feel his body begin to shake and he tried to steady himself. An image of the girl he had been with during the night came into his mind. He winced and tried to push the empty feeling out of his body. He began to shiver.

He looked at the bare section of wall directly beside the lithograph. As he stared at it, he could feel the beginnings of nausea stirring in his stomach and chest. His head began to throb. Again he thought of the girl and winced painfully.

He went into the living room and looked around. His eyes took in the entire room and then went slowly from object to object. He observed each item of hand-crafted furniture, every piece of sculpting, each lamp and vase, every painting, the two large tapestries. He felt no relief. The pain in his head was now almost unbearable and he knew he was about to throw up.

He ran to the bathroom and leaned over the toilet bowl, trying desperately to control himself. The nausea dissipated but Kerner knew it was only temporary. He washed his face with cold water then swallowed two 292s.

He turned and stood in the doorway of the bathroom. The blank space on the wall beside his newest possession glared out at him. He could feel the heaves coming. He sat down on the edge of the bathtub beside the toilet bowl and rested his head in his hands. Again he thought of the girl who had been with him during the night.

What did I do to deserve this? Kerner wondered as tears began to flow from his eyes. He had never hurt anyone. Why couldn't someone help him? Why couldn't Dr. Lehman help him? He felt a sudden surge of anger for the doctor.

He looked up at the blank patch of wall. He had to fill it. He knew exactly what had to go there. It had to be another lithograph by the same artist. A mate for the one he had purchased the previous day. Kerner's heart began pounding. He pressed his elbows down on his knees to try to stop the tremors in his arms.

He glanced at his watch. The stores wouldn't be open for another hour and a half. He pictured himself in the store taking possession of the work. His heart was pounding. He glanced up at the wall. He wanted the blank space filled now! He cursed the art dealer aloud. Why did they have to open so late? Some stores were ready to do business at eight-thirty. But those bastards had to open at ten. Arrogant sons of bitches. He tried not to think about the litho, but in spite of his efforts his eyes were inexorably drawn to the wall. He could feel the wave of sickness coming. He turned and threw himself towards the toilet. On his hands and knees in front of the bowl and gripping the edges with both hands, he began to heave. He prayed for relief.

Again the wave of nausea was momentarily dissipated. He leaned his head down on the edge of the toilet bowl. He looked at his watch again. Why did the time pass so slowly? Maybe today Walton's gallery would open early. He stood up slowly, dragged himself into the bedroom and began dressing as quickly as he could. As he dressed he tried to keep his eyes averted from the wall. He threw on his jacket and headed out of the bedroom.

Suddenly there was a knock on the door. Kerner froze and held his breath. The knock came again. Kerner exhaled as slowly and quietly as he could.

Who could it be? he wondered. There was nothing in the sound to tell him anything about the person outside the door. It was a neutral knock. Three evenly spaced raps, neither aggressive nor meek sounding. Kerner had to get out. He couldn't stand there any longer.

Once again the knocks sounded.

"Yes?" Kerner said, trying to inject a light tone into his voice.

"Mr. Kerner?" the voice said.

Kerner hesitated for a moment. He didn't recognize the voice. "Yes. Who's there?" he said, moving towards the door on tiptoe.

"My name is Weisskopf – Solly Weisskopf."

Kerner went rigid against the door. Oh, no! It was Hankleman's goon. The psychopath, the killer! His body frozen, Kerner's mind groped desperately for some answer that would make Solly Weisskopf go away.

"I was asked ta come down an see you by a certain person about a madder of some money."

"Oh. I see. ... Yes. ... Well, I'm sorry but I can't discuss money matters with you today, Mr. Weisskopf."

"No? How come?" the Hawk asked.

"Well. ... I'm quite ill actually."

"Oh yeah? What's de matter?"

"It looks like I've come down with something quite bad," Kerner replied.

"Yeah? Like what f'rinstance?"

"It could be a rare form of leprosy."

"Leprosy? No kidding. I tot you could only pick dat up in de hot climates."

"Yes. Yes. That's quite true," Kerner replied hastily.

"So where d'ya tink ya got it?"

"I'm not sure."

"You were in Africa?" the Hawk asked.

"Yes, that's right. I was there on a buying trip. I must have gotten it there."

"I was in Africa once. I found it very hot dere. It's not fer me."

"I agree. I like a more temperate climate too."

"Yeah," the Hawk said, and then added, "Anyway, I'd like ta come in an talk wid you."

"Well. ... I really don't think you should, considering what I think I have."

"It doesn bodder me. I'm not worried about leprosy."

"You should be. It's quite contagious, you know."

"Yeah, but only from touching, an I don wanna touch. I only wanna talk."

"Oh, you don't have to touch?"

"No. Why should I have to touch?"

"You shouldn't. I just thought..." Kerner stopped himself in mid-sentence.

"So can I come in?"

"Well, what exactly is it you want to discuss?"

"Like I said, it's about de money dat you owe to a certain Mr. Hankleman."

"Right. Right. Uh huh. Yes. Well. Actually, the other thing is I can't discuss money matters with you today, Mr. Weisskopf."

"Why not?"

"Well, you see, I happen to be an orthodox Jew and we're not allowed to discuss money on the Sabbath. As a matter of fact, I was in the middle of my morning prayers when you knocked. I'm actually not allowed to do anything on the Sabbath. I'm not even allowed to brush my teeth or comb my hair or open or close a light switch or anything. I can't even go to the bathroom till after sundown."

"No shit?" the Hawk exclaimed, feigning surprise.

"Yes, and no piss either," Kerner replied.

"Isn't dat someting," the Hawk said. "I haven't talked to an ortidox Jew in a long time. My fadder was ortidox also. A very religious man; which is why he trew me outa da house when I wanted to join de army. He also did what you do. He wouldn do nutting but read de Bible on de Sabbit."

"Of course. That's what I was just about to do before you knocked. I actually shouldn't even be talking to you. ..."

The Hawk let Kerner finish and then continued. "De only difference is dat fer my fadder, de Sabbit was on Saturday, an fer you it's Wensday."

Kerner felt his legs buckling under him. "Isn't it Saturday today?"

"Today it's Wensday," the Hawk replied.

Kerner leaned against the door. He had thought for sure that it was Saturday. He was so involved with his buying problem and his psychiatrist that he was now losing track of the days. What would be next? he wondered.

"I was sure it was Saturday. It looks like I did all that praying for nothing."

"Well, it couldn't hurt."

Kerner knew he had to get out of the apartment even if it meant taking a beating. Maybe the psychopath outside the door would take it easier on him if he could establish some rapport with him before opening the door. The fact that they were both Jews was something positive. That was a good angle. He would try playing that up.

"So your father was orthodox?" Kerner said.

"Yes, he was very religious. He was actually a rabbi."

"Oh, wonderful," Kerner replied, feeling much better. Certainly a rabbi's son couldn't be all that vicious. "So I guess you must be religious too, then."

"Me? Naw. De only time I go ta Shul is on Yom Kippur so I can ask ta be forgiven for alla de sins which I committed dooring de year."

Kerner felt his heart suddenly pop into his mouth and lodge there like a large rock.

110

"Well, anyways, it's always nice talking to another Jew, but you'll have to excuse me now, Mr. Weisskopf, so I can get back into bed. My doctor told me that lots of rest is the best thing for leprosy."

"He didn't tell you to drink lots of fluid?" the Hawk asked.

"Yes, that too. As a matter of fact, I think I had better take a drink right now. Why don't you call me tomorrow at the office. Okay?"

Kerner pressed his ear against the door. He couldn't hear anything. He began to ease away from the door on tiptoe.

"Mr. Kerner," the Hawk said suddenly.

Kerner froze again. "Yes," he replied.

"You're a religious man, so you must know some of the famous old Jewish sayings which have come down to us troo de ages. Right?"

"Well, yes ... some. I mean, there are some I forget."

"Well, maybe you know dis one. It says dat a nail can't stay lost in a sack. Eventually it's gotta come out. If not today, den tomorrow. D'ya know dat one?" the Hawk said, smiling to himself.

"Yes, I think I've heard that one," Kerner said, his voice cracking.

"It's a good one, eh?"

"Yes." Kerner's voice was choked to a whisper.

"I tink our forefadders were smart, Mr. Kerner. Dey made up like a lotta smart sayings. Anudder one I remember is, 'It's easier to get in den to get out.'"

Kerner could feel his legs giving out under him. What did the psychopath mean by that? Kerner wondered in a sudden panic. He must know. Somehow he knew about his buying sickness. He knew that he had to get out and get down to the art gallery. He'll stay here all day and torture me. The more Kerner thought about this, the greater was his urge to get out. He knew he had to get out of the apartment soon or he would crack.

What could this man Weisskopf do to him? Beat him up? How badly? A broken arm? A broken leg? A broken jaw? All three?!

Kerner could feel himself cringing. He tried to steel himself. He had to take his chances with the goon. Even a completely broken body would be better than to continue feeling the way he felt at that moment. Anything was better than that. If the pain and nausea went on much longer, he would go into a state of shock. He prayed that Weisskopf wouldn't punch him in the stomach. He'd take a broken jaw any day before that.

He reached for the dead bolt, but as he did so something told him to hold on just a bit longer. Maybe, just maybe, if he could force himself to make one last effort, he might be successful in persuading the man to leave.

He withdrew his hand from the lock. With his head lowered and his eyes closed, he summoned up all his will power in an effort to control himself. If he was smart he would stay on the same verbal wavelength as the goon. It might be wise if he now used an aphorism of his own to convince the man to desist. He searched his mind for the appropriate saying.

"I don't want to seem rude, Mr. Weisskopf, but this is the worst possible time for me to discuss this with you. As a matter of fact, to quote an old Jewish expression... you sort of caught me standing on one leg."

"Well, you shouldn't complain because like de old Rumanian saying goes: One leg is better den none."

Kerner's blood curdled. "I thought the expression was: Two heads are better than one."

"Dats a different one, Mr. Kerner. Deres anudder one also dats very similar: One head is better den no head. I tink dats also an old Jewish one."

"It sounds like it."

"Wouldn't you agree wid dat one, Mr. Kerner?"

"Yes, definitely. It makes sense," Kerner replied quickly, biting on his knuckles.

"And one head an two legs is better den one head an only one leg. No?"

"Yes, yes. That's true. That's logical all right." Kerner felt his eyes popping in their sockets.

"An one head an one leg an two arms is better den one head one leg an one arm. ... Right?" the Hawk asked.

"Right," Kerner replied. "Is that an old Jewish one as well?"

"I tink so but I'm not sure. It could be Ukrainian."

"I see."

"An would you not agree dat one leg an one arm is better den one head, no legs an one arm?"

"I would agree."

"An dat one head, one leg an one arm is better den no head, one leg an two arms?"

"Yes. Definitely, yes. I couldn't say no to that."

"You sound like you have a good head on your shoulders, Mr. Kerner, so lemmie ask you dis. ... Which is better – one head, two legs, one broken arm an one good arm, or ... one head, two legs, one good arm, one broken arm an only one ear?"

"That's a tough one," Kerner said, pondering the problem. "Let me mull that over for a moment or two."

"Don take too long on it, Mr. Kerner. Like dey say ... time flies."

"Give me a chance, eh! This is a toughie."

"I don see why you're making it so hard for me, Mr. Kerner. De way you're acting you would tink I was asking for an arm an a leg."

"You're not?! ... I mean ... well, look ... I don't see why I should have to let you in. This is my apartment. As far as I'm concerned, we can talk like this ... through the door."

"Sometimes when you talk troo a closed door whatever is said goes in one ear an out de udder," the Hawk said.

Kerner couldn't think of a reply.

"Are you there, Mr. Kerner?"

"Yes, I'm here."

Kerner decided on a last desperate gambit. He would try to make the goon leave by taking an offensive posture. He would attempt an indignant and outraged approach. Maybe this might succeed where meekness had failed. If threats failed to drive the man away and he was forced to let him in, what could he lose? The punishment would probably not be any worse than if he allowed him in at that very moment. He decided to go for broke.

"Look, who the hell do you think you are, anyway? Eh? I mean, who do you think you are? What is this! Coming up here and threatening me! I mean ... as far as I'm concerned, you're a criminal. I could have you prosecuted. There are laws against this kind of thing, you know!"

Kerner waited for a response which he expected would be immediate one way or the other. For several seconds there was silence. Then:

"Mr. Kerner," the Hawk said, "I would like to suggest dat before calling me a criminal you should take de bean out from your own eyes."

"It's not a bean ... it's a beam."

"A beam?"

"Yes, a beam."

"If you had a beam in your eye, I doubt if you could take it out by yourself. I doubt if you would need to even have it removed."

"It's not a beam, like a two by four."

"No?"

"No."

"So whad is it?"

"I think it means a small particle or a piece of dust or something like that."

"Hmm. Live and learn. An I always tot it was a bean. ... Mind you, not a big bean like a lima bean or a kidney bean but ... you know, like a liddle bean. Of course, I always wondered how someone could get even a liddle bean stuck in dere eye. A pea, a very small pea ... maybe ... like from a peashooter ... but in dose days dey didn't have peashooters."

Kerner detected a conciliatory note in the man's voice. Perhaps his show of outrage had made a dent in the man's psychic defenses. Perhaps now if he said the right thing it might be possible to force the man into having a sudden in-

114

sight into the shallowness of his line of work. If he could achieve that, then it was possible that the man might have a change of heart and leave him in peace.

"Don't you find this kind of job somewhat unsatisfying?"

"Unsatisfying? No. Why should it be?"

"Well. I mean. After all ... look what you have to do."

"Well, I don wish to get involved in a philosophical discussion wid you, Mr. Kerner, but to me it's a job. You understand. It's a way of making a living. It's better den being on unemployment, an like dey say, a bird in de hand is wert two in a bush."

"It depends what kind of bird," Kerner replied cockily.

"Yes, dats true. It depends on what kind of bird. A dead bird in de hand isn't wert much."

Kerner felt his face contort into a sick grimace. Was the man threatening to kill him? No! That couldn't be. Dead men didn't repay debts. Still, just hearing the words made him tremble.

"Deres anudder old saying... dat a half of a bird in a bush is wert more den five in a hand if de hand is not connected to an arm. Would you not agree?"

"Yes," Kerner replied, happy that the subject had returned from talk of death to simple physical maiming.

"In fact," the Hawk went on, "a dead bird in a bush is wert more dan five dead birds in a hand wid all de fingers broken."

"That makes sense. That sounds like an old Jewish one."

"No, dats Polish," the Hawk said.

"Oh, I see," Kerner replied hesitantly.

There was a long silence which was finally broken by the Hawk. "So where do we stand, Mr. Kerner?"

"Stand? Well, to repeat what I first told you, I'm still more or less standing here on one leg."

"Well, den maybe it would be easier for you an your leg if you put your ass on de table ... or maybe you tink you have enough on your plate already?"

"I have more than enough on my plate, without putting my

ass on it as well," Kerner replied.

"I'm not asking you to put your ass on your plate, just on de table, Mr. Kerner."

"I don't know if that will accomplish anything at this point," Kerner said.

"You never know. ... Maybe it will give you some food fer tot," the Hawk replied.

"Food for what?"

"For tot," the Hawk said.

"Tot?"

"Yeah, tot."

"What's tot?"

"Tot, tot," the Hawk said.

"How do you spell that?" Kerner asked, puzzled.

"Tot! T-h-o-u-g-h-t ... tot!" the Hawk said emphatically.

"Oh! Tot!" Kerner exclaimed, realizing he had made an error.

"Dats right, tot," the Hawk said.

"That's what I tot you meant," Kerner replied.

"Just remember dis, Mr. Kerner, as the old Jewish saying goes: As much as you have on your plate, you still can't eat wid someone else's teet."

Kerner's resolve broke. He knew he had to get it over with one way or the other. He had to get out.

Kerner turned the dead bolt and opened the door. As he did, he was almost afraid to look at what he was certain would be a hard, vicious face. He pulled the door open all the way and forced himself to look up. He was surprised by the appearance of the man standing before him. Instead of a gigantic, wrestler-type goon with a heavily scarred and punched-up face, he saw a thin, well-dressed man of about average height, with a slightly scarred and punched-up face.

Solly the Hawk smiled wryly at Kerner. "I won't keep you long as I know you're a sick man."

"Well, actually, I may not be as sick as all that. They're not quite sure what it is. They'll have a better idea after they get the results back from the lab."

The Hawk nodded noncommittally. "Can I come in?"

"Yes, come on in."

The Hawk entered and was surprised as he observed the apartment's interior. He knew that something was very wrong somewhere. One quick glance into the living room told him that. In an instant he had evaluated the contents of the room and he knew without any doubt that they were worth at least fifty thousand dollars. The Hawk didn't know what to think.

Kerner, meanwhile, was observing the Hawk's face, waiting anxiously to see how he would react to the total effect of that one room.

Solly, however, as taken aback as he was, allowed no emotion to register on his face. After a moment, he turned slowly and looked directly at Kerner. "Is dis your place?" he asked in a soft, matter-of-fact voice.

The thought of saying no flashed through Artie Kerner's mind. But then he thought, *What's the use of lying?* Even if he talked his way out of this situation at that point, he would only succeed in putting things off for a day or two. One way or the other, Morrie Hankleman would find out about his possessions. Then lying wouldn't help him. More importantly, he knew he had to get out of there soon, before he passed out or went mad from his sickness. He might as well get it over with as fast as possible. Maybe he would be really lucky and somehow avoid a physical assault.

Of course, it was more likely that he would be unlucky and have his face bashed in. In that event, Kerner thought, it might be a good idea to repeat a few key Hebrew prayers. This might remind the goon of his rabbi-father and induce the man to go easy on him. Then again, if he only went to synagogue on the High Holy Days, as he had said, it was possible he was anti-religious. Maybe he even disliked his father. Then the prayers would only make things worse. Kerner felt his mind spinning out of control.

"So is dis your place?" the Hawk repeated.

"Yes. Yes, it's my place," Kerner replied, watching the Hawk's face closely.

The cramps in his stomach were now making it difficult for him to stand erect. He tried to straighten himself out and succeeded only partially.

"You don look so good, Mr. Kerner. Maybe you should sit down," Solly said, his face impassive.

"No, I'm fine."

The Hawk nodded his head slowly several times. Then he pursed his lips, stared around the room again and turned back to Artie Kerner. "Anyway, so you know why I'm here, eh?"

"Yes, you said you were representing Mr. Hankleman."

"Dats a nice way of putting it," Solly said, smiling broadly. "Usually dey don say it so nice like you jus said it."

Kerner was happy to see the sudden good-natured grin on the Hawk's face. If he can smile like that, he must have empathy, Kerner thought. Maybe if he limped around the room as though he were crippled, the man would feel sorry for him and not hit him too hard.

He could limp around and, at the same time, perhaps even hold one of his arms in such a way as to give the impression that it was paralyzed. At least that might save an attack on those two limbs. But what about the other arm and the other leg, and his jaw? Maybe he could make his jaw crooked or, better still, start talking funny as though he had a speech impediment. That still left one good arm and one good leg. He could hold both arms funny, as though they were paralyzed or at least semi-paralyzed. That still left one leg available for punishment. The only solution was to walk around on his knees. He could stumble around like that, holding both of his arms crooked and talking funny. That would cover his arms, legs and face, but would leave the stomach as open territory. Maybe he could retch at the same time to show that he had stomach trouble. There was no way he could take a shot in the stomach. The mere thought of it made him break out in a cold sweat.

Again he felt his mind spinning out of control. He felt dizzy. He had to get out and down to the gallery. The Hawk's voice suddenly broke into his thoughts.

"Someting doesn exactly figger here, Mr. Kerner," the Hawk said and paused, waiting for a reply. Kerner remained silent. "Like, fer instance, I see over dere like near dat liddle table what looks to be a piece of sculpting from Hans Klepper ... which I would estimate is wert maybe two ... tree gees. Am I right?"

Kerner nodded, more than a little surprised at Solly the Hawk's accurate appraisal of the object.

"Also," the Hawk continued in a slow, nonchalant voice, "I see next to it on de wall what looks like a limited edition print by Chagall which, at t'day's prices, goes for maybe fifteen, sixteen hunnert. ... Also, I see anudder sculpting ... de bronze one dere ... what looks like it's by Bruno Martinelli, which should not have cost you more den two gees. Also, I see dat small green statuette on de marble table dere which looks like jade, which means by de size alone, if it's good-quality jade which from here is hard to tell, but I tink it is by de deep colour, although I could be wrong which I don tink I am, dat it's wert maybe two gees. Also, I see lots of udder stuff which I won bodder to mention."

Kerner stared at the Hawk.

"Like I would figger dat you got here in dis room alone fifty tousand wert of stuff ... which makes me wonder why you're like trying ta stiff my client."

"I'm not trying to stiff him," Kerner protested.

"So why don't ya pay em?"

"I can't pay him right at this moment."

"Why not?" the Hawk asked, cocking his head slightly.

"I just don't have the money right now. But I told him I'd pay him in a few weeks."

The Hawk's eyebrows went up in whimsical manner. Kerner watched Solly's face.

"Are you going to beat me up?" Kerner asked in a hesitant voice.

"Whaat?" the Hawk replied, blinking with surprise. This was the first time in all his experience that someone had asked him that question.

"I just asked if you were going to ..." Kerner grinned sheepishly, "... you know... if you were going to lean on me, as they say."

"As who says?" the Hawk asked, unable to keep the astonishment from his voice.

"I don't know ... I just thought, from what Morrie Hankleman said to me in my office the other day, that you were going to ... you know... sort of force me to pay up."

"Hankleman said dat?" the Hawk asked angrily.

Kerner nodded. "Yes, he said you were going to put me in the hospital."

The Hawk was suddenly fuming inside. Where did this Hankleman get off? he wondered. Who was he to make threats on Solly Weisskopf's behalf. That was something only he himself had the right to do! No one had ever dared to do that before. Hankleman wasn't even supposed to have had any contact with Artie Kerner. Big Moishie was right about that Hankleman. He was a mooch and he definitely could not be trusted.

"When did Mr. Hankleman tell you dat?" Solly asked, trying to retain an appearance of calmness.

"The day before yesterday."

The Hawk nodded several times. Kerner watched as the Hawk's eyes narrowed.

"I don lean on nobody ... unless dey start wid me. You know whad I mean, kid?"

Kerner nodded. "I think so. I'm not exactly sure, but I think so," he said quickly.

Kerner didn't know what to think. Maybe the man was telling the truth. Maybe he wasn't a ruthless psychopath as Morrie Hankleman had said he was. The man's face, in fact, suggested perhaps the opposite of cruelty. No, he didn't look mean. He had the features of a big angry bird but now, as he observed the two little black eyes that stared out at him from between the thin slitted eyelids, Kerner sensed a certain softness in them.

"Anyway, you can take my word for it. I'm not here ta

120

muscle you. I'm here ta find out why you don wanna pay back Hankleman; so if you got a story, kid, like lemmie hear it already."

Kerner hesitated. What could he possibly say that would be in any way acceptable.

"I mean, deres no doubt you could come up wid de scratch by hocking a few items from here," the Hawk said, making a sweeping gesture with an arm.

"Well … I wish it were as easy as that," Kerner replied.

"No? … It's not?"

Kerner shook his head and then shrugged. Who but a crazy psychiatrist like Dr. Lehman would possibly believe him. Even if this man did believe him, what good would it do? He didn't care about Artie Kerner and his problems. All he cared about was getting the money he had come for. He must have heard thousands of hard-luck stories, each one more pitiful than the next, and for sure had never been affected by any of them. Men like this Weisskopf couldn't afford to feel empathy or compassion, Kerner thought. It was their business to be hard. Kerner figured that he'd best say nothing. However, he knew that their meeting had to be concluded very quickly, one way or the other, because he couldn't take the pressure very much longer. He was on the verge of losing all control.

"Like I don unnerstan," the Hawk said. "What's de problem? You don own dis stuff here?" He gestured about the room again.

Kerner nodded reluctantly. "Yes … I own it."

"So what's de big problem?"

"It's not a big problem. I just can't sell it."

"Why not?"

Kerner felt panic pushing behind him. He had to get out. He couldn't take it anymore. A picture of the blank bedroom-wall space kept flashing through his mind.

"I just can't," Kerner protested, glancing at the door.

"Look," the Hawk said quietly. "You got a fortune of stuff in here. You probly got even more in dere. Right?" The Hawk pointed towards the bedroom.

Kerner nodded. Suddenly the events of the preceding night came into his mind again. His stomach started churning wildly.

"So like talk ta me, kid. Tell me why you can't sell some of dis stuff."

"I just can't," Kerner said, trying to get a grip on himself. He glanced furtively at the door.

The Hawk noticed Kerner's nervousness and the sickly appearance of his face. That was normal for this kind of situation but there were other signs which were abnormal. Usually he would get a hard-luck story poured out without any encouragement. Kerner was the opposite. He didn't have the usual bullshit patter and he didn't have the face of a mooch. He didn't even seem scared in the normal way. The Hawk couldn't figure it.

"Lissen, kid. You gotta gimmie a reason if you say you can't sell dis stuff."

"I can't give you a reason."

"You mean, you jus don wanna sell it, right?"

"I can't! Believe me, I can't!" Kerner half-shouted.

The Hawk watched as Kerner put a hand to his stomach, as though in pain.

"Look, I have to get out of here. If you have to beat me up, could you please do it right away?"

"Whatsa matter wid you, kid? Are you nuts or someting?" the Hawk said in amazement. "I told you I'm not gonna do nutting ta you. I jus wanna know why you can't sell some of dis chazerai here. Level wid me, kid. We'll work someting out. You'll see. I'll get you top dollar fer dis stuff. I got good connections."

"I've got to make a buy!" Kerner yelled, moving towards the door.

"What? What did ya say?" the Hawk shouted, making no move to stop Kerner.

"I have to go right now. If you want to hit me, hit me, but I have to go. I'll be back. I'm not trying to get away," Kerner said, the words spilling out of him as he yanked the door open and headed along the corridor.

Solly went out after him, shutting the door. He trotted along the corridor behind Kerner who was moving quickly towards the elevator.

Kerner reached the elevator and pressed the down button. He leaned against the wall for support. The Hawk came up beside him.

"What d'you mean ya hafta make a buy? You're a junkie?"

Kerner shook his head. "No, not with drugs."

"So what is it?" Solly asked as the elevator doors opened.

Kerner rushed in, followed by the Hawk.

"You won't believe me," Kerner said, trying to catch his breath.

"I'll believe you, kid. What is it?"

"I have to buy."

"Buy what?"

"Just buy. Anything. Things. Anything. Jewellery, clothes, artwork, furniture. Anything that looks nice. Anything that won't melt."

The Hawk looked at the pain on Kerner's face and could see that it was real. He had never heard of anything like this but somehow he knew the man wasn't lying. There was a desperate gleam in his eyes. It was the same look that Solly had seen over the years on the faces of certain gamblers who were at the end of their rope.

"Dats where you're running now? To buy someting?" the Hawk asked.

"Yes, I have to make a buy. I swear I'm not conning you. You can come with me. Then you can come back with me to my apartment and beat me up if you still want to."

"Look, enough already wid de beating up. Okay? Dat fucking Hankleman's got a too-big mout on em."

The elevator doors opened and Kerner headed quickly across the garage towards his car. The Hawk followed close behind. Kerner reached his car, ripped the door open and jumped inside. Solly got in the other side. Kerner peeled away towards the garage exit, hardly waiting for the Hawk to close his door. They shot out into the daylight.

The Hawk looked over at Kerner who was hunched over the wheel and driving with frantic concentration. He'd had a feeling that the last collection might be a strange one. The way it was developing now, there was no doubt it would be. Who had ever heard of such a thing? It was crazy. Still, anything was possible. Some people were addicted to alcohol, some to gambling, some to eating. So why not to buying? Anything was possible in this crazy world, he thought.

The Hawk buckled on his safety belt and settled back in the seat. The car hurtled along the road towards downtown.

Chapter Fifteen

Teddy Regan and Jerry Shmytxcyk were driving along Dorchester Boulevard. Regan was behind the wheel. Shmytxcyk was staring at the knuckles of his right hand which were scraped and bleeding.

"I handled that one pretty good, eh, Teddy?"

"Yeah," Regan muttered morosely.

"I did that one all by myself. You didn't fucking help me at all."

Regan said nothing.

"And I set it up, too. ... Fuck! That's four in a row that I got us."

Regan said nothing.

"Christ. I oughta get more than half. I oughta get sixty percent."

Regan made no reply. His eyes remained fixed on the road.

"Christ! You ain't lined up a job in months. ... When are you gonna get us some work? Eh?"

"Don't you fucking worry about it. Any one of these days I'll get us something big. Not one of your fifty-dollar jobs."

"Yeah. I'll believe that when I see it."

"You'll fucking see it."

"Well, don't take all year about it, eh," Jerry Shmytxcyk said snidely.

"Just fuck off, eh, Jerry."

Jerry Shmytxcyk rubbed his bleeding knuckles and smiled.

Chapter Sixteen

Artie Kerner sat in Dr. Lehman's waiting room, feeling as though he were split in two. When he thought about his encounter with Solly Weisskopf, he felt happy. He had really expected to be beaten to a pulp by that Mr. Weisskopf. In fact, the exact opposite had happened. The man hadn't even threatened him, let alone beaten him. He had been very understanding. He had really believed him! And it was possible that he may have even felt sorry for him.

Solly Weisskopf had left him on an up note. For some reason, Kerner now felt hopeful. Before parting, Weisskopf had suggested ... no, more than that ... he had almost promised that something would be worked out. Yes, he was hopeful, something he had not been for many months. Maybe with a bit of luck he'd be able to beat his sickness, pay off Hankleman, and get his business back on its feet. He needed some luck. He prayed that his creditors wouldn't pressure him into bankruptcy. If only he could make one substantial sale to keep going for another few weeks.

While he was thinking these things, another part of his mind was grinding dully on the events of the evening which had preceded Solly Weisskopf's visit. He didn't want to think about that but he couldn't help it. He kept seeing flashes of the evening and the girl, and although he angled these thoughts off to a corner, he couldn't avoid their effects. A chill passed through him and he shuddered.

He looked at his watch. The doctor should be through in a few minutes. Kerner got up and tiptoed to the office door. He eased himself forward and placed his ear against the door panel.

"Kerner, get away from the fucking door!" the doctor screamed from inside the office.

Kerner raced back to his seat.

Chapter Seventeen

"An even more ... dis is really amazing ... if he tries to sell anyting, he right away has ta run out an buy twice as much as what he sold."

Big Moishie sat hunched in his seat listening to Solly the Hawk with a look of disbelief on his face. "It sounds too crazy to be a lie," the big man said, shaking his head.

The Hawk nodded vigorously. "Yeah, yeah. Anyway, I say to him at one point dat he could save himself like a lotta scratch if he bought wholesale. So whad does he tell me? He tells me, 'No! Wholesale is no good and a store sale is no good.' Like dere not for him. Why? Because he found out dat whenever he bought someting wholesale or if he got like a bargain somewhere, den de effect didn las long. He had to pay top dollar to get de maximum effect. Also, de more wertless an item is, de better de effect. Like a two-hunnert-dollar piece of decorative glass which stands an does nutting is like wert more den a five-hundred-dollar coat."

"Incredible ... incredible," Big Moishie said, shaking his head.

The Hawk gestured with his hands as though reluctantly having to agree with his partner.

"Anyway, so I go wid de kid to where he's running. We

come ta Walton's Art Gallery. On de way he picks up a nice speeding ticket. We go inta de gallry. He's running ta get a special litagraph which he saw dere like de day before. So, anyway, we go inside. He's running. I'm walking. Right away he rushes to de manager. He's like shaking, he's so nervous. 'Where's de picture?' he asks him. He says, 'I'm jus now showing it to Mrs. Jerkoff.' De kid goes like apeshit. He runs over ta dis liddle ole lady dats looking at de picture what he wants. 'I'm buying dat picture, lady,' he tells her. She says, 'I wanna buy it.' She's a liddle ole dame, maybe seventy years old. He says, 'I saw it de udder day an it's mine.' She says, 'I saw it first an it's mine.'

"Now dis perticler picture isn wert a piece a shit but dey boat wan it like it's gold. It sells fer a hundred an eighty-five an it's not wert a double sawbuck. But dey wan it. So dey argue back an fort, back an fort. 'I'm buying it!' 'No, I'm buying it!' 'No, I'm buying it!' Back an fort, back an fort. Meanwhile, de owner is watching wid a big smile on his face, like he jus farted in a crowded subway. Finely he tells dem, 'Look, why don't you bid fer it.' Dey boat right away agree. De kid puts in a bid of two bills. She says two an a half. He goes ta tree. She comes back wid tree twenny-five. De kid doesn fuck aroun. Right away he goes ta four bills. De ole dame is starting ta fold. She tinks fer a minute an den makes a counter of four twenny-five. He goes ta four an a half. De ole dame folds. She trows a few anti-Semitic insults an fucks off. De kid peels off four an a half yards, dey wrap de picture which I lug out fer him because he's so excited he can hardly stand up, an we fuck off."

Big Moishie dragged on his cigar and stared out across the office, shaking his head slowly and deliberately. "He's a strange kid," he said, exhaling a thin stream of cigar smoke.

"Yeah, he's a strange kid, Moishie, but he's like a nice kid. Very nice manners. Polite. You know whad I mean?"

Big Moishie nodded. "So how did you leave it?"

"I left it like ... open," the Hawk replied.

"So then, what do you intend to do?"

The Hawk shrugged. "I dunno."

130

"What do you mean, you don't know?"

"I dunno. ... Like ... wid reference to what we talked about yesterday, maybe I ... Ah! I dunno. Like I jus don have de heart ta pressure dis kid. It bodders me ta tell you but like I feel sorry fer him."

Big Moishie nodded again. "Look, Solly, I don't have to tell you that I don't like this Hankleman. I mean, I can't stand his guts. You know?"

"Yeah, I know."

"So if you want to call this deal off, it's okay with me. We can tell Hankleman that we don't want his business and let him go fuck himself."

The Hawk shrugged.

"What? What is it?"

"Ah, I dunno ..." the Hawk replied, pursing his lips.

"What?" Big Moishie asked again.

"Like I had de idea ta make one last collection," the Hawk said.

"Yeah, so?"

"So nutting."

"What d'you mean, so nothing? What is it?"

"It's nutting. I told you. I feel sorry for dis Kerner kid, especially when I tink what a putz dis Hankleman is. ... D'ya know dat after he came here an agreed to our conditions about de job, he went right away ta see Kerner an told em dat I was coming ta put em in de hospital?"

"A lousy mooch!" Big Moishie exploded, slamming a huge fist down on the desk top. "Kerner told you that?"

"Yeah."

"A fucking mooch!" Moishie muttered. "I told you he couldn't be trusted, eh?"

"You did."

"I told you! I smelled that mooch out the minute I laid eyes on him. He's a sniffer," Moishie Mandelberg said.

"You were right as usual," the Hawk replied.

"I'd like to shaft that prick. I'd like to shaft him good."

"I was tinking ..." Solly began, and then stopped.

"What?"

"I was tinking dat maybe ... you know ... wid reference to what we discussed yesterday... maybe we should let de kid off de hook for our end. Dat means he only has ta come up wid about eight gees for Hankleman. It's crazy, I know!" The Hawk raised a hand as though to protest in advance against an imminent criticism from his partner; but Big Moishie said nothing. "I wanted ta make one last collection, but now I don give a shit. I'd radder give dis kid a break. I tink he could use a break de same way like I needed one when I was pissing away my life at de track. ... You remember, Moishie?"

"Yeah, I remember."

"Dis kid's not a stiff. He's like legit. I can tell. I know it. Can you imagine, he tells me, 'Hit me already. I gotta get outa here an make a buy.'"

"Look, Solly, you want to let him off for our end, it's all right with me. I'm getting sick and tired of that Hankleman. Would you believe that he called the office three times since this morning to find out if you collected yet. Do you believe it?"

The Hawk shook his head. "I wish *he* owed somebody. I would pay dem ta let me collect on him."

"If he owed, I would take over the collection," Big Moishie said.

The Hawk chuckled. "So, it's okay wid you den?"

"It's fine with me."

"Okay, I'll call de kid an tell em what we decided. We're doing someting good here, Moishie. We're doing someting very good."

Big Moishie nodded whimsically.

"You'll see. He'll come up wid Hankleman's end. He'll come troo."

Solly reached for the phone and dialed Artie Kerner's number.

Chapter Eighteen

"Well, Mr. Kerner, to tell you the truth, I'm very surprised that the goon believed you," Dr. Lehman said.

"He's not a goon," Kerner replied quickly.

"Well, you call him what you want but I'm still surprised."

"I was surprised too."

"Yes, I'm sure you were," the doctor said. "It's possible that you might have met a decent person, eh, Kerner?"

"Yes, he's a nice man."

"And that makes you feel better?"

"Yes. He could have bashed my face in, which was what I expected him to do. But he didn't. He really believed me."

"Maybe he was just conning you, Mr. Kerner. Maybe he showed you some sympathy, figuring it would make you more inclined to sell some of your possessions and pay him the money you owe."

"No," Kerner said emphatically. "I explained my situation to him. He knows that if I sell anything I immediately have to go out and buy three times as much. He understood that very well."

"Of course he understands that. But that doesn't mean he isn't conning you."

"There's no reason for him to con me when he could just as easily put me in the hospital."

"Putting you in the hospital wouldn't get him his money, would it?" Dr. Lehman said with a smirk.

"He's not a con man!" Kerner said angrily. "He came across as an exceptionally nice person to me."

"Okay. Relax, Mr. Kerner. Don't get excited. You seem to have some strange attraction for this man but don't let it get out of control. Another outburst like that and I may have to calm you down with a good rainstorm," Dr. Lehman said, pointing at the control panel on his desk.

"Look, I don't have any strange attraction, as you put it, for this Mr. Weisskopf. I just think he's a nice man."

"Well, I just think you may be trusting him a bit too much. Don't misunderstand me; I believe in trusting, but one has to use discretion. In any case, I'm glad it made you feel better... however ... you don't really look better. In fact, you seem somewhat depressed ... and you're holding your nuts again."

"I'm not!" Kerner half-shouted, quickly shifting his hands so that they rested on his knees.

"Kerner, Kerner," the doctor sighed. "I told you in our last session that I know a ball-holder when I see one."

Kerner shrugged, lowered his head slightly, and said nothing.

"So what is it, Mr. Kerner?"

Kerner looked up for a moment and then quickly lowered his head again.

"Kerner, I'm going to count to five and if you don't start talking by then, you get the wind and the rain; and in case you're wondering, I can also make snow."

"I'm going to talk. I'm just finding it difficult again."

"Look, I'm not interested in your problems, Kerner. I just want to know what's on your mind. Now, I'm going to start counting."

"Okay, okay. I'm going to talk."

"So talk."

"Okay. Don't rush me."

134

"Talk!" Dr. Lehman yelled, springing up from his seat.

"Okay, okay. I'm talking."

Dr. Lehman slammed a hand against his forehead.

"Here, look, I'm starting right now," Kerner said. "Here I go. Okay. Let's see. ... Okay. It has to do with something that happened after I left here yesterday. I felt a lot better after that session. I felt hopeful, especially because I realized the connection between the start of my craziness and the fact that Estelle Bercowitz... left me. Then also, you asked me, if you recall, at the end of the session, how my buying sickness had affected my sex life and I said that I hadn't given it much thought. Do you remember that, Doctor?"

"No," Dr. Lehman replied.

"But you asked me that question just yesterday."

"So I forgot; but I'll take your word for it. Now go on," Dr. Lehman said, leaping down from his seat which had been rising slowly for the last minute or so.

"Well, like I said, after the session ended I felt better; you know... hopeful. I really believed that you were going to help me beat this thing." Kerner paused for a moment as he watched Dr. Lehman move across the room towards the little hut and enter it.

"Keep talking, Mr. Kerner. I'm listening," he said from inside.

Kerner turned to face the hut. He felt a bit foolish now talking to someone he couldn't see.

"Just talk to the walls," Dr. Lehman chortled from inside.

"Fuck you," Kerner muttered under his breath.

"Did you say something, Kerner?"

"I was just clearing my throat," Kerner replied quickly.

"Is it all clear now?"

"Yes."

"So continue, please."

Kerner could hear shuffling sounds coming from inside the hut.

"Well, when I left here, like I said, I felt better, and as I was on my way down to Walton's Art Gallery ..."

"To where?"

"To Walton's Art Gallery."

"What were you going there for?"

"To buy something."

"I thought you said you felt better."

"Yes, I did, but not that much better."

"All right, so you were on your way to Walton's."

"Yes. And while I was running along the street…"

"Running! Why were you running?"

"To get there before they closed."

"I see. All right, go on."

"While I was running, I began to think about what you had asked me at the end of that session – you know, about how my buying habit affected my sex life – and I realized that it had affected it very much. I had answered you, if you recall, that I hadn't given very much thought to sex lately, but while I was on my way to Walton's, it hit me very clearly that I had been in a kind of daze regarding sex since the start of my buying addiction. As soon as I realized this, I started to feel a bit… uh … horny."

Kerner paused, waiting for some comment from Dr. Lehman. The shuffling noises continued inside the hut.

"Don't stop, Mr. Kerner," the doctor said, still hidden from view. "I'm listening."

"Well, anyway, after I had made my buy, I decided to find someone to share this suddenly revived feeling with."

"You mean someone to take it out on."

"Well, whatever," Kerner replied in an aggravated tone.

Suddenly Kerner went rigid in his seat as Dr. Lehman came out of the hut wearing a red Speedo swim suit.

"Keep talking, Mr. Kerner. I'm just going to take a little dip in my pond to cool off."

The doctor approached the edge of the pond and suddenly flung himself racing style into the water. Kerner watched dumbfounded as the psychiatrist did a fast butterfly across the pond. Dr. Lehman stood up, wiped the water from his face and pulled himself up into a sitting position on the stone rim of the pool.

"It's deeper than you thought, eh?" he asked.

Kerner nodded, gape mouthed.

"Next year I may rent the apartment directly below so I can make the pool about ten or twelve feet deeper. Then I'll be able to set up a diving board and I'll also be able to do some scuba diving. Pretty good, eh?"

Kerner nodded dazedly.

"Anyways, keep talking, Mr. Kerner."

Kerner tried to recollect where he had left off, feeling a sudden dissociative flash such as had occurred on his first visit to the doctor's office.

"So I picked up a girl."

"A girl?"

"Yes."

"You mean, like ten or eleven years old?"

"Of course not! I'm not a pervert!" Kerner said angrily.

"That's a matter of opinion; but in any case, what I meant was, be specific when you talk. You meant to say, you picked up a woman, isn't that right?"

"Yes," Kerner replied. "She was probably about thirty. ... So she came back to my ..."

"Hold it! Hold it!"

Kerner looked up at the doctor who was now jogging around the pond.

"How exactly did you pick her up? What was your technique?"

"I don't see the importance of that."

"It's not important. I'm just curious."

"Well, I used my standard method," Kerner replied.

"Yes?" Dr. Lehman said, now running in place next to the hut.

"I just walked up to her and asked her if she felt like fucking."

The doctor stopped running. "And she said yes?"

137

"Yes, she did."

"Kerner, you make me sick," the doctor said, disappearing into the little hut.

"Look, it's a good technique. It saves a lot of talk and I've had a lot of success with it."

"Okay, so you took her home. Get to the good part already," the doctor said angrily.

"Well, we were in the bed and ..."

"What did she look like?"

"Very nice."

"I don't mean very nice. I mean, give me some details."

"Like what?"

"You know what I mean," the doctor shouted from inside the hut.

"Well, she had a big pair of tits."

"Yes?"

"And a beautiful ass."

"Yes?"

"And a beautiful face."

"All right, continue."

"Well, anyway..." Kerner began, and then hesitated.

"Go on."

"This is very hard for me," Kerner replied.

"It will be even harder if a thunderstorm should descend on you. I have a set of controls in here as well, Mr. Kerner."

"Okay. I couldn't get it up!" Kerner shouted.

"Aha!" the doctor yelled, bursting out of the hut, naked and clutching a towel. "You see! We've come full circle, haven't we? If you remember, I suggested in our first session that you had a problem getting it up, but you lied and said you didn't."

"I didn't lie," Kerner protested. "At that time I didn't have this particular problem," he said vehemently.

"Well, in any event, you have it now, and it's just another part of the overall syndrome. Now tell me exactly what happened."

"Nothing happened. I was completely impotent. The only way I could have gotten it in was to have stuffed it in like a piece of soft putty. It wouldn't get hard."

"I can make mine hard in sixty seconds flat," the doctor said matter-of-factly.

Kerner ignored the remark.

The doctor went back inside the hut. A moment later music began emanating from the various speakers located all about the room. Kerner recognized the song as "Ba Mir Bist du Shane," sung by the Andrews Sisters.

"Go on with your story, Mr. Kerner," the doctor called from inside. "What did you do next?"

"Well, finally I told her that I had to go to the bathroom. I went in there and tried to ... well, you know ... to fantasize about some particularly erotic situation. I mean, I was terrified. That was the first time in my life that I was completely impotent and what was worse was that the girl was the type I had always found the most stimulating. I racked my brain to try and visualize one girl from all my experiences over the years who had been especially good. I'd had hundreds of girls, but as I tried to picture just one of them in my mind, I found I couldn't. I couldn't distinguish one face or one body from another. They were all one huge mass of ... of flesh.

"Then finally I remembered back to when I was about fourteen or so and. ... There's no sense in me telling you the rest, it's not really important."

"Uh, uh, uh! No, no, no, Mr. Kerner. You're not going to stop now, just when you're getting to the good stuff. Just keep talking and let me decide if it's important or not. Okay?"

"All right, but I just don't see ... all right. So I finally remembered back about this Mrs. Braun. I had the hots for her when I was about fourteen or fifteen. I used to fantasize about her."

"Why?"

"You know," Kerner said, angling his head.

"No, I don't know. Explain."

"You know ... for uh ... you know!"

"I don't know."

"It's very embarrassing."

"Tough!" Dr. Lehman said, now emerging from the hut fully dressed. He walked over to a small, grass-covered mound beside the pond and sat down.

"All right, Kerner, I'll make it easier for you. You were trying to say that, as a youth, you fantasized about Mrs. Braun for purposes of masturbation. Is that correct?"

"Yes."

"The old wankeroo, eh, Kerner?" Dr. Lehman snickered.

Kerner smiled sheepishly.

"So describe the fantasy to me, please."

"Well, it's nothing much really..."

"Kerner, if you hold back now, just as you're getting to the real good stuff, then as far as I'm concerned this will be our last session."

"Okay, I won't hold back."

"Good, good," the doctor said, rubbing his hands together.

"Usually I pictured her coming over to my parents' house to have a friendly chat or something. Of course when she got there, only I would be there. I'd be sitting in the living room. She'd come in and sit down on the couch. I'd be sitting in a chair opposite her. She'd start talking to me about how I was doing in school and bullshit like that. After a few minutes, she'd raise her feet up onto the couch while continuing to talk in a seemingly innocent way."

Kerner began to giggle nervously. "This is very embarrassing," he said, blushing.

"Kerner, if you stop now, I'll somehow find a way to have you committed."

"I'm not stopping. Just give me a chance here, eh?... Okay, so she'd be talking and sitting with her legs up and, while she was talking, I would suddenly notice that she wasn't wearing any underpants and I'd see..."

"The old snatcheroo?"

Kerner nodded, blushed and laughed nervously.

"What happened then?"

"I don't remember exactly, but not too long after that I would have her with all her clothes off and..."

"And?"

"And I would screw her. ... Sometimes it was in the bathtub, sometimes on the diningroom table, sometimes on the floor."

"But never on the bed?" Dr. Lehman asked.

"No, never on the bed. It was always some place a little out of the ordinary."

"It looks like you thought of every place but the bed and the kitchen sink."

"Oh, I thought of the kitchen sink but it didn't really appeal to me."

Dr. Lehman pursed his lips and gave a few patronizing nods of his head. "Was this sex relatively straight or were there elements of what we might call sado-masochism involved?"

"Well, sometimes I'd whip her a bit when she asked me to. Sometimes I'd tie her up and then I'd have her saying things like, 'Hurt me, Arthur.'" Kerner began to laugh with embarrassment. "Then also, for some reason, whenever I was giving it to her, I'd always have her on her hands and knees."

"The old doggie style, eh?" the doctor said with a half-sneer. "Did you have any other positions?"

"Well, occasionally I'd have her being lowered onto my cock by a block and tackle while I sat on a chair and read a comic book."

"What was her husband doing while all this was going on?" the doctor asked sharply.

"I don't know. He was at work, I guess."

"You guess! Didn't you know? Weren't you a little worried? He could have killed you if he'd caught you with his wife!"

"Pardon?"

"Weren't you worried about being caught?"

"But, Doctor, I told you this was only a fantasy. It didn't really happen."

"What? Oh yes! Of course. I was just testing you to see if you could distinguish between reality and your fantasies. Sometimes the two merge in a patient's mind. All right, continue."

"Well, as I was sitting in the bathroom, I tried to recall these particular fantasies about Mrs. Braun, but they didn't work. In fact, all I could think about was the painting I had bought a few hours earlier. The harder I tried to think of something stimulating, the more I thought about the painting. It just stayed in my mind and finally I told the girl I was sick and sent her home."

"Well, one thing comes out of this in stark haut relief, Mr. Kerner, that is one thing other than the fact that you can't get your petzel up; and that is your desire to put women in degrading positions. You obviously don't want to face them, symbolically speaking. That's why you always have them on their hands and knees. That should be quite obvious to you, I would imagine."

"Yes, I see what you mean," Kerner said.

"In any event, this sudden impotency is directly related to your buying addiction. They're both manifestations of a deeper problem. A hidden guilt. Let me recap the last three sessions. First of all, your craziness seemed to start when your girlfriend Estelle, whom you perhaps loved, left you. The reason she left you, however, was because you let her go. The reason you let her go was because you were afraid of making a close contact with anyone. Now what we have to find out is why you are afraid. Once we know this we ... you will be on your way towards being cured. There is some guilt somewhere, Mr. Kerner."

"But I don't feel guilty," Kerner said.

The doctor stood up and approached the couch. He looked down at Kerner who was reclined on his side.

"In this world, Mr. Kerner, everyone feels guilty whether they know it or not."

Kerner stared up at Dr. Lehman. "Well, I'll take your word for it."

"Good. Now what I'd like to do is try and speed things up a bit. To try and uncover the source of your problem more quickly."

"I'm all for that. That's what I'm here for," Kerner replied, sitting up on the couch.

"We may be able to progress more quickly if we were to try hypnosis on you. What do you think about that?" Dr. Lehman asked.

142

"That's fine with me. Do you think it will really help?"

"Look, Kerner, if it helped the Wasp, it'll help you," Dr. Lehman said curtly.

"Okay, I'm sorry. I was just asking."

"And I was just telling! Okay?"

"Okay, I'm sorry," Kerner said contritely.

"You're making a nervous wreck out of me, Kerner. By the time I'm finished with you, *I'll* need therapy."

Kerner was about to suggest to the doctor that he was already in need of treatment but held his tongue.

"All right then, Mr. Kerner. If you've agreed, we can proceed now with the hypnosis."

"I'm game."

Dr. Lehman turned and walked to a point several feet away from the couch. He motioned for Kerner to come over. Kerner stood up and approached the psychiatrist, wondering what he was up to.

"Now before trying to put you under hypnosis, it's essential that I establish whether you trust me or not. If you don't trust me, then you'll resist my efforts to put you in a trance. Now the way I'm going to determine whether or not you trust me is as follows: I'm going to stand directly behind you. When I say 'Go,' you will let yourself fall straight back until I catch you. Do you understand? I will catch you before you hit the floor. Do you trust me to catch you, Mr. Kerner?"

"Yes," Kerner replied, nodding.

"All right then, let yourself fall now without stopping yourself at all. Fall straight back now. Go!"

Kerner took a breath and let himself topple backwards. As his head smashed against the floor, a series of starlike flashes danced through his eyes. Dazed, he picked himself up, holding the back of his head.

"Why didn't you catch me?" Kerner asked in an injured tone.

"Why? Because it wouldn't have been a true test of your confidence in me. Now if I tell you to do it again and you're still prepared to fall back, *then* it will *really* show that you have confidence in me and then I'll be able to put you under with ease. Are you ready to try again?"

Kerner nodded grimly. What did he have to lose?

"Okay, let yourself go then. Don't worry, I promise I'll catch you this time." The doctor yelled, "Fall back!"

Kerner let himself fall. As his head hit the floor for the second time, he almost lost consciousness. When he regained his senses, he rolled over on his side. The doctor stood over him, looking down sternly.

"That was to teach you self-reliance. An overly trusting mind is the mind of a fool, my friend."

Kerner shook his head, trying to clear it.

"Now we're ready for hypnosis," the doctor said. "Go lie down on the couch."

Kerner staggered over to the couch and fell onto it. The doctor seated himself on the little chair and leaned over towards Kerner.

"Now then, you will begin slowly counting backwards from ten. By the time you reach one, you will be in a deep trance. All right, begin counting."

"Ten … nine … eight …" Kerner said.

"Your eyelids are becoming very heavy," the doctor said in a slow, ponderous voice.

"Seven … six … five … four …" Kerner said.

"You are now almost asleep," Dr. Lehman intoned.

"Three … two … one. …"

"You are now asleep. You are in a deep trance, Mr. Kerner. Do you hear me?"

"Yes," Kerner replied, wondering why he felt exactly as he had before his countdown. He had expected to feel as though he were in a dream, but aside from the dizziness and pain caused by his two falls, he felt much the same as thirty seconds before.

"Now the purpose of this session is to find out certain things about your past which for some reason you've been unable to recall or are otherwise reluctant to discuss. For example, you

144

haven't said anything about your feelings towards your parents. You seem to be fighting me on that and I want to get to the bottom of it. Do you understand?"

"Yes," Kerner replied, wishing he felt more asleep.

"All right. Now when I snap my fingers at the end of this session, you will wake up feeling refreshed and remember nothing. Do you understand, Mr. Kerner?"

"Sure, Doctor, whatever you say."

"You have a glib mouth even when you're in a trance," Dr. Lehman said sharply.

"I'm sorry, I was just answering your question," Kerner replied, opening his eyes.

"Shut up, Kerner. You're in a trance, which means you can't talk freely unless I tell you to!" the doctor yelled.

"Okay, okay. Take it easy. I didn't know that. You should have explained that before you put me under and I wouldn't have said a word. How was I supposed to know?"

"Ah! You're not even hypnotized," Dr. Lehman said in a choked voice.

"You mean, I'm awake now?"

"Well, that's debatable, Kerner. ... You might have a hard time proving it to anyone else but, yes, you're as awake as you'll ever be. You must have been resisting me."

"I tried my best," Kerner said, gesturing with open hands.

"Well, sometimes it doesn't work," the doctor said sullenly.

"Can't we try it again?"

"No, I don't want to do it now," Dr. Lehman snapped. "Maybe we can try some word association?"

"What's that?"

"I say a word or a series of words and you say the first word or words that come to mind. By your response, I may be able to obtain some clue, some insight into the cause of your perversion. Do you understand?"

"Yes," Kerner said, sitting up on the couch.

"All right then, here we go. The first word is ... dog!"

"Buy."

"Cat!"

"Buy."

"Buy!" said the doctor, leaning forward, a sly grin on his face.

"Cunt," Kerner replied.

"Money!"

"Shit."

"Shit!"

"Buy."

"Shit! Shit! Shit!" said the doctor.

"Buy, buy, buy!" was Kerner's response.

The doctor paused as though thinking. "Enough," he said.

"Buy," said Kerner.

"That's enough!" the doctor yelled.

"Shit!" screamed Kerner.

"Okay, stop already!"

"Buy, buy, buy, already!" Kerner shouted.

"No! Enough! Stop it!"

"Buy! More! Shit!" Kerner screamed.

The doctor stopped. In a very low voice, he said, "Mr. Kerner..."

"Buy," Kerner replied.

The doctor ran over to Kerner and placed a heavy hand over his mouth.

"No more, Mr. Kerner. This part is finished. I keep getting this connection between money, sex, buying and shit, but I know that already. I don't think this particular technique will take us any farther."

"I couldn't think of anything else to say. Those were the only words that came to mind."

"Never mind. We'll move on to something else."

"I was thinking, Doctor..."

"Yes?"

"I've heard they've cured people of things like alcoholism and smoking and so on by making the patient associate their addiction with a bad experience."

"Oh, very good. I see now you're an expert in psychology," the doctor sneered.

"I'm not trying to tell you anything. I just happened to have read a few things on that."

"You read a few things and right away you're an expert, eh? Well, let me tell you something, I don't believe in all that crap. And just for the record, Mr. Psychology Expert, the behaviourists try to effect cures not only by giving the patients bad experiences but also good experiences. For example, a colleague of mine who is very big on behaviour therapy once had a Mrs. Greenberg as a patient. Maybe you know her – Sally Greenberg, the wife of Jack Greenberg, the paper magnate?"

"No, I don't know her."

"They live in Westmount," the doctor said.

Kerner shook his head. "Don't know them."

"From the paper mills," the doctor said.

"No," said Kerner, "I don't know them."

"Well, in any event, she had a frigidity problem, this Mrs. Greenberg; was absolutely terrified of sex. During a word association session such as we've just had, it became apparent to my colleague, who doesn't know his ass from his elbow anyways, that she had an incredible desire, bordering on lust, for mint candies. He would say 'Fuck' and she would immediately reply 'Mint candy,' slobbering at the mouth every time she said it. So he advised her husband to give her a mint candy every time they had intercourse. Within a relatively short period of time, she began wanting to screw constantly."

"So she was cured?"

Dr. Lehman shrugged. "Let's put it this way: Before her therapy she was afraid of sex; now apparently she's not, but now she weighs three hundred and sixty pounds as compared to a hundred and twelve before. Every time she has intercourse, she finishes a half-pound box of mint candies. Soon they'll have to push her around in a wheelbarrow."

"I see," Kerner said, nodding understandingly.

"That's not for you, Mr. Kerner. Besides, I don't believe in all that shit. I'm not against working on eradicating the symptoms of a disorder through an attack on the symptoms themselves, but at the same time we have to find the root cause of it and that can best be done through the psycho-analytic method. Now we've already made some very good progress with you, wouldn't you say?"

"Yes. Yes. Definitely," Kerner said eagerly.

"Now I already have a good idea of what your problem is. However, I should like to use two more tests on you in order to validate some of my conclusions about your disorder. At the same time, these tests may give you some further insight into your problem. The thing that I find puzzling is that you haven't as yet blamed anything on your parents or your teachers, or anyone in fact. Surely there must be someone you can blame for having screwed you up."

Kerner shrugged and made no reply.

"Well, maybe these next tests will open things up a bit more. Now the first is the Rorschach test. Let's go over and sit at the table near the pond."

Kerner got up and walked over to the table. The doctor went into the hut and came out a moment later with two Manila folders. He sat down opposite Kerner and withdrew several sheets from one of the folders. He passed one across to Kerner who looked down at it and observed a large ink blot.

"All right, now what do you see there, Mr. Kerner?" the doctor asked, pointing at the sheet.

Kerner studied the blot for a moment. "It looks like a painting by Lambert Groulx."

"But what do you see there?" Dr. Lehman said testily.

"It looks like a car," Kerner replied.

"A car?"

"Yes, it looks like a car to me."

"Well, for your information, it's a cunt!" the doctor snapped.

"It doesn't look like a cunt to me," Kerner said.

"No, I don't imagine it does considering how fucked up you are. If you were normal, you'd see a cunt; but since you're not normal, you see a car."

Kerner shrugged. "Well, I can't help it. It looks like a car to me."

"Well, just take my word for it, it's a cunt all right."

"Look, I know I'm not normal, but anyone who sees a cunt in that blot isn't either, as far as I'm concerned."

"Don't philosophize, Mr. Kerner. Just tell me what you see in this second blot," Dr. Lehman said, pushing another sheet over towards Kerner. "What do you see there?"

"A cunt?" Kerner said hesitantly.

"A cunt!" the doctor screamed.

"Well, yes, look. See. There's like the lips and there's the little jigger up here," Kerner said, tracing his finger along the blot.

"That's not the little jigger, my friend; that's the front fender of the car. It's a 1972 Maseratti, for your information."

"It looks like a cunt to me."

"Oh, Kerner, leave me alone already," Dr. Lehman muttered, grimacing as though in pain.

"Look, I'm sorry. I'm just trying to be honest."

"Okay. Never mind. It's just that you get on my nerves, Kerner. I know you can't help it, but you do."

"Well, you know, I'm not exactly crazy about you either."

"Don't start with me, Kerner, because verbally I can make mincemeat out of you."

"I'm not starting anything. I just don't think it's right of you to insult me all the time."

"Look, in this office I can do whatever I want! If I want to insult you, I can insult you; if I want to shit on my desk, I'll shit on my desk; if I want to piss in my pond, I can piss in my pond. Okay?"

Kerner nodded.

"Okay?" Dr. Lehman repeated.

"Yes," Kerner replied.

"Yes what?

"Yes, Doctor."

"Okay," Dr. Lehman said with a satisfied nod of his head.

"Now let's get back to business here. Let's see ... Let's see ... Enough of this Rorschach shit," he said, throwing the sheets into the waste-paper basket. "I think we'll try some thematic apperception." He pushed another sheet across the table. "Do you understand how this works?"

"No."

"Well, there is a vaguely defined picture in here," the doctor said, pointing at the paper. "There is something happening in here. I want you to tell me what went on prior to the event or events in this picture; then I want to know what is actually taking place in the picture itself; and then tell me what happened afterwards. Do you understand?"

"Yes."

"Well then, go ahead."

Kerner stared down at the picture. "Well ... Let's see ... I think it has to do with an old couple," he began.

"Yes? Yes?"

"They were quite old. Too old, in fact, to have children. Then one day the old woman decided to bake some gingerbread cookies. She made one in the shape of a little man."

Dr. Lehman was now eying Kerner suspiciously.

"When she opened the oven, the little cookie man jumped out, yelling, 'Run, run, as fast as you can, you can't catch me, I'm the gingerbread man!'"

"Mr. Kerner," the doctor said in a quiet but firm voice.

Kerner looked up at Dr. Lehman.

"Do you really see all that in that stupid little picture?"

"Well ... not exactly."

"Then why are you making it all up?"

"Well, I saw a cookie in there."

"And that started you off?"

"Yes."

"Do you know what a cookie is?"

"Pardon?"

"A cookie, a cookie! Do you know what a cookie is?"

"It's a biscuit."

"A cookie is another name for a cunt, Mr. Kerner. You have cunt on the brain. For you a cunt is symbolic for love and you are chasing it. Don't you see?"

Kerner nodded. The doctor was right.

"I'm telling you, sometimes these little pictures are quite helpful for separating the crazies from the normal types. For example, if I looked at it, what would I see?"

The doctor retrieved the card and glanced at it. "Now here's the difference. When I look at it, I see a little girl and three bears. ... But that's beside the point. What I see doesn't count; it's your vision that is important."

The doctor glanced at his watch. "Well, that's about it for today, but just let me leave you with this. It's obvious to me, and should be to you, that your addiction is completely psychological and is a direct result of your attempt to replace love with sex. We've seen quite clearly that you're afraid to love. Why? ... That we don't know. However, at this point I feel confident in saying that you must now begin making a serious effort to control your buying habit. This should be easier now that you've gained a certain insight into yourself. Furthermore..."

Dr. Lehman suddenly put a finger to his lips, indicating a desire for silence. He tiptoed quickly to the door and yanked it open. Mrs. Griff toppled forward into the room. The doctor waved a finger at her as she picked herself up off the floor.

Kerner sidled past the doctor and headed into the waiting room.

"That's the second time I've caught you, Mrs. Griff," Kerner heard the doctor say. "You know you can't fool the old doctor, don't you?"

Kerner pulled open the door and quickly walked away.

Chapter Nineteen

"...Then at approximately nine-twenty A.M., the subject, Mr. A. Kerner, came out of the apartment garage driving a red Corvette, license number 3C84-CL. He was accompanied by another man who had entered the apartment building approximately thirty minutes earlier."

"What did this other man look like?" Morrie Hankleman said, interrupting the burly man seated opposite him.

The detective shuffled through the several pages on his lap and pulled one out.

"Yes, here it is. ... This subject was middle-aged. Late forties or early fifties. Approximately five-foot-eight. Thin build but larger-than-average shoulders. Slight greying of hair at the temples. Sharp features. Prominent nose ..."

"All right, go on," Hankleman said curtly. The description was more than enough to tell him that it was Solly Weisskopf in the car with Kerner.

The man continued where he had left off. "I followed the subject at high speed to Walton's Art Gallery, located on Sherbrooke Street West near the corner of Crescent Street. On the way, the subject was stopped for speeding and given a ticket by a motorcycle policeman. He then proceeded at the same high speed to Walton's where he parked the car in a no-parking zone and ran very quickly into Walton's. The subject appeared frightened or in a state of semi-panic as he ran in, followed by the other man whom I described a moment ago.

"I entered the store and saw the subject purchase a painting for which he paid over four hundred dollars. This was carried out of the gallery by the second man. They got back into the subject's car and proceeded..."

"Wait a minute! Hold on! ... You say the other man was carrying the painting?"

"Yes, that's right."

"You're positive?"

"Yes. Very definitely so," the man replied.

"All right, go on," Hankleman said, scowling.

"Well ... then, unfortunately, I lost track of the subject for a while."

"Whatta you mean, you lost track?"Hankleman yelled angrily.

"Well, sir... you see, I was trailing the subject in traffic and I was trying to keep a few cars back of them. The car directly in front of me was a taxi. ... Well, for some reason, he suddenly had to hit his brakes and I ended up rear-ending him."

"So you should've kept going!" Hankleman shouted.

"Well, hey, look. That would have been a hit-and-run. I could lose my investigator's license for that. Besides, the taxi driver flew out of the car from the impact and fell onto the street. He was out cold; they had to take him away in an ambulance. I couldn't leave until the police came and filled out a report. Then I had to fill out my own report about the accident to give to my boss. See, here, I had to fill all of this out on the spot," the man said, holding a sheet out towards Hankleman. "Here's the guy's name and everything about the accident. See, here! Gabor Pelzic, that's the guy I hit. It's all here in black and white, just in case you think I was goofing off or just lost him through inefficiency."

"Never mind, never mind! I'm not interested in your problems!" Hankleman snapped. "Did you pick him up again?"

"Well, I went back to his apartment but the doorman said

153

he hadn't returned. I then went to his office, the address of which you had given me, but he wasn't there either."

"So where the fuck was he? What the fuck am I paying for anyway?" Hankleman shouted. He stood up and began pacing around the office.

"I returned to his apartment and waited there. The subject returned at approximately six P.M."

"So for half a day you lost track of him. During that time he could have got on a plane and left the country," Hankleman said.

"Well, he didn't," the investigator replied.

"Yeah, and you're just lucky that he didn't."

The burly man made no reply.

"Anyway, is that it, or is there more?" Hankleman asked.

"No, that's it. I left his apartment at six-thirty and came straight here."

Hankleman nodded and gestured to indicate that the meeting was over. The investigator stood up and headed for the door. Hankleman followed him. The man stopped at the doorway and turned to Hankleman. "Do you want us to continue the surveillance on this guy?" he asked.

"I'll speak to your boss in the morning and tell him what I want done," Hankleman replied.

"Very good, sir," the detective nodded, turned and went out. Hankleman closed the door after him and walked back towards his desk. He smiled grimly to himself.

His instincts had been right. He had done well to hire an agency to keep tabs on Kerner. He was certain now that Solly Weisskopf was up to something. What was he doing accompanying Artie Kerner into an art gallery and then coming out with a painting? What was he up to? He had to be up to something. Hankleman knew it without any doubt. Either Solly Weisskopf and his partner had made a deal with Kerner or they were doing an extortion number on him. Maybe they would force Kerner into paying them the whole bundle and then frighten him out of town so no one would be the wiser.

It was something like that, he knew it now. They had

probably had that idea in mind the minute he had come to their office with his proposal. It was strange how quickly they had agreed to take on the collection job for him. They were almost too eager; in fact, he had expected them to say no and had been surprised when Weisskopf had said yes.

The more he thought about it, the more certain Morrie Hankleman was that they were out to shaft him. He laughed aloud and shook his head several times. No, no, there was no way he was going to allow himself to be taken. Not by Kerner and not by Solly Weisskopf and his partner. He would have to move fast. He would go and see them first thing in the morning. He would sound them out. He would tell them that he wanted things sped up; that he wanted his money within forty-eight hours.

Yes, he would sound them out. He would find out what they were up to. He would tell them what to do and if they put him off, then he would move on his own. He wasn't going to be screwed. No way! He was going to get his money. All of it. He was glad they were trying to screw him. That made his agreement with them invalid. He owed them nothing. He could do whatever he wanted now. He could do what he should have done in the first place.

He would get all his money. Every cent. It was his. Not Kerner's and not those two hoods'. Just his. He was going to get it. All of it. One way or another.

Chapter Twenty

Artie Kerner arrived home at six P.M. He went into his bedroom, took off his shoes and lay down on his bed. He began to
think. He thought over his past life. He thought about the
ambitions and the dreams he'd had; the compromises that
he'd made. He thought about the present and the problems he
was faced with. He thought about the emptiness of his life.
Then he thought about the future.

Some time past four in the morning, he knew what he was
going to do.

Chapter Twenty-One

Hankleman arrived home at eight P.M. Only the maid was home. She informed Hankleman that his wife had packed half a dozen suitcases, taken the child and left for parts unknown.

Hankleman fixed himself a double Scotch and went into his den. He put on the T.V. and sat in front of it wondering where his wife could have headed off to. He got up and went into her bedroom. He opened all her drawers and her cupboard. He gave a short laugh of sardonic admiration when he observed how she had cleaned things out.

He went back into the den and watched some T.V. A short while later he went out and tried to fuck the maid. She refused. Hankleman fired her. Then he went to bed alone. He thought about Artie Kerner and Solly Weisskopf and Moishie Mandelberg for a few minutes. He felt very calm as he told himself that they were not going to screw him. There was no doubt about it in his mind. He would be the screwer and they would be the screwees.

Hankleman fell asleep. He slept soundly.

Chapter Twenty-Two

Solly the Hawk and Moishie Mandelberg were having their morning coffee and discussing several legitimate business ventures when their secretary announced the arrival of Morrie Hankleman. Big Moishie winced disgustedly. Solly stood up and forced a smile as Hankleman entered the office.

"Morning," the Hawk said.

"Good morning," Hankleman replied with a curt nod. He turned to Big Moishie who gave a short nod to Hankleman and said nothing.

"Have a seat, Mr. Hankleman," the Hawk said, motioning towards the chair in front of his desk.

Hankleman sat down.

"What can we do for you, Mr. Hankleman?" Solly asked.

"Well, I was just wondering how you're progressing with our friend Kerner."

"We're making very good progress," the Hawk replied.

"Uh huh. I see. How good is good?"

"Good is very good, Mr. Hankleman."

Hankleman hesitated for a moment. "Well ... you know, I had hoped I might have had some ... some feedback by now, if you know what I mean. I mean, I don't exactly understand why it's taking so long."

"Long? We only took dis ting on two days ago. Dats not long."

"Well, maybe I was over-optimistic but I had really expected something definite by now, if you know what I mean."

"We understand," Big Moishie said. "But sometimes these things take time," he added.

"Of course, of course ... but how much time?" Hankleman asked, turning to Moishie Mandelberg.

"I already had a liddle talk wid dis Kerner," the Hawk said, passing over Hankleman's question. "An I can guarantee you dat he'll come up wid de scratch."

"Well, yes. Of course. That I take for granted, but I'd like to have an idea of when. I mean, what exactly did you say to him?"

"Tings," the Hawk replied.

"Things?"

"Yeah, tings."

"I mean, could you be a bit more specific?"

"Jus tings. I have certain tings dat I say. Each case is different. Deres tings what I say to one person which I don say to anudder," the Hawk said patiently.

"I'm sort of curious ... I mean. ... Did you suggest how things might turn out if he didn't pay up quick?"

"I told em whad had to be told to him, Mr. Hankleman. He got de message."

"I see," Hankleman replied with a heavy note of dissatisfaction in his voice.

"Mr. Hankleman," the Hawk said quietly. "Don worry. You'll get your money. I always deliver."

"Fine. Yes. I know. I know that, but I thought that if maybe you ... like ... you know, put some pressure on him, he'd come through faster, if you know what I mean."

"Sure, sure. I know what you mean. Don worry. I put on plenny pressure."

"Well ... it depends what you mean by pressure," Hankleman said.

"I had a very good liddle talk wid de man."

"Well, I didn't mean that kind of pressure. I meant... something a little bit different."

"Like what?" the Hawk asked innocently.

"Like if you broke his fucking arm or something!" Hankleman suddenly half-shouted.

Big Moishie remained silent, puffing calmly on his cigar.

"Dats not really necessary, Mr. Hankleman," Solly replied. "Besides, dats illegal, you know. Especially now wid de crime commission investigating shylocking, you have to be careful dese days."

"Well, the way I feel about it, something drastic has to be done with this guy. He's trying to stiff me. For all I know, he's planning to blow town. He's a con man. I've been around long enough to know that. If he can get away without paying up, he'll do it, so ... as far as I'm concerned, if he doesn't pay up very soon, I'll look for some other way to get my money."

"Whadda you mean, Mr. Hankleman?" the Hawk asked.

"I mean, I'll have to do it my own way."

"But you already hired us."

"I know that but I haven't had any results yet."

"You'll have results."

"Well ... fine ... but I'm worried."

"We have a gentlemen's agreement, Mr. Hankleman," Big Moishie said suddenly.

Hankleman turned to face him.

"We have a reputation here, you know."

Hankleman was about to reply but he held himself in check in spite of his desire to press the point further. He nodded several times. "Yes. Okay. That's true. We do have an agreement. I just would like to have some idea of when you think you'll collect."

"Soon, Mr. Hankleman," the Hawk said.

"What do you think? A week? Two weeks?"

"It's hard to say exacly but it will be before de turdy days are up. Dats fer sure."

Hankleman forced a resigned nod. "All right. I'll wait to hear from you then," he said, rising.

160

"As soon as I have someting definite, I'll give you a call," the Hawk said, smiling.

"Good," Hankleman said.

"We'll be speaking wid you," Solly said as Hankleman turned and headed for the door.

"Goodbye," Hankleman said.

Big Moishie nodded. Hankleman opened the door and went into the outer office.

"Have a nice day, sir," the secretary said as he passed by her desk. Hankleman ignored her and went out into the corridor, slamming the door behind him. He spat against the corridor wall and headed towards the bathroom at the end of the hall, trying to recapitulate the brief meeting.

He had played his cards well in spite of his anger and frustration. He had accomplished what he had gone there for. He knew now, beyond any doubt, that they were playing some game where they would try to make him the loser. They were cute, real cute, he thought; but he was cuter. It was frustrating to have an edge on someone as he did and not be able to use it to any advantage. In terms of the frustration it had caused him, it would almost have been better not to have known about Weisskopf's strange meeting with Kerner. The only way he could have used his information about that meeting would have been to confront them directly with it. But that would have been foolish and would have accomplished nothing. It would have given him some momentary satisfaction to see their surprise; but what was that worth? Then they would realize that he hadn't trusted them from the start and they would feel justified in going all out to shaft him. It was better that he had controlled his frustration and said nothing. Let them think he was stupid. In the long run he would get them, and his satisfaction would be far greater when they realized he had been on to them from the very beginning.

Hankleman reached the men's room and went in. He went up to the urinal and unzipped his fly. He glanced about the small room and saw that he was alone. Chuckling to himself, he began to urinate on the floor.

Yes, he thought, Weisskopf and Mandelberg were real cute, but he was cuter. He had shown them that he wasn't a pushover, that he wasn't afraid to stand up to them. He had put some pressure on them and let them know who they were dealing with. He had threatened to dispense with their services just to the right degree. Just enough to get them a little nervous and maybe give them some second thoughts about any games they were planning to play, and not too much to force the issue to the point where face saving was necessary, or to the point where they might suspect he was on to them. Yes, he had played his cards perfectly. He was glad he had controlled himself.

Hankleman zipped up his fly and stepped around the puddle he had made on the floor. He went over to the sink. Now Weisskopf and Mandelberg would have to move fast. Whatever it was that they were planning would have to be done within the next few days and he would be ready for them. He would know what they were up to almost as soon as they knew themselves.

Hankleman washed his hands then yanked several paper towels out of the dispenser above the sink. He wiped his hands and threw the towels into the sink, leaving the cold-water tap on. He walked to the door, opened it and started to go out. Suddenly he froze. He was certain Artie Kerner had just passed by. Hankleman peeked his head around the corner of the doorjamb. It was Kerner, and he was obviously headed for the office of Weisskopf and Mandelberg. Hankleman watched as Kerner stopped outside their door, buttoned his jacket and went in.

Hankleman could feel his chest tighten. He began to laugh to himself. He went out into the corridor and headed towards the elevator. Another bit of information to confirm what he was already convinced of.

It made him feel good to see Kerner go into that office. He was glad Kerner had gone into that office! Hankleman stopped in front of the elevator and pressed the button.

A few minutes before, he might have had misgivings or doubts concerning his next move but not anymore.

162

Chapter Twenty-Three

After Solly Weisskopf had introduced Artie Kerner to his partner, he motioned for Kerner to take a seat on the large leather sofa between the two desks. Kerner sat down and the Hawk joined him. Big Moishie remained at his own desk.

"Would ya like a coffee, Arter?" the Hawk asked.

"No, thank you," Kerner replied.

"Maybe a tea?"

"No. Nothing, thanks."

The Hawk gave a little nod. "Anyway, I'm glad you came down here, Arter. I tried ta reach you yesterday but I couldn't. I wanted ta talk wid you some more about your problem wid Hankleman."

"Well, that's why I came down here."

The Hawk lifted his eyebrows slightly.

"I've done a lot of thinking since yesterday morning when ... we met. As a matter of fact, yesterday morning seems like weeks ago. Well, anyway, I'm going to have Mr. Hankleman's money in about a week."

The Hawk turned slowly and deliberately to face his partner. He pointed a finger at him. "Ahh?" he said to Big Moishie.

Big Moishie nodded slowly.

The Hawk chuckled gleefully, still pointing at his partner. "I told you de kid had class, eh?"

Moishie Mandelberg nodded again.

Kerner's eyes darted back and forth between the two men as he tried to make some sense out of what was going on.

The Hawk turned back to Kerner. "I'm really glad t'hear what ya jus told me, Arter; but wid reference to what we discussed yesterday, can I ask like how yer gonna manage it?"

"Well, I decided to make a big change in my life."

"A big change?"

"Yes, I've decided to sell everything."

"Everything?" the Hawk said, dumbfounded.

"Yes, everything."

"But it's gonna make you feel very sick, no?"

"Yes, I guess so, but I decided to go all the way. I can't go on like I've been doing. It's really crazy."

"Lissen, Arter, it's not really necessary ta do dat. It might be better ta do it like slower. In fact, dats what I wanted ta talk wid you about. We decided ta do someting here which might make it easier fer you. ... Ya see, like when we took over dis collection, our end was gonna be turdy-five percent of what we got from you. You unnerstan?"

"Yes."

"Dat means our end is like aroun five gees. Right?"

"Yes," Kerner said, nodding.

"But now we decided, me an my partner, for our own personal reasons, which you shouldn bodder yerself wid, dat we're not interested in our end. You unnerstan?"

"I'm not exactly sure," Kerner replied.

"It means dat you only gotta come up wid about eight gees. De rest you can forget."

"Jesus! That's very nice of you," Kerner exclaimed.

"It's no big deal," the Hawk replied, shrugging.

"It is," Kerner replied.

The Hawk shook his head. "Naw."

"Well, I appreciate it. It's hard to believe. It's ..."

"It's no big deal," the Hawk repeated. "But now maybe you should tink about only selling enough ta make de eight gees."

"I don't think it'll make any difference if I sell eight-thousand-dollars' worth of my stuff or all of it. Either way it's going to be hard, but I have a feeling it may be better to go for broke. In any case, what I'm really trying to do is change my whole way of life. I'm selling my business too, for what little it's worth right now."

"Whadda ya gonna do?" the Hawk asked with amazement.

"I'm going to pack it all in here and move to Israel. I'm going to change my whole life. I'm going to work on a kibbutz and see what it's like."

The Hawk shook his head. "That's a very big step, a very big step."

"Yes, I know. But I'm going to do it. That's why I have to settle all my accounts here. In fact, that's why, even though I really appreciate your offer to let me off for the five thousand dollars, I'm going to pay it all back. I owe Mr. Hankleman thirteen thousand and I feel I have to pay it all up. I'm just sorry I caused this whole bloody problem for everyone."

"Look, dats life, Arter. Dese tings happen. You know?"

"Yes, that's true. I just hope you're not offended by my wanting to pay it all back."

"We're never offended when someone offers to give us money," Big Moishie said.

Kerner turned towards the big man. "I just don't want to owe anyone," he said.

"We unnerstan, Arter."

"But I really appreciate your offer. It's the most generous thing I've ever heard of."

"Forget it. We had our reasons for it," the Hawk said.

"What about your business?" Big Moishie asked.

"I'm going to sell that as well. Mind you, it's not worth very much. right now. I've got a few debts which I'll pay off and then I'll try to sell it."

"How much do you owe?"

Kerner shrugged. "About twenty thousand. I had hoped to make a couple of big sales in the last few weeks but it doesn't seem very likely right now. Anyways, in view of my new plans, it doesn't really matter."

"Maybe you should bail out," the Hawk said.

"Declare bankruptcy?" Kerner shook his head. "No, I couldn't do it. I thought about it but now there's no point. When I sell my stuff I'll have the money to pay back what I owe."

"By the time you're finished wid your business and wid Hankleman, you'll be left widout a jit," the Hawk said.

"Well, I won't need it on the kibbutz," Kerner replied with a shrug.

"Look, bankruptcy is nothing to feel guilty about. The act was written expressly to help people when they get into a jackpot," Big Moishie said.

"I realize that; but I got into this jackpot myself and I don't feel right about not paying what I owe, especially if I'm going to have the money."

The Hawk nodded slowly. "Well, you know what ya gotta do. But if you change your mind, it's okay wid us."

"Thank you. It's really very generous of you," Kerner said, rising.

He shook hands with the Hawk and then with Moishie Mandelberg.

"Thank you again," Kerner said. "Thank you very much."

"No problem. We'll see ya around eh?" the Hawk said as Kerner opened the door.

"I'll see you. Thanks. Thanks a lot." He went out, closing the door behind him.

As he passed the secretary, Kerner glanced down at her, staring directly and unabashedly at her breasts. She looked up, caught his eye and smiled slyly at him. Kerner smiled back.

"Goodbye, Mr. Kerner," the secretary said, purposefully moving her tongue slowly along the length of her lips.

"Bye," Kerner replied and went out into the hall. As he headed for the elevator, he was suddenly surprised and elated as he realized he had an erection.

166

Chapter Twenty-Four

Morrie Hankleman sat at his desk trying to work his way through the pile of papers in front of him. To his left were letters, leases and other documents pertaining to his apartment buildings. To his right was a large, black loose-leaf folder with the word 'Proposals' taped across the front cover. This binder contained an outline of the various ideas and inventions that Hankleman had been actively soliciting for possible financing over a period of several months. Some of the presentations in the book were quite good. A few were potentially real moneymakers, in Morrie Hankleman's opinion; and before his problem with Artie Kerner had arisen, he had been close to deciding which proposal to back. After having studied several hundred submissions, he had managed to narrow the field down to three.

Hankleman pushed the folder away, swivelled his chair and put his feet up on the desk. He pulled a cigar out of his pocket and lit it. He was almost ready to roll again. For the first time in weeks, he was able to concentrate on something other than his problem with Artie Kerner. Since that difficulty had developed, he had ignored everything else.

Now, however, as he sat at his desk, he realized that although the anger that had been fuming inside him was still there, it had settled and he was on top of it. He felt calm, almost relaxed, yet at the same time very sharp and lucid.

He suspected that this unusual state was partly due to the fact that his wife had left. He had known she would leave. He had almost planned it that way. He hadn't planned to get her pregnant, but he knew that his insistence on her having an abortion would force her into leaving. He felt free – in a way, more free than he had felt after his coup on the stock market. He knew this was it. This time she wouldn't be back. He was sure a letter or call would soon arrive from her lawyer informing him that divorce proceedings had been initiated.

For a moment he tried to estimate what he'd have to shell out in the way of alimony. Hopefully, if his accountant and his lawyer were worth their salt, he might get away with five or six hundred a month.

Yes, his wife's departure was one very good reason why he was now so relaxed. The other reason was that he knew he would soon have the upper hand with Weisskopf and Mandelberg and Kerner. Another twenty-four hours and he'd be laughing. After he'd finished with them, he would shoot down to Vegas for a week and then perhaps take a little cruise or head for some resort where there were a lot of unattached women. After that he would get back on track again. He had to keep his money working for him. He had to keep things rolling. Just a little bit longer and he'd finish with them. Then he could start moving again. He'd decide on an idea to back and go on to something new. Another twenty-four hours and he'd have the upper hand. He just knew it.

He sat up in his seat. He didn't want to work anymore that day. He would go home early and relax. He wouldn't have to hear the kid squawking. There was no one there to bug him. What a pleasure, he thought. Maybe he'd go out for supper with someone and then check out the action on Crescent Street. He wondered who he would call. At one time he'd had a few friends, but after scoring on the market he had gradually broken off contact with them. The only person he had socialized with since that time was Eugene Carlin, the man who had originally given him the tip on the market. Not that he particularly enjoyed Carlin's company, but at least they thought along the same lines.

He tried to think of someone else whose company pleased him but he could come up with no one; and suddenly for the first time it occurred to Morrie Hankleman that there was no one in the entire world that he cared for in the slightest. This thought gave him comfort.

Chapter Twenty-Five

Artie Kerner could feel a tension building up inside him. He had called each of his creditors and informed them that he was going to clear his debt within a few days. From the way they had all sounded, he realized that his decision to sell everything and pay them off had been well timed. They all had given the impression that they were about to jump on him with both feet.

Kerner sighed despondently and stood up. He left his desk and walked into the warehouse area. It's too bad, he thought, that the business was a total write-off, but then, so what? He had made his decision, and it didn't really matter. He was going to pay up and get out. That's what mattered. He was going to get himself together. If he didn't have a nickel left when it was all over, that wasn't important, he told himself.

He was starting to feel sick. He looked at his watch. It was twelve-thirty. The time was passing so slowly, he thought, but at least he was having some success in controlling himself. Usually by that time he would have already been downtown for a good hour and have made at least one and maybe two or three buys.

He took a deep breath and walked back into his office. He sat down on the desk top. Yes, he was going to beat his sickness. He was going to make a new start. He didn't need the business, he didn't need money. He knew he would be better off without it. No one needed it. It made most people crazy. He thought about Solly Weisskopf's offer of a few hours earlier. Amazing. Truly amazing. He couldn't figure it out. How many people would offer to give up almost five thousand dollars without a second thought? Why would he do it? Kerner wondered. In a way, there was something almost unreal about it. He couldn't figure it out. It was hard to believe but yet it was true.

It took a superior man to make an offer like that, he thought. It would take a superior man to conquer the sickness that he himself was now struggling with. But he would do it. He dreaded to think of the agony which he would have to go through. But he would do it. He was going to beat it. He would not make a buy today. If only his mind would stop flashing the image of the bronze sculpting he had seen in La Galerie d'Or the other day.

Kerner could feel a headache coming on. He looked down at his hands which were now beginning to shake. Soon the nausea would arrive with full force. He was surprised that it hadn't already overtaken him. Just as he thought this, he felt a light pressure moving from his throat to his stomach and he knew that soon he would not be happy.

Chapter Twenty-Six

Big Moishie was more than a little surprised when the phone rang and he found Mendy Garelick on the line. He had not heard from Mendy Garelick in a long time. Several years before, Garelick, also known as Busfare due to the fact that he had once been run over by a provincial bus, had come to Moishie in a desperate state.

He had become involved in a major bankruptcy swindle and had been arrested. Fortunately for Busfare, the presiding judge was found to be broad-minded about monetary persuasion. Busfare was given to understand through his lawyer that ten thousand dollars might help considerably in keeping him out of jail.

He had come to see Big Moishie. Big Moishie had always liked Busfare and considered him a straight type. He had loaned him the ten thousand interest free. Busfare went to trial and was acquitted. Two months later he had repaid Big Moishie in full.

That had been three years ago and since that time, although Big Moishie had heard about Busfare, he had not heard from him.

Now, suddenly, here was Busfare on the phone talking as though the last three years had never happened. Big Moishie hung up the phone and turned slowly towards the Hawk.

"Solly, do you remember Mendy Garelick?"

The name didn't register. Solly shook his head. "No."

"Sure you know him," Big Moishie said emphatically. "You know – Mendy! Skinny Mendy Garelick."

The Hawk thought for another moment and then shook his head again. "I don remember em," he said.

"Of course you do. You know him as well as I do. You remember, when he was a kid he got run over by a bus near de Bullion Street."

"Oh! Busfare! Sure I remember Busfare," the Hawk said, nodding vigorously.

"Right … Busfare," Big Moishie said.

"Was dat him on de phone?"

"Yes. He says he has a favour to repay me. Some important information. He wants to come up here right away."

"So he's coming?"

"Yes, he'll be here in about twenty minutes."

"I wonder what he has?"

Big Moishie shrugged. There was no sense in even trying to speculate about what information Busfare might be bringing him.

"I remember him when he was about sixteen or seventeen. He climbed up on de cross on Mount Royal and turned off some lights so it spelled out 'Fuck.' You remember dat, Moishie?"

"Yes, I remember. It made the third page of the *Star*."

"He was always doing someting a liddle bit different, eh, Moishie?"

"Yes."

"I wonder what he's got?"

Big Moishie shrugged indifferently once again. "We'll know soon enough," he said, and getting up from his seat he began pacing about the room.

Chapter Twenty-Seven

Artie Kerner stood in front of La Galerie d'Or making a last ditch effort to control himself and hoping that Dr. Lehman would meet him there as he had promised.

Kerner looked at his watch. It was two-fifteen. He had done well, exceeding by far the limit of restraint that he had thought was possible.

He looked up and down Sherbrooke Street for some sign of Dr. Lehman. Then he looked up into the large show window of La Galerie d'Or. He could see one of Verland's bronzes there. Kerner knew he could not hold out anymore. It was too much. Too much for anyone. Perhaps tomorrow he could progress a bit further. Eventually he would beat his addiction, but today he was through.

He scanned the street again for Dr. Lehman. Then he rushed up the stairs into La Galerie d'Or.

Chapter Twenty-Eight

"Where's our six draught?" Teddy Regan shouted at the waiter. He turned back towards the T.V. set.

"We really worked that queer over the other day, eh, Teddy?" Jerry Shmytxcyk said.

"Yeah."

"You really got em good."

"Yeah."

"He was fucking tough for a queer, eh?"

"Yeah."

"Maybe he wasn't a queer."

"He was. Every time I hit em, he kept tryin' to grab me by the balls."

The waiter placed another six draughts of beer down on the table.

"Pay em for the beer, Jerry," Teddy Regan said.

"Hey, fuck! I paid for the last three rounds."

"Will you just pay him!"

"That's my fourth round," Shmytxcyk protested.

"Tough shit! Just pay em," Regan said and turned back towards the T.V. set.

Shmytxcyk grudgingly reached into his pocket, extracted a handful of change and threw it onto the waiter's tray. "I'm always fucking paying," he complained.

"Hey, will you shut up! I'm trying ta watch this program."

"Who gives a shit?" Shmytxcyk said.

"I do."

"Yeah! Well, I don't."

"Too fucking bad!"

"It's too fucking bad for you because I'm gonna change the fucking channel!"

"If you change the channel before I find out if she wins the fucking washing machine, then you're dead, Jerry."

"Fuck you, I'm changin' it."

Jerry Shmytxcyk got up and headed for the T.V. set. He placed a chair under the set and got up on it. A patron sitting a few feet away suddenly shouted, "What the hell are you doing?"

"I'm changing the channel," Shmytxcyk replied.

"Hold on. I wanna see her win the washing machine," the man called out.

"I don't give a shit about her washing machine!" Jerry Shmytxcyk retorted.

"Don't change that fucking channel, buddy," the man said threateningly.

"Change the channel!" Teddy Regan suddenly yelled from the back of the room.

Jerry Shmytxcyk changed the channel and got down from the chair. He walked back to his table.

"Who was that prick?" Regan asked.

"I dunno. Just some prick."

"He's got a fucking big mouth."

"Yeah."

"I'd like to punch that prick out."

"Yeah. Me too," Shmytxcyk said, looking at his friend.

"Hey, prick!" Regan suddenly shouted.

The man turned hesitantly towards Regan and Shmytxcyk. They began heaving chairs at him.

Chapter Twenty-Nine

Whatever it was that Mendy Garelick had to tell Big Moishie, he was coming around to it very slowly, leading up to it step by step.

First he inquired about Moishie's and Solly's health, then he moved on to ask about their wives. After that, Busfare talked a bit about his own children and how they were growing up and so on. Then he slipped back three years and explained how, after he had been acquitted due to Big Moishie's generosity, he kicked around aimlessly for almost a year looking for something to get into.

He explained how he finally got a few dollars together and became involved as a partner with a private investigation firm in the East-End of the city. At this point he paused, as though savouring the last remaining moments of his indebtedness to Moishie Mandelberg.

"We handle anything you can think of," Busfare said.

"I see," Moishie Mandelberg said.

"It's very rare that we get any work from the English-speaking side of the city. Our clientele is mostly French."

"I see," Big Moishie repeated with a little nod.

Solly dragged on his cigarette.

"Just the other day, though, we got a call from a guy who wanted someone tailed." Busfare paused again.

"Yeah, so?" the Hawk said quietly.

"So that's why I wanted to talk to Moishie. I never forgot what you did for me, Moishie, so now maybe I can do something for you."

Big Moishie said nothing. He just kept his eyes fixed on Mendy Garelick and puffed on his cigar.

"This guy wanted someone tailed. ... Okay. So we put a tail on the guy and we gave him a report on the guy's activities the same night. I mean, I wasn't handling this. It was all arranged by my partner, Armand Lachaine, but I look at all the files on any job we do. Anyway, the morning after we gave him the report, this guy calls back and tells us that now he needs an office bugged. My partner tells him okay and he takes down all the information. Then he gives it over to me because I'm the one who arranges for that kind of thing.

"Now I study the information. There's no name of who owns the office that we have to do. Just the address. But I always like to know where I'm going, which I think is a wise policy. So I check out the address in Lovell's directory and I see that the address is listed as being rented by Mountbatten Holdings Limited, which is you and Solly."

Mendy Garelick stopped talking. Big Moishie continued to puff on his cigar and said nothing. The Hawk remained silent as well.

"I don't know what this guy's interest is in you but I figured I had to let you know."

"Who is it?" Moishie Mandelberg asked.

"The guy's name is Morrie Hankleman."

"Jee-sus Christ!" the Hawk said incredulously.

"And the guy he had tailed the first day was who? Arthur Kerner?" Big Moishie asked.

"Yes. Right. How did you know?" Busfare asked.

"I'm starting to see the picture," Big Moishie said, leaning his chin in his hand and ignoring Busfare's question.

"I hope this information will help you," Busfare said.

"Yes. This is very good."

"I just figured ... you know ... forewarned is forearmed, as they say."

"Yes. Yes, that's true," Big Moishie muttered, hardly listening. He turned to Solly. "Didn't I tell you about this Hankleman?"

"It's like a joke. Like he's not fer real, dis Hankleman," the Hawk replied.

"Oh, he's for real all right. He's a mooch. He didn't trust us from the minute he left our office when he first came to see us. A guy like that doesn't trust anyone. He wouldn't trust his own mother and father. I spotted him for a yentz the minute he walked into our office and opened his mouth. Do you see the picture, Solly?"

"Yeah, I tink I see it. He musta got it in his head dat we were gonna like do a number on him wid Kerner. Like maybe make de collection and make Kerner disappear, or maybe even make a deal wid Kerner."

"Right," Moishie said. "Something like that."

"A fucking mooch," the Hawk cursed.

Big Moishie turned to Busfare. "When is your man supposed to plant this bug?"

"He's supposed to come in tonight and plant it. He'll pick up anything that goes on in here on tape. Then, at noontime tomorrow, he's supposed to bring the first tape to Hankleman's office. In other words, Hankleman wants to know what's going on every five or six hours."

"De man is a messhug."

"Yeah, he is, but he went a little too far," Big Moishie said, scowling. "He went just a little bit too far."

"If you want, I can cancel this job, or you can just stay out of your office while it's bugged. I can let you know when it's clean. You just tell me what you want."

Moishie Mandelberg gazed down at his desk as though thinking. After a moment, he looked up. "You say your man is going to plant the bug tonight?"

"Yes. He'll come in around eleven, twelve. You know, maybe with the cleaning staff."

"Okay. Let it ride like nothing happened, and tell your man

that if he has any trouble getting into our office, I'll come down personally and open the door for him. Just let it ride. Okay?"

"Fair enough," Busfare said with a grin. "I won't ask you what you're going to do but, knowing you, I'm sure it'll be one for the books."

"I'm not sure yet myself what I'm going to do but, between me and Solly here, we'll think of something."

Big Moishie looked over at Solly the Hawk. "What d'you think, Solly?"

The Hawk stared back at his partner with a sour grin on his face. "Nutting ta worry," he said. "Nutting ta worry."

Chapter Thirty

"Oh, Mr. Kerner. How nice to see you again so soon. Can I help you?" Mrs. Crawford, the owner of La Galerie d'Or, asked.

"No, it's all right, thanks. I'm just browsing today," Kerner replied, struggling to keep a smile on his face in spite of the cramps in his stomach.

"I remember you mentioning an interest in one of Verland's bronzes when you were in last week. Mr. Verland is in the gallery today if you'd care to meet him."

Kerner nodded. "Sure, I'd love to meet him."

"Oh, fine. He's around somewhere. I'll just go and track him down. I'll be back in a jiffy."

"Fine," Kerner grunted.

Mrs. Crawford walked away towards the back studio.

Kerner put a hand to his stomach. He knew he would have to make a buy soon. He was trying desperately not to give in but he knew he couldn't hold out much longer. Still, he had put up one hell of a good fight. He never would have believed that he was capable of such self-control. He felt proud even though he knew he was just about finished.

The nausea was getting worse. Kerner looked around for the bathroom. He wanted to know exactly where it was in case he had to make a sudden dash for it. He was at the breaking point. But still he knew he had done well and was certain he was on his way to conquering the strange addiction which had been his master for so many months now. Even though he would have to make a buy, his expenditures for that particular day would be significantly less than they had been in a long time.

If only Dr. Lehman would show up. He had promised to do his best to get down there but he was already half an hour late. Why wasn't he coming? Artie Kerner wondered, starting to feel angry. With the psychiatrist's assistance, it might be possible to get over the hump and not have to buy anything. If he could just hold on for another ten or fifteen minutes, maybe Dr. Lehman would show up and help him.

He prayed that he wouldn't throw up. Suddenly he was aware of Mrs. Crawford approaching. She came up to him.

"I told Mr. Verland that you were interested in that bronze, Mr. Kerner. He'd very much like to meet you." She took Kerner by the arm. "He's in the back studio with some of his pieces." Mrs. Crawford began leading Kerner towards the back of the gallery.

It's all over, Kerner thought. The moment he laid his eyes on the bronze, he would be finished. He could feel his insides constricting. With great effort, he forced himself more-or-less erect and walked along with Mrs. Crawford. She led him into the back studio.

Where the hell is Dr. Lehman? Kerner wondered. He looked into the room. His eyes immediately centred in on the bronze. It rested on a desk-high pedestal on the left side of the studio. Next to it stood a gangling man of about fifty, dressed in a jean suit. Mrs. Crawford approached the sculptor, dragging Kerner along with her.

"This is the gentleman I was telling you about, Mr. Verland. Mr. Kerner, Mr. Verland."

Kerner's head was spinning. He had a great urge to scream, *Okay, I'll buy it! I'll buy it!*

"Yes. How do you do," the sculptor said, extending a white-gloved hand.

182

"Nice to meet you," Kerner replied, taking Verland's hand.

"Well, I'll just leave you two gentlemen to talk by yourselves," Mrs. Crawford said with a smile. She turned and walked away.

"So, I understand you like this piece here," Verland said, releasing Kerner's hand and pointing to the sculpting.

Kerner nodded, afraid to speak. He knew he was going to be sick and the more he thought about it, the sicker he felt. He had to talk, not think. Maybe he should ask the sculptor about his work. Perhaps he'd have some interesting things to say about his techniques. They might be really fascinating and hearing about them might distract him.

"I'm curious to know how you work with these bronzes," Kerner said.

"Oh, yes. Very good," the sculptor said enthusiastically. "I'll tell you. It's very difficult what I do. No one else can do it. You see, it's my own invention. I thought it up all by myself. I can't tell you too much about it, you understand. Just the superficial idea. Don't get me wrong. Don't misunderstand. But it's a very valuable idea. I'm getting it patented. But even if I told you, I don't know if you'd understand it. It's very complicated. Very tricky. No one else can do it. You follow?"

Kerner tried to pay attention to the man's patter but it was just a drone in his head. His eyes were fixed on the sculptor's mouth, which now seemed like some strange pink squirming tire tube. Kerner put a hand to his head and tried to concentrate on what the man was saying.

"... Don't get me wrong. But this is something very new. You follow? Never been done. They all want to know. They come to me. Every day they come. They all want to know. From everywhere they come. From England, from France. Every day. From Germany, Sweden, you name it. They all want to know. 'How do you do it?' they ask. 'Tell me what's the secret,' they say. 'Let us in on it. What is it?' ... You follow?"

Kerner rubbed his eyes which were now almost completely out of focus, and the thought occurred to him that this man's mouth might succeed in hypnotizing him where Dr.

Lehman had failed. Again he heard the scream inside his head: *I'll buy it! I'll buy it! How much?* The more this yell banged around in his head, the more nauseous he felt. The yell kept turning one way and the sculptor's mouth kept spinning the other way. Kerner tried to concentrate on the man's words.

"... So that's it, Mr. Kerner. But, anyway, that's enough of me talking about me and my sculpting. Now let's hear what you think about us," Verland said, resting a gloved hand on the bronze.

Kerner was about to reply when he heard a booming shout.

"Hold everything!" Dr. Lehman called, striding into the room. He came up alongside Kerner. "Okay, what's going on?"

"Thanks for coming," Kerner said.

"Have you bought anything yet?"

"No, not yet, but I don't think I can hold out much longer."

"Who's this?" Dr. Lehman said, pointing at Verland.

"This is Mr. Verland, the sculptor."

"How do you do, sir," Verland said, extending his hand.

"What the hell is that?" Dr. Lehman asked angrily.

"Oh. That's my special glove for touching my works."

"Well, you can touch your works with it but don't try to touch me with it. I don't shake hands with gloves."

"Oh, well, I'll take it off."

"It's too late. You should have taken it off before. Now I don't want to shake hands with you," Dr. Lehman said curtly, turning away to face Kerner. "So how are we doing, Kerner?"

"I don't think I can hold out any longer."

"Just hang in there."

"I'm trying."

"Well, try harder."

"I am. I am. But it's very difficult."

"And just what is so attractive in here that's making it so difficult to resist?"

Kerner pointed at the bronze next to him. "That piece of sculpting."

"That?!" Dr. Lehman gasped.

Kerner nodded.

"You call that a sculpting? That piece of shit?!"

"Excuse me, sir..." Verland began in an angry tone, but Dr. Lehman cut him off.

"I've seen better sculpting done by chimpanzees using balls of elephant crap."

Kerner blanched and threw a furtive look at Verland whose eyes were now bulging out of his head.

"I must interject here, sir," Verland said.

Dr. Lehman ignored him and turned away so that his back was completely towards the sculptor.

"Just hang in there, Kerner."

"I'm trying."

"Just ride right on through it."

Kerner nodded several times in quick succession.

"You've almost got it beat. It would be a shame to quit now and buy a piece of shit like this."

"Now hold on!" Verland yelled, stepping around in front of Dr. Lehman.

"Please don't interfere," the psychiatrist said sharply.

"I don't like the way you're talking about my work," Verland said, waving a finger in the doctor's face.

"I assure you, it's nothing personal. I'm dealing with a sick man here, so I'd appreciate it if you wouldn't interfere."

He turned towards Kerner. "Look. You've almost got this thing beat. Wouldn't it be a shame if you couldn't resist the temptation to buy what is essentially a piece of garbage. They wouldn't take this at the Salvation Army."

"Okay! That's it! I've had it with your insults, mister!"

"It's Doctor, not mister."

"Okay, Doctor. I don't care what the hell you are. I've had enough out of you. I think you're looking for a fight."

"A fight?" Dr. Lehman said, squinting.

"Yes, a fight," Verland replied, stepping towards Dr. Lehman.

The psychiatrist scratched his head. Kerner was frozen in place.

"What's the matter, Doctor?" Verland sneered. "You chicken or something?"

"Chicken? No, I'm not chicken. I just happen to think fighting is irrational."

"Yeah, I heard that one before," Verland laughed.

"Well, if you're really all that anxious to fight, Mr. Verland, I guess I can accommodate you."

"What?"

"You heard me. I'll fight if that's what you want."

Verland studied Dr. Lehman's face closely for a moment. "You're sure about that now?"

"I'm ready," Dr. Lehman said, taking off his suit jacket and dropping it on the floor.

"I don't want to break your glasses," Verland said hesitantly.

"Don't worry about that," the doctor replied, taking off his glasses and dropping them on the jacket.

Kerner looked on with disbelief, rooted to the floor.

"Okay," Verland said. "Boxing or wrestling?"

"What? When I fight, it's rough and tumble – no holds barred!"

"Okay, but if someone wants to give up, he just says so and the other guy has to stop fighting. Okay?" Verland said quickly.

"No, no. When I fight, it's a fight to the finish."

"Well, maybe we shouldn't fight in here. I don't want to break any of my sculptings."

"Well, you decide."

"Forget it. I don't want to injure my hands."

"Good enough," Dr. Lehman said and picked up his glasses and jacket. "Come on, Kerner. Let's get out of here and head back to my office."

"Aren't you going to consider this piece, Mr. Kerner?" Verland asked, stepping up to him.

"He doesn't want it," Dr. Lehman said.

"Well, how about letting Mr. Kerner decide for himself?"

"There's no way he could want a piece of crap like that. I wouldn't take it if you paid me."

"I'll ignore your insult. Mr. Kerner obviously has an aesthetic sensibility which is lacking in you," Verland replied.

Kerner was trying to speak but he couldn't get the words out.

"What do you think, Mr. Kerner?"

"Don't buy!" Dr. Lehman commanded.

"Let him decide!"

"Don't buy!"

Kerner struggled to say something.

"What do you think, Mr. Kerner?"

"You don't need it!"

"It's one of my best works."

"It's garbage."

"Some people consider it a minor masterpiece."

Dr. Lehman suddenly doubled over with laughter.

"What do you think, Mr. Kerner? What's your opinion of this piece?"

Kerner opened his mouth to speak but the only sound that came out was *ahhhgh!* as he threw up all over the sculptor and his work.

Chapter Thirty-One

The more the Hawk thought about Hankleman and what he was planning to do, the more ludicrous it became. He couldn't take it seriously. Hankleman was out of his mind. The man was insane. The whole thing was too incredible; so incredible that the Hawk couldn't feel even the slightest anger. He just wanted to laugh.

Moishie Mandelberg didn't see things quite the same way. He was in a fury. "I'll tell you, Solly, if this was ten, fifteen years ago, I'd put out a contract on this piece of dreck and have him hit in the head. I swear to you, that's what I'd do."

"De man is a messhug, Moishie. You shouldn let it bodder you."

"Bother me?" the big man said, shaking his head for added emphasis. "This yentz bothers me so much that if he was here in this office at this minute and I had a piece, I'd blow him away myself."

"Relax, Moishie, relax. De man's a putz. It's not wert getting upset over."

"I'm going to get this Hankleman, Solly. I'm going to get him good."

The Hawk shrugged. "Why waste your time on em?"

"Why? Because he deserves it."

"De man is a nebbish, he's not wert any aggravation."

"I'm going to fix his wagon, Solly."

"He's a lemmish, a nutting."

"I don't know exactly what I'm going to do but I'm going to do something."

"Why waste your time on dis shmendrick?"

"Because it's going to make me feel good when I fuck him."

"My own idea is dat since Kerner is gonna pay, den we jus carry on an do our part."

"We were doing our part but that cocksucker didn't trust us!" Big Moishie shouted.

"Big deal. A guy ly dat will never trust no one."

"I know. But he went too far. I knew he didn't trust us the minute he walked in here the first time. I knew it before he knew it. He probably didn't know it till the next day, but I knew it the minute I saw him; before he even opened his mouth."

"So whadda ya wanna do?"

"I don't know exactly but I'll think of something."

"I mean, you don wanna do nutting wid muscle, right?"

"No. No violence. I want to hurt him in such a way that as long as he lives, whenever he starts thinking what a big mavin he is, he'll remember me and he'll know he's a pisher. That's how I want to hurt him."

"It's not wert de aggravation, Moishie."

"It's worth it. Believe me, it's worth it."

The Hawk sighed deeply.

"You remember when we were talking the other day, Solly?"

"Yeah."

"You remember how you were telling me how you felt about Saltpeter ... how you wanted to crush him ... to break him?"

The Hawk nodded.

"That's how I feel about this Hankleman. I'm going to teach him a lesson that he won't ever forget."

"You're sure dats what you want?"

"That's what I want. ... You wanted your last collection; I

want my last gaff ... and I'm close to it. I know I have him somehow. I just can't quite see it yet. But I know I have him."

"Yeah, you have him, Moishie."

"What d'you mean?"

"I mean, you got em. At least I tink you got em."

"How?"

"It just came to me. Like jus now, in one seccun I saw de whole picture in my head. De minute you mentioned Saltpeter's name, I saw de whole picture."

"What is it?" Big Moishie asked, edging forward in his seat.

In a very low voice and with a droll smile on his face, the Hawk replied, "We jus found a new mooch for de telephone gaff."

Chapter Thirty-Two

Kerner was lying on the little couch in Dr. Lehman's office. Beside him a light rainshower was in progress. The doctor was hidden from view somewhere behind his desk.

Kerner watched the rain coming down.

"That was very significant, what you did back there," Dr. Lehman said, still out of sight.

Kerner turned and stared at the big desk. "I couldn't help it. It just came out all by itself."

"It's all right. Don't apologize. That was very good."

Kerner could see the top of Dr. Lehman's head coming slowly into view above the desk top.

"What you did back there at the gallery was very symbolic ... very significant. Don't you realize that?"

The upper half of the doctor was now visible.

"I guess so ... I'm not sure," Kerner said hesitantly.

"Well, it was. Take my word for it. Within the context of your particular problem, your act of barfing on that piece of crap was in effect a classic catharsis. You were expressing a point of view. Whether you know it or not, you had decided to put an end to your craziness and, when you brecched on that guy and on his sculpting, which you had been so tempted to buy, you were in effect giving concrete and tangible form to your inner decision. You were expelling, as it were, your past sickness. ... Just to prove my point ... don't you feel better now?"

"Yes, I do. Mind you ... I still feel very nervous ... uneasy. ... You know?"

The doctor's chair continued to rise so that his legs could now be seen dangling above the level of the desk.

"Yes, yes. I know. But don't worry. Something's clicked somewhere in your head and you're going to be all right."

"Do you really think so?"

"Kerner," the doctor said tersely, "don't start with me today. Just take my word for it. Okay?"

"I'm sorry. I just wanted a bit of reassurance. ... Look, I'm insecure."

"Okay, Mr. Kerner, I understand. But just take my word for it – you're going to be all right if you want to be. ... Now just come over here and press that white button on my desk. This fucking chair has gone out of control," the doctor said as his head gradually approached the ceiling of the room.

Kerner got up and went over to the desk. He pressed a white button. Dr. Lehman's chair suddenly began spinning wildly.

"Not that one, you fool!" Dr. Lehman shouted, gripping the sides of his chair. "The other white one ... on the left."

Kerner pressed the smaller white button on the console. The chair stopped turning and began to descend. Kerner watched it come down.

"Okay, stop," Dr. Lehman ordered as his feet touched the floor.

Kerner released the button. The doctor got up from the chair.

"Did you do that on purpose, Kerner?"

"No, I swear. There were two white buttons. I saw the bigger one first. It wasn't my fault."

Dr. Lehman scowled. "If you weren't sure, you should have asked."

"I'm sorry."

"Okay. Forget it. Go back to the couch."

Kerner went back to the couch. Dr. Lehman walked over to the table near the hut and seated himself.

"In any case, as I was saying, you're going to be all right if you want to be. I think your decision last night to sell everything and live on a kibbutz was very important and what you accomplished today was a direct offshoot of that decision."

"I'm still quite nervous about the idea of selling all my stuff. ... You know... I'm afraid of how I might react. Maybe I'll get completely crazy and have to buy ten times as much as I've sold."

"I don't think that will happen. You've proved that you can overcome your obsession with buying. Now it's just a question of retaining and reinforcing your decision to change your life. I have confidence in you, Mr. Kerner. I believe you'll be fine. However, I'm not telling you that you're cured. You still have a ways to go and I trust you'll continue these sessions up until the time you're ready to leave for Israel."

"Oh, yes. I still intend to see you regularly. It'll probably be a few months before I get everything straightened away here, so I hope to be able to see you as much as possible during that time."

"Good, good," Dr. Lehman said, getting up from his seat and looking at his watch. "Anyways, we've gone over our time here. We'll carry on tomorrow."

Kerner got up from the couch and moved towards the door.

Dr. Lehman walked over to his desk. "Oh, just one minute, Mr. Kerner."

Kerner stopped and turned around.

"I might as well give this to you now so you can study it for a while," the doctor said as he opened a desk drawer and withdrew a folded sheet from inside. He walked over to Kerner and handed the paper to him. "I want you to look this over. Study it during the next while. There's no rush. Look it over, change it around a little bit to put it in your own words. Then write it up on your own stationery... in a natural way... let it flow; let it come from the heart. Then sign it and give it back to me before you leave Montreal."

Kerner unfolded the sheet.

"Just use this as a general guide," Dr. Lehman said, pointing at the paper in Kerner's hands.

Kerner scanned the sheet. It read:

Dear Dr. Lehman:

I can't begin to tell you how gratified I am for all you've done for me. Before meeting you I had heard the word genius bandied about. You know, people would say this one's a real Einstein, that one's a real Einstein, this one's a genius, that one's a genius. The way people abuse that word, a person might have thought there were a million geniuses running around. Well, let me say this, in all honesty. I've been around. I know and have known thousands of people, be they doctors, lawyers, accountants, physics professors, mathematicians, biologists, neurosurgeons, chemists, anthropologists, biochemists, urologists, philosophers, gynecologists, neurophysiologists, psychiatrists, and whatever, and, until I met you, I had not yet met a genius.

When I first stepped into your extraordinarily beautiful and imaginatively designed office and had the honour of meeting you, I knew then that I was face to face with 'The Genius.' The fact that you cured my illness is, I think, one of the most incredible accomplishments, if not the major accomplishment, of the modern age and far exceeds anything that was done by Freud, Jung, Adler and people of that ilk.

I thank you from the bottom of my heart.

(signed) With eternal gratitude,

P.S. I have enclosed with this little note a cheque for five thousand dollars as a very small token of my great admiration and appreciation. I know that you will say you have been paid for your services and that this extra amount is quite unnecessary; but please, please keep this and perhaps it may be of some small help in aiding you in the extensive research you have been doing over the years to try and help sick people like myself.

Kerner finished reading the letter. He looked up at Dr. Lehman, who was smiling broadly.

"It's just a little testimonial, Mr. Kerner. You don't actually have to send me a cheque for five thousand dollars. Just write it up in your own words, sticking pretty much to this model as a general guide. Letters such as this from my patients are very helpful."

"Sure, I'll do it," Kerner said.

"Thank you, Mr. Kerner. It'll be much appreciated."

"It's no trouble," Kerner said as he walked to the door and opened it. "I'll see you tomorrow." He headed across the waiting room.

"Oh, one other thing," Dr. Lehman said.

Kerner turned.

"In case I forget, remind me tomorrow and I'll give you the address of the Wasp. He started his own kibbutz in Israel. Maybe you can look him up when you get there."

"Great," Kerner said. "I'll remind you."

Dr. Lehman waved goodbye.

Kerner went out and closed the door. From inside he could hear the doctor's voice.

"You can come out of the closet now, Mrs. Griff. He's gone."

Kerner walked away.

Chapter Thirty-Three

At eight P.M., Morrie Hankleman was seated at a table in the front room at Ruby Foo's, listening to Eugene Carlin discuss his new real estate venture. Hankleman no longer felt as calm as he had several hours earlier. His anger was beginning to stir again and Hankleman was becoming increasingly agitated.

The fact that Carlin was fully involved and rolling fast with an exciting and apparently lucrative business deal made Hankleman that much more aware of the time he had lost on account of his problem with Artie Kerner.

Hankleman snapped his fingers at the waiter who was passing by. The waiter turned.

"Where's our bloody food?" Hankleman demanded angrily.

"It's coming, sir."

"You said that ten minutes ago. Now c'mon, speed it up, eh. We haven't got all night."

The waiter nodded curtly and walked away.

"Fucking arrogant prick," Hankleman muttered. "We'll see how he acts when I don't leave a tip."

"That's one thing I never do," Eugene Carlin said.

"What?"

"Tell off the waiters."

"Why not? Some of them need to be told off sometimes."

"It's not worth it," Carlin said. "If you get them pissed off, they spit in your food. I'm sure they all do it. ... When he brings your food, you just better examine it closely."

Hankleman shrugged. "This one wouldn't have the guts to do it."

"Maybe not but just check anyways."

Hankleman looked at Carlin sceptically.

"Did you hear from your wife yet?" Carlin asked.

"I heard from her lawyer. He called just before I left the office."

"Who's she using?"

"Sampson and Rothman."

Carlin nodded. "That's who my ex-wife used. You remember?"

"Yeah."

Eugene Carlin rubbed his mustache. Then he dragged on his cigarette, exhaled, and sipped slowly at his martini. He put the glass down.

"That Rothman's a real smiling whore," he said.

"Oh yeah?" Hankleman replied, trying to sound disinterested.

"Yeah."

Hankleman waited for him to add something, but Carlin remained silent.

"Why do you say that?" Hankleman finally asked.

"He just is," Carlin replied offhandedly.

"Why do you say that?" Hankleman asked again, trying to sound as nonchalant as possible.

"He's got a thing about trying to make all his female clients."

"Yeah? Where did you hear that?"

"I heard it from this woman I was taking out. She got her divorce through him. I also heard it from a few other people."

"It's probably just talk," Hankleman said.

"No, no, it's more than talk," Carlin replied.

Hankleman shrugged and picked up his drink. For a while

neither of them spoke. Hankleman looked around for the waiter.

"You feel like checking out the action at George's after we eat?" Carlin asked.

"Yeah, sure. Why not?"

"I picked up a real nympho there last week. She takes it any way."

"Nice?"

"Yeah, not bad."

Hankleman looked around again for the waiter. "Ah, the prick's finally coming," he said, spotting the man moving towards their table with a tray.

The waiter approached, removed the plates from the tray and placed them on the table. "Bon appetit, messieurs," he said with a smile, and moved off.

"Check your food," Carlin suggested matter-of-factly as he began to eat with gusto.

Hankleman looked down at the food on his plate. He turned it around in front of him. There, next to the thick slice of roast beef, almost camouflaged by the scoop of mashed potatoes, Hankleman saw what looked surprisingly like a gob of spit.

Chapter Thirty-Four

Early that evening, Solly and Big Moishie went over to Artie Kerner's apartment. They told him what they had found out from Busfare. They filled him in on Saltpeter and the entire background of the telephone gaff – how they had set up the office; the manner in which the telephone line had been installed to intercept the calls headed for the office of the Quebec Roads Planning Department; how they had held the plan in abeyance. They explained that everything was still set up and that they were going to use the same basic plan to teach Morrie Hankleman a very expensive lesson. Big Moishie outlined the strategy.

"How do you know he'll bite?" Kerner asked.

"How do I know he'll bite? ... I don't know how I know, Artie ... but I just know. I know a mooch and I know when a mooch is going to bite."

Kerner nodded.

"Lemmie explain you why Moishie knows, Arter. I'll give you like de classic story about Moishie's judgement," Solly the Hawk said. "Dis happened maybe ... what? ... I dunno, maybe fifteen years ago, Moishie?"

"You mean the watch story?"

"Yeah, wid de watch."

"Yeah, fifteen years ago," the big man replied.

"So fifteen years ago, one day me and Moishie were taking like a lunch break, dooring de day. We're like shopping. I tink I was looking fer someting fer de wife. So like we go into a store an we're like, you know, looking aroun. Moishie, at de time, is wearing a watch which he smuggled in from, I tink, Switzerland a year before. Dis watch cost him over dere like a g-note. A tousand bucks. Over here it was wert like maybe double. Okay? Show em de watch, Moishie."

Moishie Mandelberg drew back the cuff of his shirt sleeve and revealed a large gold watch. Kerner could see that the case was studded with what appeared to be several small diamonds.

"It's beautiful," he said.

"Dose are real diamins in case yer wondering," the Hawk offered.

"It's really something," Kerner said.

"Anyway, so he's wearing dat same watch at de time," the Hawk continued. "We're like leaning over de showcase in de store when all of a sudden a salesgirl comes over. She spots de watch on Moishie's hand. 'Hey, dats some good-looking watch you got dere, mister,' she tells Moishie. Moishie says, 'Oh yeah, you like it, miss?' At de same time he gives me like a nudge wid his foot, like to say 'Watch dis.' So I watch.

"'Yeah, I like it very much,' de bear says to Moishie. 'Are dose like real diamins?' she says.

"'Yeah, dere real,' Moishie says.

"'Tell me,' de bear says, 'how much costs a watch ly dat?'

"'Ehh! It's not dat expensive,' Moishie says. 'Why? You wanna buy it?'

"'Yeah, if I could afford it, I'd buy it,' de broad says.

"'It's not expensive,' Moishie tells her. 'You wanna buy it, I'll sell you it. Make me an offer.'

"'Are you serious?' she says.

"'Sure. What's it wert to you?' Moishie says.

"De broad tinks fer a minute. Den she says, like wid a liddle laugh, 'Fer fifteen bucks, I'll buy it.'

"Moishie makes like he's tinkin fer a secun an den he tells er, 'It's a deal.' He takes off de watch. 'Gimmie fifteen an de fob is yers.'

"De bear looks at em fer a minute like somebody just gave er a bite in de beaver. Den she rips out her wallet like fast an she pulls out fifteen and holds it out fer Moishie. 'Are ya serious?' she says.

"'Sure, gimmie de scratch,' Moishie says.

"'Yer jus joking,' she says.

"'Naw, c'mon. It's a deal,' Moishie says. 'Here, take de watch.' He shoves de watch in her shirt pocket, managing ta cop a quick feel at de same time. I remember she had a big pair of bazookas, eh, Moishie?"

"Very big," Moishie replied, nodding. "Like watermelons... big watermelons."

"So she gives em de dough," the Hawk continued. "Meanwhile, I'm looking at Moishie like he's nuts.

"'C'mon, let's go,' Moishie tells me. We walk outside. 'Moishie, are you crazy?' I say. 'Don worry, Solly,' he says. 'C'mon, let's go.'

"'Whadda ya talking?' I say. 'I'm going back in an getting back de watch.'

"'Don worry, Solly,' Moishie tells me, an he starts to pull me along de street. Okay. Dats what Moishie wants, dats what we do. We walk. We walk half a block. Moishie is like whistling, happy, like he don give a shit. He don know from nutting. ... Me, I don feel so good. We walk anudder half block. Moishie is singing now. He's singing Mein Yiddishe Mama, an I'm like, ya know, jerking myself off." Solly made the appropriate hand motion. "All of a sudden, I hear like someone screaming. It's a broad.

"'Hey, mister! Hey, mister!' she's yelling.

"I turn aroun; Moishie, he's like still singing. I see de bear from de store like running down de street. 'Hey, mister! Hey, mister!' she's yelling. Moishie, he don even bodder to turn aroun. He's like looking in de store windows. De broad comes running up.

"'Hey, mister!' she yells to Moishie.

"Moishie turns aroun slow like. You know, like he's very surprised. 'What's de problem, liddle lady?' he says like he's out ta lunch.

"'I was tinking,' she says, like holding up Moishie's watch. 'I tink I paid too much fer dis watch.'

"'Oh yeah?' Moishie says. 'Okay, so give it back.' She gives em back de watch, he gives er back de scratch. She fucks off an we start walking, and Moishie's still singing Mein Yiddishe Mama like nutting ever happened. Ever since dat time, I trust Moishie's judgement. He knows a mooch when he sees one. Dey don even have ta talk an Moishie can tell. So when he says Hankleman will bite, I guarantee you, he will bite."

"Well, from that story, I'll put my money with you," Kerner said, looking at the big man.

"So you'll do your part?" Solly asked.

"Yes, of course. After the way you've treated me, how can I refuse."

"Okay, very good. So let's get down to work," Moishie Mandelberg said, pulling several sheets out of his briefcase. "I'll make notes and then we'll each have a copy. It'll be like a T.V. show. We'll start off tomorrow like a regular day. I come into the office and my secretary blows me like usual."

"Yes," the Hawk said. "Everyting has ta be like natural."

Chapter Thirty-Five

"Go right in, Mr. Kerner. They're expecting you," the secretary said.

Artie Kerner took a deep breath, gulped and walked into the office.

"Oh, you're finally here, Kerner," Big Moishie said angrily.

"I'm sorry. I had some trouble with the car," Kerner said meekly.

"Did you hear, Solly? He had some trouble with the car," Big Moishie said with fierce sarcasm.

"Nex time take a bus. We don like ta be kep waiting," the Hawk snapped.

"I'm sorry..."

"Never mind!" Solly said, rising and moving towards Kerner. "Jus gimmie de dough."

"I still don't have it," Kerner replied.

"Well den, my friend, you're like up shits creek widout a paddle."

"I just need another few..."

"You don't need sweet fuck all, friend!" Big Moishie growled. "We told you what we were going to do to you, Kerner."

"It's not like we didn give you fair warning," the Hawk added.

"Look, you can't get blood from a stone," Kerner whined.

"No? No? You don tink so? It's bin done. We did dat lots already. We can do it. Take it from me, we can do dat; very easy like. Okay?" the Hawk sneered.

Big Moishie, orchestrating from behind his desk, pointed at Kerner.

"Please, Mr. Weisskopf, maybe you could talk to Mr. Hankleman and just give me a few days more."

Solly the Hawk laughed menacingly. "Listen, shmuck, lemmie like explain you someting here. At dis point I don care whad dis putz Morrie Hankleman tinks or whad he's ready ta do fer you. It's out of his hands. He gave it over ta us. Y'unnerstan. Whad he tinks now don interest me. We got like turdy-five percent coming ta us on what you owe. Dats what we want number one. Den number two, we want Hankleman's sixty-five percent. Dats what we want. Dats what you were supposed ta bring us here dis morning; an if I hafta break every bone in yer fucking body den dats what I'll do. Y'unnerstan, shmuck?"

"Please, just ..."

"Look, Kerner!" Big Moishie shouted, standing up suddenly. "We're through fucking around with you!" He slammed a huge fist down on the desk top.

"Look, if you give me another few weeks I'll pay you double what you're getting out of this," Kerner yelled.

"Did you hear, Solly? All of a sudden he's going to pay us double. ... He can't come up with the thirteen gees, but all of a sudden he's going to find twice as much."

"I mean it," Kerner protested.

"Did you hear, Solly? He means it."

"Yeah, I heard, I heard."

"I promise you, it's true!" Kerner pleaded.

"You promise?" the Hawk said with quiet menace in his voice. "I'm gonna tell you what *I* promise, my friend. I promise you dat if by five o'clock today you don come up wid de scratch what you were supposed ta bring to us here dis morning, den I will put you in de fucking hospital for like a year. Y'unnerstan what I'm talking?"

"Yes... but if you would only give me just another week, or even ... let's say another few days, then you could make twice as much."

"We're not interested, Kerner," the Hawk snarled. "We want what's coming. Now!"

"Wait. Wait a minute," Big Moishie said quietly. "Let's give the man a chance here. ... You have something cooking, Kerner?"

"Well ... sort of ... yes."

"You sort of have, or you do have?" Big Moishie asked.

"Well, yes, I do have."

"So let's hear about it."

"I can't talk about it, but if I have a little while longer it'll pay off big."

"You mean, if you have the use of the money you owe us a little while longer then it will pay off big?"

"Yes, that's right. But I can't discuss it."

"Did you hear, Solly? The man says he can't discuss it. Did you hear?"

"I heard. I heard," the Hawk replied softly. "He has a proposition wid our money but he can't discuss it."

"Look, this thing is worth a lot more than what I owe," Kerner whined.

"So let's hear about it already," the Hawk said.

"I don't see why you have to hear about it."

"He doesn see, Moishie. Did you hear? He doesn see why we have ta hear about it."

"I heard but I'm not sure I heard right."

"I swear to you, I'll pay you double. There's no point in me telling you about it."

"Lock the door, Solly," Moishie Mandelberg said quietly.

"What are you locking the door for?" Kerner asked, forcing a note of panic into his voice.

No one replied.

The Hawk went over to the door and opened it. He looked into the reception area.

"Eileen, if you hear any noise from inside, it's nutting. Jus ignore it," the Hawk said. Then he closed and locked the door.

"Why did you lock the door? What's going on here?" Kerner whined.

The Hawk walked over towards Kerner.

"What's going on?" Kerner repeated.

"Let's hear about the deal you have cooking," Big Moishie said.

"It's my own thing. It has nothing to do with what I owe you."

"At this point, my friend, everything you do has to do with what you owe us. ... So let's hear about it already, before I lose my patience."

"Can't you just leave me alone for another week?"

Big Moishie turned to the Hawk. "Solly, what do you think?" he asked.

"Dis is what I tink!" the Hawk shouted, and he slapped his hands together hard.

"Ahhh!" Kerner screamed.

Again the Hawk smashed one palm against the other and again Kerner yelled.

"Leave me alone! ... Please. Get off me."

"Dats what I tink," the Hawk said viciously.

Kerner continued to whine. "Jesus. What was that for? ... You loosened my tooth. Christ! What did you hit me for. Look, you made me bleed."

"An I can make you bleed a lot more."

"It's enough for now, Solly," Big Moishie said.

"My teeth are loose," Kerner said in a frightened voice.

"Soon dey might be on de floor wid yer head tagedder!" the Hawk snapped.

"It's enough. It's enough," Big Moishie said. "Am I right, Kerner?"

"My teeth are loose," Kerner replied.

"Just be thankful that you still have them. ... Now let's hear what you have cooking."

"Okay, okay, I'll tell you but it's worth a lot more than what I owe."

"Look, Kerner, don't give me bullshit. Just tell us about it!" Big Moishie shouted, slamming his fist down on the desk top.

"Okay! All right, I will. I'll tell you but I think I should get something out if it."

"Did you hear, Solly? He wants something out of it. He's telling us what he wants."

"I heard but I'm not sure I heard right," the Hawk replied with a hard chuckle.

"Don't tell us what you want, friend!" Big Moishie bellowed, smashing against his desk and pushing it aside. "We'll tell you!" He rushed up to Kerner. "You owe us. You got something that we want to know about. So talk and talk fast before they have to take you out of here on a stretcher!"

"Okay, I will. I'll talk. I said I will. But I just think if you use this, then I deserve to get something out of it."

"Deserve? Dis is what you deserve, you piece of dreck!" Solly yelled and slammed his fist into his palm.

Kerner screamed again while Big Moishie began knocking his desk around the room. "Leave me alone!"

"You piece of garbage!" the Hawk shouted.

"Okay. Hold it, Solly," Moishie Mandelberg said.

"I'll break your fucking head!" the Hawk snarled.

"You don't have to hit me," Kerner whined.

"I'll break your fucking arms, you lousy mooch!" the Hawk continued.

"Enough. Enough, Solly," Big Moishie said.

"Don fuck wid me, you mooch!" the Hawk sneered.

"I didn't do anything," Kerner howled. "You didn't have to hit me. Christ, this tooth is almost falling out now."

"Are you ready to talk to us now?" Big Moishie asked quietly.

"He hurt my jaw," Kerner replied.

"You asked for it," Big Moishie said.

"In a minute I'll break it," the Hawk added.

"Enough, Solly. Okay, let's hear about it, Kerner. Do yourself a favour and talk fast."

"If you use this, could I get a piece of the action?" Kerner asked.

"You know what you'll get. You'll get like a small plot in de cemetery. Dats what you'll get," the Hawk said with a sharp laugh.

"Okay, okay, take it easy. I'll tell you."

"So tell," Big Moishie said.

"An if you open yer mout one more time about a piece of de action, so help me I'll break boat yer fucking arms," the Hawk added.

"Just talk," Big Moishie said quietly.

"An talk straight!" the Hawk said.

"Okay. All right. ... I just happen to have some information about the new autoroute extension."

"Which one?" Big Moishie asked.

"The Laurentian."

"Oh yeah? So let's hear already."

"There's one main guy who's in charge of determining the final route. His name is Guy Gervais. He's the head of the Quebec Roads Planning Department."

"So?" Solly asked.

"So for the last three months he's been planning the route for the new extension. It's supposed to go from St. Jovite to Mont Laurier."

"So?"

"So I happen to know him."

"So?"

"So I know that he can be bought without any trouble."

"He takes a shmear?" Big Moishie said interestedly.

"Without any questions," Kerner replied.

"How d'ya know dis, Kerner?"

"Well, I ran into him by accident a few years ago when they were building phase two of the extension. We were both spending a week skiing up north at Gray Rocks Inn. I met him on the hill. Later we had a few drinks in the bar. We got friendly. One thing led to another. Before I knew it, he started suggesting that he could sell me some information on the extension. A week later I met him in the city. I paid him $4,000.00. He gave me what he called one zone. The new route passed right through the middle of it. I bought the land involved for $100.00 an acre. Three months later the government paid me $325.00 an acre. I made a profit of $22,000.00. I paid him ten percent.

"Now there's been talk of a new eighteen-mile extension. I know for a fact that it's true. In a few months the government will start buying up the land. This guy is still in charge."

"What's his name?" Big Moishie asked.

"Guy Gervais."

"An dis guy is like de big cheese?" Solly asked.

"Yes, he's the head man."

"How do you know he can still be gotten to?" Moishie asked.

"He called me a few weeks ago to ask if I wanted a piece of the new action. Since then I've been trying to get the money together. That's why I couldn't pay what I owe Hankleman."

"How did he come to you?" Big Moishie asked.

"I told you. I met him at Gray Rocks and we got friendly and then he made me his proposal."

"Yes, I know that. What I mean is why he should have chosen to give this information to you."

"That's very simple. He's from a very old fancy-type family. Okay? But they haven't got a cent to their name. And he likes money. But because of his name and who he is, everyone figures he doesn't need the dough and can't be bought. So no one ever approaches him. Right? And actually if anyone from his society, you know, the people he socializes with, did approach him, he wouldn't deal with them anyways. That's because he wants to keep his clean fancy image. You know what I mean? Among the high-class Québecois society. So what he does then is make his deals with a few guys like me, who have no real contact with his milieu. That way he figures he'll keep his clean image with the people that he mixes with socially."

"Yeah, okay," Big Moishie said. "So how does someone like me get to this guy? Do we have to go through you?"

"No, not really. He'll deal with anyone who identifies himself to him in the right way."

"What do you mean, the right way?"

Kerner hesitated for a moment.

"So c'mon, we're waiting!" the Hawk snapped.

"There's a certain word ... like a code word ... that he gave me, and I guess to whoever else he deals with. If someone calls him and uses that word, then he knows what they want and so then he sets up a meeting with them."

"So what's de code word?" the Hawk asked quietly.

Kerner remained silent.

"What's the word?" Big Moishie asked.

"If you use this information, could you cut me in?" Kerner asked.

"Cut you in? I'll cut yer troat!" the Hawk yelled and began slamming his palms together while Big Moishie began kicking his desk.

Kerner screamed. "I'll give you the word. I'll give you the word. You're breaking my arm! Okay! Leave me! I'll tell you the word!"

"All right, Solly. Leave him."

"Fucking mooch," the Hawk muttered viciously.

"Now what's the word; or should I say, what's the good word?" Big Moishie said with a chuckle.

The Hawk laughed. "Yeah, give us de good word already."

"You almost broke my arm," Kerner moaned.

"Too bad!" the Hawk replied. "In anudder minute I'll break boat of dem in tree places."

"So what's the word, Kerner?" Big Moishie asked.

"It's not a word; it's actually an expression."

"Okay, so give it."

210

"Québec sait faire."

"Quebec knows how?" Big Moishie asked.

"Yes, but in French," Kerner replied.

"And then he sets up a meeting with us?"

"Yes."

"You're sure we don't need you to front for us?"

"Yes. As long as you have the code word and the cash, he'll be ready to deal with you direct."

"How come you didn't tell dis ta Hankleman?"

"Him! If he had given me half a chance I would have offered to pay him back double what I owed him; but he never gave me a chance to even open my mouth."

"Well, I'll tell you, for our sake we're very glad he never gave you a chance to make that offer," Big Moishie laughed.

"It's much better dis way, Kerner," the Hawk said with a little cackle.

"Yes, much better," Big Moishie said. "We're not anxious for Mr. Morrie Hankleman to make any extra money. It's much better if we make it."

"Do you think I could get something out of this, if you use my information?" Kerner asked again, trying to inject a slight degree of hopefulness into his voice.

"What do you think, Solly?"

"I tink I don wanna discuss dat now. If we get in touch wid dis guy and everyting works out, den we'll see. Not now. Now I don make no promises about nutting ... except I'll promise you if dis isn't legit, you'll wish you were never born. Right now, jus be satisfied dat you're still in one piece. You got it?"

"Yes," Kerner said dejectedly.

"Okay. Now give me all the information so I can take it down on paper," Big Moishie said. "The guy's name is Guy Gervais?"

"Yes."

"And he's the head of ...?"

"Of the Quebec Roads Planning Department," Kerner answered.

"Okay. Now where's his office?"

"In the Confederation Building on Bleury Street. Forty ten Bleury. The entire Roads Planning Department is in there on the second floor."

"And we reach him at the office?"

"Yes, but only by phone."

"What's the number there?"

"Eight, four, nine, three, six, two, four."

"And where does he like to meet?"

"He won't meet you in his office. He lives up in Ste-Adèle. That's where he has all his plans and everything. That's where I dealt with him the last time around."

"What's the address of his place there?"

"It's a hundred and eighty St. Hilaire Street in Ste-Adèle."

"So if we call him at de office like tomorrow, he'll be ready ta talk business right away?" the Hawk asked.

"Yes," Kerner replied.

"Is there anything else we should know about this deal?" Big Moishie asked.

"No, you know all there is."

"Okay. Very good. This sounds very interesting."

"Maybe you could at least let me off for part of what I owe?"

"Don push, Kerner. Don push," the Hawk said. "So far we got nutting from you excep talk."

"Well, you will. This is legitimate."

"It better be or like I said before, you're gonna be very sorry."

"Don't worry."

"I'm not worried," the Hawk replied. "It's you what gotta be worried if dis don werk out right."

"It'll work out. ... I just think it would be fair to let me off for something."

"Jus be tankful you're still in one piece, my friend," the Hawk sneered. "Now take a walk!"

Kerner turned and headed for the door.

"Don't talk to anyone," Big Moishie shouted. "You understand?"

"Yes."

"We'll be in touch with you soon, so be where you can be reached easily. You understand?"

"Yes."

"That means in town. You understand?"

"Yes."

"Okay, here, the door's unlocked, now goodbye," Big Moishie said.

"Yeah," Kerner said disgustedly and walked out, slamming the door behind him.

Big Moishie began to chuckle. Solly joined him. In a moment they were both laughing hard. They continued on this way for a short while. Finally Big Moishie said, "I think we have something very good here, Solly."

"It sounds very good to me."

"If this is legit, we can make a bundle."

"It's legit. Did you see how scared he was? He was shaking like a leaf."

"Yeah, you gave him some good shots, Solly."

"I shoulda broken his arm," the Hawk said angrily.

"What for? He talked. If this isn't legit, then you can put him in the hospital for a year. Now let's go downstairs and have a coffee."

"Good idea," the Hawk said.

They walked out of the office and went downstairs where they could talk normally again.

Chapter Thirty-Six

As the tape ended, Morrie Hankleman began to laugh wildly.

"I got them!" he yelled out loud. He slammed the side of his fist down hard on the arm of his chair. He jumped up and started pacing around the room.

"I got them!" he shouted again. "I got them! I got them! I got them!"

Chapter Thirty-Seven

Dr. Lehman leaned back in his chair and pursed his lips.

"That's very interesting, Mr. Kerner," he said. "Quite a clever plan ... this telephone gaff, as you call it ... if it works."

"Well, it seems to be working so far," Artie Kerner replied off-handedly.

"Really?"

"Yes. This morning Mr. Weisskopf phoned me to tell me that Hankleman had already called our ... his man, Claude Lemay ... the man he thinks is Mr. Guy Gervais, the head of the Roads Planning Department. They've already set up a meeting for tomorrow afternoon at which time Hankleman will pay four thousand dollars for the plan of Weisskopf and Mandelberg's land. So you can see that Hankleman has obviously fallen for the whole thing hook, line and sinker. It's obvious he's not wasting any time."

"No, he certainly isn't," Dr. Lehman agreed.

"As a matter of fact, I'll be personally delivering the plan of Mr. Weisskopf's land to the phony Gervais tomorrow morning."

"Oh really?" Dr. Lehman said, raising his eyebrows slightly.

"Yes."

"How is that?"

"What do you mean?"

"I mean, how is it that you're delivering this plan?"

"Oh. Well ... I volunteered. As I told you, the meeting is up north, near Ste-Adèle. While I was talking to Weisskopf on the phone, he suddenly remembered that both he and his partner had a very important business appointment tomorrow morning. He realized that it could be a long, involved meeting. So I volunteered to do them a favour and deliver it up north for them. Why not? They're both busy tomorrow and I had nothing to do. So why not do that little favour for them? It's the least I can do after all they've done for me."

Dr. Lehman nodded thoughtfully, his chin resting in his hand.

"Well ... I'm not going to make any judgements about this whole thing ... but ... how do you personally feel about it?"

"Me?" Kerner said.

"No, me!" Dr. Lehman said sarcastically.

Kerner smiled sheepishly. "Well ... it's certainly helping me out," he said.

"It's helping you out?"

"Yes," Kerner replied.

Dr. Lehman scratched his nose. "The other day you told me you were going to pay this Hankleman fellow back whatever you owed him. ... Is that still the case?"

"Of course. Certainly. This new development doesn't change a thing for me. I'm going to pay back Hankleman every cent I owe him."

"That's good. ... Of course, it seems like Hankleman will end up getting screwed," Dr. Lehman said.

"Yes, I guess he will."

"And you have no thoughts on that?"

"Well, no. I mean, I'm just repaying Weisskopf and Mandelberg for their favour to me."

"Their favour to you was to let you off for several thousand dollars. If I recall, they were to get about five and Hankleman eight. Right?"

Kerner nodded.

216

"So then, with that in mind, isn't it possible that it might make more sense to simply give Weisskopf and his partner the five thousand dollars that they were prepared to forego and pay back Hankleman the eight that he was prepared to accept after he contracted Weisskopf? That way you wouldn't owe anyone anything and you wouldn't have to be a part of screwing this Hankleman. ... Unless of course you want to screw him."

"No! I'm not interested in screwing him," Kerner protested.

"You're not?"

"No, definitely not. I told you. I'm just repaying their favour. How could I not?"

"I don't know. Did my suggestion seem that unreasonable?"

"No, not really."

"Not really? ... You mean, you're not sure?"

"No, I'm sure."

"Sure of what?"

"I'm sure that your suggestion was reasonable."

"So?" Dr. Lehman asked.

"So what?" Kerner replied.

"So what do you think?"

"What do you mean? About what?"

"You know about what. About what I just suggested."

"You mean about Weisskopf and Hankleman?"

"Yes."

"Oh, right."

"So then to repeat my question: What do you think?"

"I'm not sure."

"A moment ago you said you were sure."

"I did?"

"Yes, you did."

"Are you sure about that, Doctor?"

"I'm positive about that."

"I forgot what you said exactly. Could you repeat it, please?"

"No, I can't."

"Why not?"

"Because."

"Because?"

"Yes ... because."

"Because what?"

"Just because," Dr. Lehman said angrily.

Suddenly there was a knock on the office door.

"Yes? Who is it?" Dr. Lehman said.

"It's me – Mrs. Griff. ... Will my hour start on time today?"

"I don't know, Mrs. Griff," Dr. Lehman shouted back with his hands cupped around his mouth.

"Last time it started a half-hour late. Do you remember, Doctor?"

Dr. Lehman didn't reply at once. Instead he sat up in his seat and reaching into his desk drawer he withdrew a microphone. He pressed a switch on the control panel in front of him.

"What are the chances of getting under way on time today, Doctor?" Mrs. Griff shouted through the door.

Dr. Lehman held the mike up to his mouth and spoke into it. "I don't know, Mrs. Griff. Let's just play it by ear, shall we?"

The sound of Dr. Lehman's voice burst out of the dozen or so speakers concealed about the room with such startling intensity that Kerner almost yelled from the pain and shock. His hands flew to his ears.

"We may end on time or we may go well over our hour, Mrs. Griff," Dr. Lehman continued.

"But that's not exactly fair, Doctor, is it?" Mrs. Griff shouted back.

Dr. Lehman grimaced angrily and fiddled with a knob on the control panel. "No, not exactly, Mrs. Griff," he replied.

The sound of his voice was now so overpowering that Kerner could feel his eardrums popping despite the fact that his hands were pressed tightly against his ears.

"But that's the way it is," he added, and then fiddled with the dial once again.

"I'll do my best to finish on time with Mr. Kerner here, but if we have to, we may go over the hour. Is that all right, Mrs. Griff?"

Kerner could feel the floor shaking under him.

"Yes! Yes! Yes, Doctor! That's fine!" Mrs. Griff shouted back hysterically.

Dr. Lehman played with the volume knob again. "So you don't mind then?" he screamed into the microphone.

Kerner was sure that the office walls were about to collapse. It was as though there was an earthquake all around him.

"No! No! I don't mind! Take all day! I don't mind at all! Take a whole hour! It's all right! I can wait! Take the whole day! Don't worry about me!" Mrs. Griff screamed back.

Dr. Lehman grunted, whistled and hissed into the mike several times. Then pressing the control switch, he put the microphone back into the desk drawer. He turned back to Artie Kerner, who now removed his hands from his ears.

"I can't stand so many questions," Dr. Lehman said sourly.

"No?" Kerner replied.

"Mr. Kerner, control yourself," Dr. Lehman said, his eyes narrowing.

"What did I do?" Kerner exclaimed.

"Enough questions, Mr. Kerner."

"What questions? Who's asking questions?"

"Let's get back to what we were discussing, please," Dr. Lehman said, rubbing his eyes and sighing wearily.

"What was that?"

Dr. Lehman reached into his pocket and pulled out a small, white rectangular-shaped object. "Mr. Kerner, do you know what this is?"

"No. Should I?"

Dr. Lehman grimaced and clicked the gadget in his hand. "Four hundred and twenty-seven, " he muttered to himself.

Kerner looked at the doctor quizzically.

"This, Mr. Kerner, is an apparatus similar in concept to

those used by baseball umpires for recording balls and strikes. ... I use it for recording the number of questions asked by certain patients."

"Why?" Kerner responded.

"Four hundred and twenty-eight," Dr. Lehman muttered, clicking the device again. "You, Mr. Kerner, up to this moment in five sessions with me have asked a total of four hundred and twenty-eight questions. That means four hundred and twenty-eight questions in a period of five hours. That means approximately one question every four seconds."

"That much?"

"Four hundred and twenty-nine," Dr. Lehman said, ignoring Kerner and clicking the white plate. "I have had people committed for far less than that," he continued. "It is a theory of mine that certain relationships can be made between the number of questions asked by certain people within a given period of time and the degree of their sickness. I won't go into it now, but for the sake of fairness let me say that if, by the time you leave here today, this little meter registers ... say ... five hundred ... I may begin to have serious doubts about you. So with that in mind, let's get back to what we were involved with."

"All right, but before doing that, can I ask you one simple question?"

"Go right ahead. ... Four hundred and thirty," Dr. Lehman said.

"Hey. C'mon. You're not going to count that, are you?"

"Four hundred and thirty-one," Dr. Lehman said, nodding.

"Isn't that a bit unfair?"

"Four, thirty-two," Dr. Lehman said, shaking his head and clicking his device.

"You don't?"

"Get a grip on yourself, Kerner."

Kerner took a deep breath. "Okay, okay, I will. No more questions. I'll talk. ... Let's see now..." Kerner said, pensively, "I was talking about Weisskopf ... and you suggested that maybe the best thing to do would be to pay off Weisskopf so that I wouldn't owe him any favours and..."

"I didn't suggest anything. I simply raised that as a possibility for you to consider."

"Yes, right. I understand."

"Just before you continue, I think I should raise one more possibility," Dr. Lehman said, holding up a finger. "Let me say this. When you first mentioned how nice this Mr. Weisskopf was being to you, I suggested that perhaps ... only perhaps ... you were being conned. Do you recall that?"

"Yes, I do, but he wasn't conning me. He was sincere," Kerner said vehemently. "I know when someone is acting sincere. He was being straight."

"Perhaps. But then again who knows. Maybe he had decided to pull this telephone con, as you call it, on Hankleman some time ago and figured he could use you to help him accomplish it."

"No, no." Kerner shook his head. "No way. You're way off track."

"I'm only mentioning this as a possibility, just so that you'll be aware of it. It's something to think about, isn't it?"

"There's no way. I know when someone is acting sincerely."

"Weisskopf may not have even thought his plan out at the time. It may have just been fermenting somewhere in his unconscious mind. It's possible that this may have been the motivating force behind his ... altruism towards you. In his own subconscious mind he may have been planning to use you for his benefit all along."

Kerner laughed sarcastically and shook his head.

"I'm just raising this as one of several possibilities," the doctor continued.

"Sometimes I think this whole shrink business with its conscious, subconscious, unconscious, whatever, is all a pile of shit."

Dr. Lehman shrugged.

"And, besides, what does it matter?" Kerner half-shouted. "At this point it's too late to do anything. I already did my part and Hankleman has already gone for the bait, so any of your suggestions now are a waste of time. It's too late for me to do anything at this point, wouldn't you say?"

"That's something you'll have to work out by yourself."

"Don't you have any ideas? You're supposed to help me! What am I paying you for?"

"You're paying me to come here and talk," Dr. Lehman replied.

"You're doing all the talking but you're not telling me anything. How about letting me do some talking, eh?"

"So talk," Dr. Lehman said.

"Okay, I will."

"So talk."

"Okay, okay, I'll talk in a minute."

Dr. Lehman pressed a button. His chair suddenly reclined and he disappeared from sight behind his desk.

Kerner, with his hands folded in his lap, sat without moving or speaking till the end of the hour.

Chapter Thirty-Eight

Morrie Hankleman drove towards his home in good spirits, knowing that in twenty-four hours, two days at most, he would be prepared to allow himself the luxury of total abandonment from pressure. Till then he would be content with just feeling good. Hankleman smiled. So far it had been unbelievably easy. All it had taken was one simple phone call to Mr. Guy Gervais. Soon he would be in a position to screw Weisskopf and Mandelberg. After that became a fait accompli, he would deal with Artie Kerner.

Hankleman put his hand to his breast pocket to reassure himself that the envelope with the four thousand dollars for Gervais was still there. He had withdrawn the money right after his brief chat with Gervais that morning. Tomorrow Gervais would have the envelope and its contents and he would have the plan of the land slated for purchase by the government for its autoroute extension.

Gervais had sounded very sincere on the phone – as sincere as anyone could sound under the circumstances. He had assured Hankleman that the particular tract of land which he was concerned with was available for purchase and that it could be bought for very little without any problem.

Hankleman knew that there was always a chance that

complications could develop when it came to actually buying the land, but he decided very quickly that it was a risk well worth taking considering the potential returns.

The major unknown factor was Guy Gervais himself. Could he be trusted? Putting himself in Gervais' shoes, Hankleman reasoned that as head of the Roads Planning Department, Gervais could not afford to play games with him. If he burned Morrie Hankleman, Morrie Hankleman could burn him much worse. Yes, Morrie Hankleman felt very good about the whole thing. Again he put his hand to his jacket and touched the bulge in his breast pocket.

He smiled and turned onto his street. His smile faded quickly as he saw his wife's car in the driveway.

He was not really surprised. Since she had walked out, he had given a lot of thought to what her future actions might be. It had occurred to him that she might return contrite, but this did not seem likely based on his knowledge of her.

As far as he was concerned, there would be no reconciliation. He had tried to visualize the two of them together again, and each time he felt himself growing tense and angry. He knew he couldn't take being married to her any longer. The very idea of it made him ill.

He was sure she was there to take possession of the house which he'd originally registered in her name. He knew that after she had thought about it, she would realize that the house was hers. This fact was obvious and even his wife who wasn't all that bright would see it eventually; and if for some reason she didn't, the various members of her family would point it out to her.

Morrie Hankleman stepped out of his car and went up the walk. He tried the door. It was unlocked and he walked in not quite knowing what to expect. As he closed the door behind him, he saw at once that she had returned with a vengeance.

Stacked in a large pile at the front of the hall were all his clothes and personal belongings. Hankleman smiled weakly as he stared down at the heap in front of him.

"Hello," he called in a loud voice.

His wife came out of the den and stood near the doorway with her hands resting against the jamb.

"There's your stuff," she said, pointing at Hankleman's things.

"Yeah, I see. So?"

"So, you can take it and then please go," she said icily.

"I was wondering when you'd be back," Hankleman said.

"Surprised?" his wife replied.

He shrugged and snorted. "I got the letter from your lawyers."

"Good," she replied, drumming her fingers on the doorjamb.

"Where's the kid?" Hankleman asked.

"Upstairs, sleeping."

Hankleman nodded thoughtfully.

"And don't go up there," his wife added.

"I'm not interested in going."

"Good."

"I've seen more than enough of him."

His wife said nothing.

"Every time he sees me he starts screaming, anyways."

"Do you blame him?"

Hankleman's mouth twisted into a sneer. He had the urge to stride over to his wife and let her have the back of his hand across the face but he controlled himself. There was no way he was going to hit her. He turned and stared down at his pile of belongings. "Is this all of my stuff?"

"Everything."

"Are you sure?"

"Positive."

"I don't see my movie camera."

"That was mine."

"Bullshit it was."

"You gave it to me, if you remember."

"I don't remember."

"Well, you did."

"Keep it. It was a crappy camera anyway."

"Like everything else you ever gave me."

"Oh really. I suppose your diamond wedding ring is crap."

"For all I know, it's glass."

"Well, if its that crappy, I'll take it back," Hankleman said.

"Hah," Gail Hankleman retorted.

"And I suppose your car is crap too, huh? And your fur coats are crap, eh? And all your other jewellery? You sure have a lot of expensive crap."

"Would you go, please," Gail Hankleman said.

"You're going to get nothing from me," Hankleman said.

"I already have the house."

"We'll see."

"There's nothing to see. It's my house. I own it lock, stock and barrel."

"What if you find out that you don't?" Hankleman said with a leer.

"Don't waste your time playing games, Morrie. You know it's mine, I know it's mine and my lawyer knows it's mine. So do you mind taking your things and getting out of my house."

Gail Hankleman left her position near the den door and moved towards him, pointing at the pile on the hall floor.

"Take your things and go."

"I guess you're in a hurry to get downtown and do some shopping for some more crap with my crappy money."

"Yes, that's right, as a matter of fact."

I'd love to smash her but there's no way I'm going to allow myself to do that, Morrie Hankleman thought to himself.

"Now please go," Gail Hankleman said, pointing at the front door.

"Or maybe you're in a big rush to get to your tennis lesson ... or is that tomorrow?"

"Today and tomorrow," his wife replied, coming closer to him.

"Or maybe I'm keeping you from visiting your lesbian friend Martha ... or I should say, Martie."

"I'm seeing her later, tonight," Gail Hankleman replied.

226

Morrie Hankleman could feel a pain in his stomach. His arms were pressed rigidly against his sides.

"You'd really just love to hit me, Morrie … wouldn't you?" his wife said.

Hankleman laughed. He knew she was right. He knew she knew she was right. He knew she knew he knew she was right, which all meant that he would have loved to bash her. The only thing that was holding him back was his realization that she would derive as much satisfaction from seeing him lose his cool as he would from bashing her. No! She was not going to get that satisfaction.

"Wouldn't you, Morrie?" she repeated, a suggestion of a sneer at the corners of her mouth.

"Don't flatter yourself. I wouldn't hit you if you paid me. It wouldn't be worth the effort."

"That's true. You never were … very energetic," Gail Hankleman said with a smirk. "Except maybe in your business things," she added, her eyes gleaming.

"Lucky for you I was energetic in my business things, as you call them, or you wouldn't have a pot to piss in," Hankleman said, stepping forward and wagging a finger under her nose.

"Get that finger out of my face," she said angrily.

"Why? Does it bother you? It's only a finger."

"Just get it out of my face."

"Don't tell me what to do with my finger."

"I'm not telling you what to do with it, I'm telling you what not to do with it … and that is, not to wave it in my face. If I told you what to do with it, I'd tell you to stick it up your nose."

"I'll stick it where I want."

"Stick it up your ass if you want to but don't stick … don't wave it … in my face."

"If I want to, I'll stick it up my ass and then stick it up your nose," Hankleman said angrily.

"In a horse's ass you will," Gail Hankleman said coolly.

"No, in my ass I will!"

"Maybe in your ass but not in my face."

"Why not? That's a good match-up. My ass and your face."

"Your ass and your face, you mean," his wife retorted.

Hankleman's mind went blank. He couldn't think of a reply. He stood there staring at his right index finger which was still raised in front of his wife's face.

"You were always very good with your finger," she said. "Unfortunately that's all you were good with."

"It's the only thing that didn't scare you," Hankleman replied with a leer, feeling a surge of satisfaction at his remark.

"I was always scared of soft, limp things," said Gail Hankleman.

A retort flashed through Morrie Hankleman's mind. He was going to say, 'Then your tits must have frightened the hell out of you,' but instead he hauled off and clunked her on the head.

Chapter Thirty-Nine

At eight o'clock that evening, Artie Kerner went for supper at Solly Weisskopf's house. There he met the Hawk's wife and daughter. Moishie Mandelberg was there with his wife as well.

After supper the three men retired to the privacy of the Hawk's den where they discussed the progress of their plan and exchanged compliments on how well things were working out.

After a while, the Hawk produced a red architectural cylinder which contained the plan that was to be fed to Morrie Hankleman. This was given to Kerner along with the address of the house where Claude Lemay would transact his business with Hankleman. The Hawk also gave Kerner a photo of Claude Lemay and a password which Lemay was to utter before the plan was handed over to him.

As soon as he had taken possession of the cylinder, Artie Kerner became anxious to get home. He felt tense in the way he usually did just prior to being overwhelmed by an attack of buying madness; but he knew somehow that in this instance he would not be forced to indulge his sickness as in the past. He had been ill all day without having lost control.

He had felt tense and irritable when he awoke that morning, and after his session with Dr. Lehman he had become even more upset. He could sense a dull aching anger growing inside him.

Kerner looked at the red cylinder in his hand. The Hawk was saying something but Kerner couldn't concentrate on the words. His thoughts drifted back to his earlier meeting with Dr. Lehman. The psychiatrist's suggestion about not becoming involved in the screwing of Hankleman came to mind. Artie Kerner winced as a wave of nausea swept through him. He pushed Dr. Lehman's words out of his mind and brought his attention back to the talk in the den.

The Hawk and Big Moishie were still discussing and laughing over their soon-to-be-accomplished coup.

Kerner joined them in this for another half-hour, then thanked everyone, said goodnight and made his exit. He drove quickly back to his apartment, knowing that only sleep would relieve his pain and give him any peace that night.

Chapter Forty

Morrie Hankleman sat at his table at Georges with Eugene Carlin and the two women that Carlin had come in with. He kept thinking of the look on his wife's face as he landed the haymaker on her head. He wondered if she really would go so far as to take out an assault charge against him as she had threatened after regaining consciousness.

Probably not. If she did, he'd go back and knock her on her ass again. Next time though he would hit her harder because it was obvious she really knew how to take a punch. She was out only for a second or two and then she bounced right back on her feet ready to fight. Hankleman had then locked her in the hall closet while he loaded as many of his belongings as possible into the car and took off.

Getting her into the closet hadn't been easy. He was amazed at her strength. While he was struggling with her, she had somehow managed to get him in a headlock and then after he had broken that hold with some effort, in a full nelson, from which grip he had been able to escape only by giving her an elbow in the stomach. That had weakened her hold enough so that he had been able to hook his right foot behind her right ankle and trip her. She had fallen backwards with his full weight on top of her. That old judo trick had knocked the wind out of her completely and allowed him to finally get her under control and into the hall closet.

He had quickly gathered up his belongings and headed straight downtown and taken a room at the Mount Royal Hotel. He knew he would be best off there for the next few days. After he had finished teaching Weisskopf and Mandelberg their lesson, he would look for an apartment.

Morrie Hankleman took a sip from his fifth glass of Scotch. It was his aim to get good and drunk. He had no intention of going into his office the next day, and since his appointment up north with Guy Gervais wasn't until the late afternoon, he knew he could sleep in late and deal with his hangover. He felt a tingle of excitement as he thought about the meeting with Gervais. He began to smile. He glanced at his watch. It was eleven o'clock. Another eighteen hours or so and he would snatch a valuable piece of land right out from under the noses of Weisskopf and Mandelberg. Oh, the satisfaction! he thought and his grin became even wider. He would get Kerner too. He was going to have Kerner put in the hospital. He had made up his mind about that. Then he would send him flowers and a get-well card. Hankleman laughed out loud at this thought.

"Let us in on the joke, Morrie," Eugene Carlin said, leaning forward across the table.

"It's nothing. It's nothing," Hankleman said, shaking his head and still grinning.

"I think you're getting a little high, Morrie, aren't you?" the young woman named Linda said.

"No, no, I never get drunk," Hankleman replied seriously. "I can drink all day and all night and nothing happens."

"Do you ever get a hangover?" Linda asked.

Hankleman shook his head. "Never. . . . I don't know what a hangover is."

"God, are you lucky," the other woman named Fran said.

Hankleman shrugged. "It's just one of those things, right, Eugene?" he said with a sly smile.

"Yes, that's right," Carlin replied.

"I had such a bad hangover last Saturday, I thought I was going to die," Fran said.

232

"Did you ever try those new anti-hangover pills?" Carlin asked.

"Yes, they don't work at all," she replied.

"All they do is make you want to throw up," Linda added.

"Fluids are the best thing," Fran said.

"Fluids?" Carlin asked.

"Yes. If you've had a lot to drink, then just before going to sleep, you force yourself to drink as much water or juice as possible. That way you don't get dehydrated during the night. It's the dehydration that gives you the hangover."

"Where did you learn that?" Carlin asked.

"From my ex-husband. He had a lot of experience since he spent most of his time drinking and throwing up."

"He sounds like he'd go well with my wife," Morrie Hankleman said. "She's very good at eating and retching."

"You sound somewhat bitter, Morrie," Linda said.

"Bitter? Not at all. I'm not the slightest bit bitter. I'm just speaking factually. . . . If she wasn't eating and retching, she was sleeping and retching. If she wasn't sleeping and retching, she was playing golf and retching. If she wasn't playing golf and retching, she was playing bridge and retching. If she wasn't playing bridge and retching, she was doing something else and retching. But don't think I'm bitter. I'm just stating a fact," Hankleman said.

Everyone just stared at Hankleman without saying anything.

"And if she wasn't retching, she was kvetching," Hankleman added.

"Kvetching?" Linda asked.

"It's just a different way of retching," Carlin offered.

Linda nodded understandingly.

"It's retching with words," Hankleman said.

"Or you could say that retching is non-verbal kvetching," Carlin offered.

"That's good," Hankleman said. "That's very good, Eugene. I like that."

He downed the last of the Scotch in his glass and signalled the waiter.

"I always say it takes two to tangle," Linda offered. "There's always two sides to every story ... at least most of the time. Ninety-nine percent of the time. Oh, I guess it's possible that there's that one percent situation where one person is mostly at fault, but I would think that generally for every bad thing a husband says about his wife, his wife can add something to match about her husband. Wouldn't you say?"

"Is that a question or a lecture, Linda?" Hankleman asked.

"It's just a theory of mine," she replied.

"Well ... you could be right ... but in my case I happen to fall into that one percent category."

Linda and Fran exchanged a quick glance across the table. The look wasn't lost on Hankleman. He raised his hand and snapped his finger at the waiter who was passing by. The waiter turned and Hankleman lifted his empty glass, signalling that he wanted another. He put the glass down and looked at Linda who was engaged in a conversation with her friend.

Hankleman's thoughts went back to the altercation with his wife earlier in the day. He couldn't get over the fight she had put up. If he hadn't been able to get his foot behind her and trip her, she might have beaten him. She was obviously in much better condition than he was. He shuddered as he thought of the humiliation he would have felt had she been able to pin him. It was definitely not a good idea for a man to be involved with any woman who was perhaps physically stronger than him, he thought.

Hankleman glanced over at Linda who was still conversing with her friend.

The waiter approached and put another Scotch down in front of Hankleman. He picked up the glass and took a large gulp. He cleared his throat and looked over at Linda. "Tell me something, Linda," he said.

She turned and leaned towards him. "Yes, Morrie?"

"How good are you at arm wrestling?" Morrie Hankleman asked.

Chapter Forty-One

Artie Kerner was aware that he was dreaming but he felt that he could wake himself at any moment.

He was in a room which seemed to be his bedroom. Then he found himself standing in the same position in an area that he recognized as the foyer of his parents' house. He was staring at a large steamer trunk which rested near the front door directly ahead of him. Suddenly he heard his mother's voice coming from somewhere beside him.

"All right, Arthur, we're ready to go now."

He turned and saw his mother and father standing next to him. He spied a strange, almost malicious look in their eyes and for a moment thought of waking himself and ending the dream, but for some reason he did not.

"Are you ready, Arthur?" his father asked.

"No," Kerner heard himself replying. "No, I'm not ready."

"Well, we are, young man," they said in unison, almost as though singing. "So let's get a move on, shall we? Get in the trunk now like a good little boy."

Kerner looked at the trunk. He dreaded getting into it but somehow he knew it would be futile to protest.

He stepped inside and the top came down over him. Just

before it closed all the way, he caught one last glimpse of his parents leering at him.

Then he was in darkness. He had the feeling that he was going to be driven somewhere but he wasn't sure where.

Suddenly he found himself in a room at the Prescott boarding school in southern Ontario. He had been going there since he was very young. He looked up and saw the school principal, Dr. Forest, standing in front of a large desk. Dr. Forest stared back at him saying nothing.

Suddenly Dr. Lehman was standing next to him. "So there you are! I was wondering where you had gone to!" he said in a booming voice.

"Do we know you?" Kerner's mother asked, having suddenly materialized with his father.

"I ask the questions," Dr. Lehman said.

"You do, do you?" Mr. Kerner said.

"Yes, that's right. I do," Dr. Lehman replied.

"Well, ask away then," Kerner's father said.

"All right then, Mr. Kerner. What is the length of your tool?"

"Which one!"

"You have more than one?"

"Well, yes. Certainly. I have several."

"On you at this moment?"

"No, I didn't bring them. They're all at home in my workshop. There's the hoe, the shears ... and of course my trusty old rape."

"You mean the rake."

"Yes, that's right, the rake. I can give you the length of all of them if you'd like."

"Shut up, Louis. Don't tell him anything," Mrs. Kerner shouted.

"You shut up or I'll cut off your nose to spite your face," Mr. Kerner replied with what Artie Kerner saw was a venomous sneer.

He suddenly felt obliged to speak. "Let's get out of here."

"Shut up, Arthur," his parents sang in perfect unison.

"Let's go home," Kerner said.

"Are you a doctor, Doctor?" Kerner's mother said, turning to Dr. Lehman.

"Yes."

"Arthur, this man is a doctor," his parents said together. "If you don't shut up, he's going to bandage up your face ... aren't you, Doctor?"

"Too many questions," Dr. Lehman said. "I ask the questions."

"Well, ask them," Mr. Kerner said.

"Let me rephrase my question, Mr. Kerner. What is the length of your prick?"

"I can best answer that," Mrs. Kerner said, opening her purse. "I think I have it right in here."

"Okay, put it on de table." Kerner recognized the voice of Solly Weisskopf and realized that he had been somewhere in the room all along.

"I think it's around seventy-eight inches long," Kerner's father said.

"Not bad," Dr. Lehman replied with an approving nod.

"Well, you know, Doc, to tell you the truth, confidentially, it wouldn't be so bad if it were a little longer."

"Oh, really. Like how much longer, for instance?"

"Oh, perhaps another five or six feet."

Dr. Lehman shrugged pensively.

Kerner's mother continued to rifle through her purse. "No, it doesn't seem to be in here. Looks like I forgot it at home."

"And my balls!" Mr. Kerner shouted angrily. "What about my balls?"

"Nine hundred and ninety-two," Dr. Lehman said.

"Are my balls in there, at least? Or did you somehow manage to forget them as well?"

"Nine hundred and ninety-three," Dr. Lehman murmured.

Kerner suddenly began to feel frightened.

"I think I must have left them at home too," Mrs. Kerner said. "Where exactly, I don't know, Louis, but we'll look for them when we get home."

"Where could they be?" Mr. Kerner shouted.

"I think I left them in a drawer."

"C'mon, get dem on de table already," Solly Weisskopf said.

"Don't you think I have enough on my plate already?" the principal, Dr. Forest, said.

"Nine hundred and ninety-four," Dr. Lehman muttered.

"Isn't it enough?" Dr. Forest said.

"Nine, ninety-five," Dr. Lehman said.

"What is all this counting, Doctor?" Mrs. Kerner asked.

"Nine, ninety-six," Dr. Lehman replied, raising a cautioning finger.

"She never brings my balls, Doc," Mr. Kerner said. "She always leaves them at home in her drawers. They're my balls but they're in her drawers."

"Did you bring your drawers, Mrs. Kerner?" Dr. Forest asked.

"Yes, I think so."

"Put dem on de table," Solly Weisskopf said.

Mrs. Kerner hitched up her dress and pulled down her underpants.

Kerner now found himself wishing desperately that the dream would end. He decided to stop it but he couldn't.

Out of the corner of his eye he could see his mother getting up on Dr. Forest's desk. He tried to figure out why she was doing that. He could feel his stomach sinking and falling away from his body. Behind her he could make out the figure of a large man smoking a cigar. He had seen the man somewhere but he couldn't recall where.

"You wanna buy a nice gold watch, lady?" he asked and then disappeared.

"Nine hundred and ninety-seven," Dr. Lehman said from somewhere in the room.

Suddenly Morrie Hankleman burst through the door. Kerner could see that his fly was undone and a large red cylinder was projecting out of it. He rushed over towards Kerner, screaming and frothing at the mouth.

"You're the biggest motherfucker of them all!"

238

"Don't bet on it," Dr. Forest said with a sly leer and he began unbuckling his belt.

"Dats right ... don bet on it," Solly Weisskopf said and began doing the same.

"I have a plan," Morrie Hankleman screamed.

"I'd like to leave," Artie Kerner said in a quiet voice.

"Why?" Dr. Lehman asked.

"I just do."

"Why?"

"Because."

"Because what?"

"Just because," Kerner said and realized that everyone had disappeared and he was now alone with Dr. Lehman in what appeared to be a different room.

Kerner looked down and saw that the red cylindrical object which he had seen a moment before sticking out of Hankleman's fly was now in his hand.

"Why do you want to leave?" Dr. Lehman asked.

"Because I have the plan," he said.

"Really. Tell me about it."

Kerner laughed slyly. "Uh, uh," he said, shaking his head slowly.

"Why not?"

"Just because," Kerner said and suddenly became suspicious. He turned and looked warily at the door behind him.

Suddenly it opened and Mrs. Griff toppled into the room.

"What's she doing here!" Kerner yelled.

"Nine hundred and ninety-eight," Dr. Lehman said with a sour smile.

Behind Mrs. Griff, framed in the doorway, Kerner could see Mrs. Braun crouched on all fours in what appeared to be a large sink.

"What do you all want from me!" Kerner screamed.

"Nine hundred and ninety-nine," Dr. Lehman said, and Kerner woke up in a cold sweat.

Chapter Forty-Two

The Hawk was lying on his back staring up at the ceiling.

He could see light coming through the opening between the window sill and the bottom of the blind. He could hear the robins singing in the back yard. He knew it was early morning. He could hear his wife moving about in the bathroom. He felt depressed but he didn't know exactly why. He knew he had been dreaming and that it had upset him but he couldn't recall the dream at all.

"Is something the matter, Solly?" his wife asked, coming out of the bathroom.

"No. Should someting be de matter?" he replied testily, without turning his head.

"No," she replied.

"So why ask?"

"Why? Because you've been lying like that for the last hour without moving a muscle."

"I was sleeping. I just woke up a minute ago."

"But your eyes were wide open for the last hour."

"So? Sometimes I sleep wid my eyes open."

"And you were also sucking your thumb."

"Whadda you do, stay up all night an spy on me?"

"I just happened to wake up early and noticed. That's all," she replied.

"I wasn't sucking my tumb. I have a habit of picking my teet sometimes when I'm sleeping," the Hawk said.

Helen Weisskopf nodded understandingly. "I just thought something was bothering you, Solly."

"No, nutting's boddering me," the Hawk replied.

He suddenly thought of Artie Kerner and felt an embarrassment that made him blush. He wondered why he had acted so understandingly towards Artie Kerner. That had been a new experience for Solly Weisskopf.

"Do you feel all right, Solly?" Helen Weisskopf asked from the walk-in closet.

"Of course! What's wid you? Leamie alone already. I feel fine."

"Okay, I'll leave you alone, but I know something's on your mind."

"Oh, leamie alone already. You're gonna gimme a headache."

"Okay, I'm not saying another word," Helen Weisskopf replied, coming out of the closet.

"Good. Make me a coffee."

"Okay, Solly," she said and left the bedroom.

The Hawk continued to lie motionless. The sound of the robins was grinding on his nerves. Usually he liked their song but at that moment he knew that had his thirty-eight revolver been in his hand rather than locked in the basement safe, he would have found it very easy to blast them into silence.

The Hawk raised his lower body slightly off the mattress and farted. Then he sank back down and continued to stare at the ceiling.

Chapter Forty-Three

Artie Kerner was driving along route 15 heading north.

The sun was shining. It was a beautiful day.

Kerner looked down at the red cylinder lying beside him on the seat.

He smiled as a wave of euphoria swept over him.

Chapter Forty-Four

Solly the Hawk and Big Moishie Mandelberg were sitting at a table in the rear of Dankoff's Delicatessen. Big Moishie took a bite of his corned beef sandwich.

The Hawk plunked a slice of dill pickle into his mouth and looked at his watch. "By dis time if everyting went off okay, our friend Hankleman has already laid out his money."

Big Moishie raised a hand with his fingers crossed. "We'll know soon enough," he said, gulping down his corned beef and glancing at the pay phone on the wall beside them.

The Hawk nodded in agreement. "I figger Lemay should call widdin two minutes," he said.

"That's if Hankleman was on time for the appointment." Big Moishie put his head back and downed a large glass of coke in one long swill.

"I have a feeling he was dere on de button."

Big Moishie nodded and bit into his third corned beef sandwich. He raised his fingers again in a good-luck gesture.

"You ever get de feeling dat like dis whole ting already happened?"

Big Moishie shrugged and chewed on his food.

"Sometimes I get de feeling like it all happened before. It's funny."

Big Moishie finished the last of his corned beef. "Bring another medium!" he bellowed towards the front of the restaurant.

"I even had a dream about it las night," the Hawk said. "I jus remembered it about an hour ago."

"Yes?"

The Hawk nodded.

"Do you tink dere's any meaning in dreams, Moish?"

Big Moishie shrugged and made an open-handed gesture. "They say a dream is half a prophet."

"Yeah ... it might be so," the Hawk replied. "I dreamed about Hankleman. Kerner too. ... I saw Kerner wid our plan ... you know, in de red package dat we gave him. He was holding it and giving it to Hankleman."

"That sounds good," Big Moishie said.

"Yeah, I guess so," the Hawk replied and then looked at his watch.

Suddenly the phone on the wall rang.

The Hawk jumped in his seat, momentarily surprised. "That must be Lemay."

He stood up and walked over to the phone. He grinned and picked up the receiver.

Chapter Forty-Five

Morrie Hankleman was driving along route 15 heading south. He took a deep, luxurious breath of air and exhaled it with a whoosh. He could feel the tension rolling off him. He looked down at the red cylinder lying beside him on the seat.

He smiled broadly and turned his eyes back to the road.

He began to whistle as a wave of euphoria swept over him.

Chapter Forty-Six

Dr. Lehman finished his twenty-fifth lap and pulled himself up onto the edge of the pond. He stood up and walked over to the hut. He went inside, dried himself and dressed. He left the hut, walked back to his desk and sat down. He glanced at his watch. Kerner was already an hour and a half late.

Dr. Lehman pressed a button on the desk and his chair shot several feet upwards, rotating as it ascended. Then he pressed the remote control button on the chair and it descended slowly, spinning in a counter-clockwise direction. He allowed it to rotate for several seconds and then stopped it. He looked at his watch again.

"Can I come in yet, Doctor?" Mrs. Griff shouted from the waiting room. "My hour should have started already."

Dr. Lehman made no reply.

"You didn't answer me, Doctor," Mrs. Griff yelled.

Dr. Lehman opened his desk drawer and reached for his microphone.

Chapter Forty-Seven

"Where to from here?" Jerry Shmytxcyk asked as he headed along Côte des Neiges Road.

"Just keep goin' straight till I tell you ta turn," Teddy Regan grunted.

Shmytxcyk accelerated and shot through a red light. "What exactly am I supposed to do when we get there?" he asked.

"You don't have ta do nothing ... unless I'm havin' trouble with this guy. ... I wanna work him over all by myself."

"Hey, shit! Can't I take a few shots at him too?"

"You stay the fuck out of it ... unless I'm havin' some trouble. ... You understand?"

"Aw, c'mon, Teddy! Shit! Lemmie take one or two shots at em, eh?"

"Jesus shit, man! You deaf or something! I said no. I got us this fucking job. Eh!"

"What about all the jobs I lined up, eh? I let you in on most of the action. I let you punch em out as much as you wanted to. You were hittin' those fuckers more than I was."

"Sure, because you asked me to, Jerry. You were gettin' punched out. You're just lucky I was there to help you ... and anyway... on the last job you did it all yourself. You had all the fun. Didn't ya?"

"Shit! You call that fun? Christ! She hardly even put up a fight. I hardly even hit her and she was out cold. She didn't even feel me kicking her."

"She musta felt the first few."

"No way! She didn't even yell once. The old cunt was out cold."

"I heard her yell."

"She didn't yell, Teddy. She just went fucking plop, right on her face."

"Okay, okay. Look," Teddy Regan said, "if I let you kick this guy one time, will that make ya happy?"

"One fucking kick! Christ, what's that! That's sweet fuck all! ... Lemmie fucking kick him a few times, Teddy. Eh? C'mon," Shmytxcyk pleaded.

"No! You get one kick. That's it. If he starts givin' me trouble, then you can boot him all ya want. Okay?"

"I don't want the fucking kick. ... Lemmie hit him on the nose one time."

"No! The nose is mine! You leave the fucking nose alone. That's my property!"

"Ya always keep the nose for yourself," Jerry Shmytxcyk whined angrily.

"So what!" Regan said, turning to glare at his friend.

"So, I want some of that!"

"The nose is mine!" Regan said with grim finality. "No one touches the fucking nose but me!"

They drove in silence for a while.

"Ah! I never get ta do nothin'."

Regan turned slowly to look at Shmytxcyk. "Oh, Christ! You're so full of shit!"

"It's true. You know it."

"Okay, okay. You can knuckle him on the back of the head."

"Ah, fuck that! Christ! Is that all you're giving me?"

"Hey, look! Fuck off, eh! It's more than you fucking deserve," Regan yelled.

"Says who?" Shmytxcyk shouted back.

"Says me! That's who!"

"Who the fuck are you, eh?"

"I'm the boss of this fucking outfit!"

"Says who, eh?"

"Says me!"

"What the fuck makes you think you're the fucking boss of this fucking outfit, eh?"

"Because I can break your fucking head if you fucking get me mad, you fucking asshole!"

"That's a fucking good reason," Shmytxcyk said meekly.

"You're fucking right it is, fuckface!"

"Okay, okay, take it easy."

"Okay, but don't fuck with me, Jerry."

"I wasn't fucking with you."

"You were fucking with me. ... So don't fuck with me, Jerry."

"Fuck! I wasn't fucking with you, Teddy."

"Eh, look. Will you just fuck off!"

"Okay, okay."

Again they drove in silence. After a minute, Shmytxcyk said, "Lemmie kick him in the balls, Teddy."

With deliberate slowness Regan turned to look at Jerry Shmytxcyk. "The balls are mine, Jerry," he grunted.

"Ah! Everything's yours – the nose, the balls. You get all the good stuff."

"What the fuck are you cryin' about? Didn't I give you a kick and a knuckler on the head? Eh?"

"Big fucking deal."

"Big fucking deal, eh? Okay, farthead, now you got nothin'! I'm takin' it all back. Now you got sweet fuck all."

"Okay, okay, I'll keep the kick and the knuckler," Shmytxcyk said quickly, slowing the car and turning towards Regan.

"No, farthead. I took em back. So shove that up your arse and blow it out."

"No, I'll take em, Teddy. Lemmie keep em. C'mon, eh."

"I thought you didn't want em."

"Yeah, I'll keep em."

"D'you want em?"

"Yeah, okay, I'll keep em."

"D'you want em!"

"Yeah. Yeah, okay."

"Well, ask for em then."

"Could I have them back?"

"Say please."

"Please."

"Say it like ya fucking mean it!"

"Please."

"Say please, Teddy."

"Yeah, okay. ... Please, Teddy."

"Okay, farthead, you got em back. One kick and one knuckler on the head."

"Big fucking deal," Shmytxcyk muttered.

"You're just never satisfied, are ya? I just gave you back the kick and the knuckler and ya still ain't satisfied. What the fuck's the matter with you, eh?"

"I'll give you back the kick and the knuckler for one shot on the nose."

"I said the nose is mine. You fucking deaf or something?"

"Okay, okay, I'll trade you back the kick and the knuckler for one shot in the balls."

"I already told ya, the balls are mine!"

Shmytxcyk scowled. He turned to his friend. "Lemmie give em a coco bump and see if I can knock out all of his teeth."

"No way, asshole. Are you kidding? If you miss his teeth, you'll end up busting his nose, and I told you, that's mine."

"I won't miss, Teddy. I swear. Shit, I've been practising – you know, butting my head against the wall. I'll just get his teeth."

"No! The teeth are mine."

"Ya see! Ya see! You get ta keep everything," Shmytxcyk whined.

"Okay, you asshole, gimmie back the kick and the knuckler and you can have ... let's see ... okay, let's say three rabbit punches to the back of the neck. Okay?"

Shmytxcyk shrugged. "The neck. Big fucking deal."

"What's the matter with the neck?"

"I just don't like it. Okay?"

"Okay. Then three in the kidneys. How's that?"

"Throw in a few kicks in the head to go with the kidneys and you got a deal."

"A few kicks! Naw, no way. One kick, okay, but not in the head – in the leg."

"In the leg?!"

"Yeah, in the leg. Whatsa matter with that?"

"I don't want the fucking leg."

"Whatsa matter, ain't the leg good enough for you?"

"No, it ain't. Gimmie the kneecap."

"The kneecap?"

"Yeah, I want the kneecap."

"Okay, you got it, prick, but only one."

"And I wanna use the big baseball bat on it."

"No fucking way! We're not using no bat."

"Okay, then I'll use the little bat."

"I said no fucking bats!"

"Okay, then I'll use the brass knuckles when I knuckle him on the head."

"No equipment, Jerry. Nothin'."

"Ah! This is for the birds," Shmytxcyk snorted.

"You're always fucking cryin'," Regan said. "You got three in the kidneys and one on the kneecap. That oughta make ya happy, prickface."

"Gimmie one more thing, okay?"

"Like what?"

"I dunno ... something good."

"Well, like what, asshole?"

"I dunno. I'm thinking."

"Well, don't take all day. We're almost there."

"Okay, I got it! An open-hand smash on the ears. Okay?"

"Yeah, okay... but don't fuck up my action. If I'm goin' for the nose, you stay clear of the ears. You get it? You go for the ears when I go for the balls."

"Okay, okay, don't worry."

Regan leaned back against the seat. "You got three things now, Jerry. ... Are ya happy?"

"I guess so."

"You guess so! You prick. You're just lucky I'm a nice guy," Regan shouted.

Jerry Shmytxcyk made no reply. He just kept on driving.

Chapter Forty-Eight

"Mr. Kerner," the doctor said, unable to keep the shock out of his voice.

Kerner turned his head slowly and looked up at Dr. Lehman.

"What happened to you?"

"I had a bit of an accident."

"A bit of an accident! ... You look like a house fell on you."

"That wouldn't have been so bad."

"What happened?"

"Nothing."

"Nothing? ... I'd hate to see you when something did happen."

Kerner smiled weakly.

"So what happened, Mr. Kerner?"

"It's not important."

"Look, you asked for me to come down here, so the least you could do is tell me how you got here."

"I told you. I had a little accident."

"What kind of accident? ... Were you in a crash?"

Kerner shrugged.

"Look, Kerner, why did you send for me?"

"I don't really know."

Dr. Lehman stared down at Artie Kerner for a moment. "It's been over three months since you were in to see me. ... How is it that you stopped coming?"

"Just like that."

"Just like that?"

"Yes, just like that."

"You still owe me a hundred dollars, Mr. Kerner."

"Don't worry, you'll get paid."

"I'm not worried, Kerner. Like I once told you ... I can buy and sell you. So believe me, I'm not worried about a lousy hundred dollars. I was just mentioning it for the record."

"Okay, so now you mentioned it," Kerner replied.

The doctor hesitated. He looked up at the ceiling as though thinking. "Mr. Kerner, I detect a change in you. You seem somewhat different from the last time I saw you."

"Maybe I am."

Dr. Lehman nodded. "Yes ... maybe you are."

Kerner turned his head towards Dr. Lehman. "Would you mind lighting me a cigarette. They're on the table beside the bed." The doctor took a cigarette from the pack and lit it. "Just put it between my lips and give me a drag," Kerner said. "As you see, I can't hold it too well myself." Kerner gestured with his head towards his arms which were both in casts from the shoulder to the tips of his fingers.

The doctor put the cigarette between Kerner's lips. Kerner dragged and Dr. Lehman withdrew the cigarette.

"You can put it out. I just wanted a drag."

Dr. Lehman stubbed the cigarette. He walked towards the end of Kerner's bed and picked up the medical chart that hung there. "How long have you been here?" he asked.

"About two months."

The doctor held the chart up in front of him and studied it. "From the look of this chart, Mr. Kerner, it appears that almost every bone in your body is broken."

"I'm not in very good shape," Kerner replied.

"No. That you're not," Dr. Lehman said, replacing the chart. He walked over to Kerner and looked down at him. "So what happened, Mr. Kerner?"

"Nothing."

Kerner averted his head.

The doctor turned and headed for the door. "I'll see you around, Mr. Kerner."

"Wait. ... Wait a minute."

Dr. Lehman stopped at the door. "Yes?"

"I'll tell you what happened."

The doctor came back to the bed. He pulled up a chair and sat down near Kerner.

"I was beaten up," Kerner said.

"Beaten up, eh? That's what I figured. ... The various bone fractures listed on your chart seem to suggest that. Anyways, they did some job on you."

Kerner glared at the doctor.

Dr. Lehman pulled his chair closer to the bed. "Who did it?"

"A couple of goons."

"I guess this had to do with your problem with this Mr. Hankleman, hmm?"

"Well ... yes ... sort of."

"What do you mean, sort of?"

"Well. ... Okay, I'll tell you exactly what happened. ... Do you remember the last session I had with you?"

"Very vaguely. That was quite a while ago."

"I told you about the plan that Mr. Weisskopf and his partner had set up to shaft Hankleman. ... Do you remember that?"

"Oh, yes. Yes. You had done a whole scenario in their office for the benefit of Hankleman who'd had the office bugged."

"That's right. And he had fallen for it, if you remember."

"Yes, I remember."

"A meeting had been arranged up north and Hankleman was going there supposedly to get the plan of a tract of land slated to be expropriated by the government for the new autoroute extension."

"Yes, I recall that. And if my memory serves me right, you were going to deliver the plan to Weisskopf's man who was posing as the director of the Autoroute Authority."

"The Roads Planning Department," Kerner corrected.

Dr. Lehman nodded.

"That evening, after I left your office, I went for supper at Weisskopf's house and picked up the plan which was in an architect's cylinder. Then I went home."

With some effort, Kerner turned his head and looked directly at Dr. Lehman. A strange smile came over his face.

"Go on," Dr. Lehman said. "You went home with the plan ..."

Kerner continued to smile strangely.

"What happened then?" the psychiatrist asked.

Kerner began chuckling. "Then I freaked out," he said.

"You what?"

"I freaked out."

"Yes?"

"Yes," Kerner replied, still chuckling.

"Would you care to amplify on that statement?"

"Sure, why not? But I'll have to go back a bit in time and explain a few things first."

"So go," Dr. Lehman said without any expression.

"By the end of my last session with you, I think it would be fair to say that I had progressed quite well. Wouldn't you say?"

"Yes, that's true," Dr. Lehman replied with a brief nod.

"I had gone ... what? ... two days without buying?"

"That's right, two days."

"And if you remember, I had decided to sell everything I owned and move to a kibbutz in Israel."

The doctor nodded.

"I owned a lot of valuable stuff, right?"

"Right."

"I was going to sell it all, right?"

"What is this, a quiz?" Dr. Lehman asked, scowling.

Kerner laughed almost gleefully and ignored the question. "But there was one other thing I owned, something I had bought during the height of my buying addiction." Kerner paused.

Dr. Lehman said nothing.

"Aren't you going to ask me what it was?"

"No," Dr. Lehman replied nonchalantly.

"Aren't you curious to know?" Kerner said, the strange smile coming back onto his face.

"No," Dr. Lehman answered.

"Well, I'll tell you anyways," Kerner said and then paused. There was a bright gleam in his eyes and he began to laugh softly as though savouring some secret thought. He averted his eyes from Dr. Lehman for a moment and stared straight ahead. His laughter stopped and he turned quickly back to look directly at the doctor. "I also owned a piece of land," he said, throwing the words out almost as though in a challenge.

"Yes, I know that," Dr. Lehman said offhandedly. "You had mentioned that in your second session with me."

For a moment there was a puzzled look on Kerner's face, as though he were trying to think of something. "Yes, I guess I did mention it to you, but I'm surprised you remembered."

"I remember everything, Mr. Kerner. I have total recall. I can remember every word you ever said to me and I can tell you at what time and on what day you said it. I can also tell you exactly what you were wearing when you said it. So don't be surprised."

"I'm very impressed," Kerner said sarcastically.

"As you should be," Dr. Lehman replied calmly.

Kerner took a deep breath. "Do you want to hear this story or not?" he said, a note of anger in his voice.

"Enough questions, Mr. Kerner. You called me down here. So if you want to talk, talk; if you don't want to, then don't."

Kerner grinned and nodded several times. "Okay, okay... so I had this land. It was a fair-sized piece which I'd originally bought for next to nothing. The really interesting thing about it though was..." Kerner was grinning broadly now. "... was that coincidentally it happened to be located in the same general area as Weisskopf and Mandelberg's land."

Dr. Lehman's face showed no emotion.

Kerner became serious. "Anyway, I had decided to sell all these things, as you know. It was a hard decision. I mean, you know what I was going through. But to be honest, during the few days immediately after I had made that decision, things weren't as bad as I had thought they would be. ... The first day that the significance of my decision really hit me was the day when I last saw you."

"Yes, I remember you said very little at that last session," Dr. Lehman commented.

"I was bugged that day," Kerner said.

"Bugged?"

"That's right, bugged. ... That morning I had a few meetings with various people who were interested in buying all of my art, sculptings, furniture, the whole works. The best offer I had was equal to about half of what it was all worth and it was obvious this would be the best price I could expect. That bugged me. It bugged me a lot. Then I began to think about my business. I knew it was a total write-off. I knew I could expect to get next to nothing for it. That bugged me too because it had been worth a lot. I had spent a lot of time building it up. I had put my guts into it. I had built up a tremendous amount of goodwill. I had fantastic contacts. That alone made that business worth a lot of money... a fortune. And it bothered me that because of my particular situation at that point in time, I'd end up getting next to nothing for it. That bugged me. It bugged me a lot. But I kept telling myself that I had made my decision to quit the whole rat race and I shouldn't let all these things bother me. But they did. I started feeling ill. By the time I got to your office that day, I was really sick. As a matter of fact, I almost didn't show up that day."

"So why did you then?"

Kerner shrugged nonchalantly and smiled. "Who knows."

"You didn't mention a word about how you felt that day," Dr. Lehman said.

"I don't remember."

"In fact, you spent the last half-hour of that session without saying a word."

"Of course. How could I? You were too busy screaming at Mrs. Griff through your crazy microphone."

"I only spoke to her for about twenty seconds, Kerner. Don't exaggerate. You had plenty of time to talk if you wanted to."

Kerner grinned and nodded. "That's true. I just wasn't interested in saying anything at that last session. As I said, I was feeling sick and by the time I left your office I felt even sicker. By the time I got to Weisskopf's house that evening, I was afraid I was going to throw up on his dining-room table. That's how bad I felt. Anyways, I finally left there about eleven with the plan, which I was going to deliver to their man the next day. I just wanted to get home and get to sleep. The minute I got to my apartment, I took a few tranquilizers and flaked out on my bed. ..." Kerner paused. "Do you mind lighting a cigarette for me?"

Dr. Lehman lit a cigarette and passed it to Kerner who took it between the two unbroken fingers of his left hand, the tips of which projected from the cast just enough to grasp the cigarette.

"I'll hold this," Kerner said. He took a long drag and exhaled slowly through his mouth. "So I went to sleep. ... Sometime during the night, I woke up. I was sweating and shaking as though I'd been having some kind of nightmare, but I couldn't recall anything. I sat there trying to remember what I had dreamt. I had a feeling it was important for me to remember. Why? I don't know. I just did. I thought and thought but everything was just one big blank. I started feeling sick again. I stood up and turned on the lights. I began walking through my apartment and looking at all my beautiful things, thinking that soon, in another day or so, they'd all be gone. The more I looked at them, the sicker I became, but in a way that was worse than ever before. Until that night, whenever I'd been ill it had been almost entirely a physical thing, but that night it was like a pain in my mind. It grew worse and worse. I thought I was going crazy. ... There seemed absolutely no purpose to living. The whole world seemed absurd, useless." A shadow passed across Kerner's face. He dragged on the cigarette.

Dr. Lehman sat motionless in his chair.

Kerner shifted his body slightly, grimacing with pain. "Then I went back into the bedroom. I had to lie down or pass out. I lay down on my bed. Something in my mind kept pushing at me to remember what I had dreamt. I had a feeling it was a key that could help me unlock some secret that could help me solve my predicament. I kept thinking about a plan. A plan. A plan. This idea kept passing through my mind. I sat up on my bed. Something told me I was close to finding the key. ... And then I looked down towards the end of my bed. Lying there was the architect's cylinder containing the plan of Weisskopf and Mandelberg's land." Kerner paused and began to laugh. He took another drag of his cigarette and then dropped it beside the bed. "Do you mind stepping on that," he said.

Dr. Lehman put his foot over the cigarette and ground it into the tile floor.

"Do you remember the day you came down to La Galerie d'Or and I threw up on that sculptor?"

Dr. Lehman nodded slowly.

"Afterwards when we were back at your office you said I was on my way towards beating my sickness. You said something had obviously clicked inside me and I was going to be all right."

Dr. Lehman remained silent and motionless.

"Well, at the time you said that, I didn't recall anything having clicked inside me, but on the night I'm telling you about now ... on that night, something did click inside my head. I could actually hear it and feel it, as though a switch had been released somewhere inside there, inside my brain. It was as though my real personality had been hidden, locked away somewhere deep inside me . . . and when that switch went *click,* it was suddenly liberated... and everything about me fell into place. In one instant, I saw everything exactly the way it was. I knew I had been fooling myself with the idea that I would change my way of life, sell everything and live on a kibbutz. I realized it was insanity. I suddenly knew I could have everything I wanted and that was how I should live ... getting everything there was to get. Everything. There was nothing to stop me. I knew for the first time in my life that I didn't owe anything to anyone. That morality doesn't exist. That we're just animals that can think. That we're not on this earth for long and that while we're here we should do everything we can to satisfy ourselves. I realized that it's only guilt that screws people up and that it's only the weak who feel guilty. I realized without the slightest doubt that there was no reason for anyone to have to feel guilty about anything ... and I mean anything!

"I saw the whole picture. It was so clear that there was no doubt in my mind. It's dog eat dog in this world. Nobody gives a shit for anyone, anyways. Everyone's out for their own ass. I thought about Weisskopf and what you had said about him in that last session. You said that maybe he had intended to use me from the first minute he'd met me. I realized you were probably right; and even if he wasn't using me for his own purposes he still wasn't doing me any favours. When he let me off paying that five thousand dollars, he didn't let me off for my sake. Maybe he did it to set me up for the telephone gaff; but if that wasn't the reason, then he did it for some other ulterior motive. Maybe he felt guilty about things he'd done in the past and wanted to ease his conscience through me. I saw that very clearly. It was obvious that I hadn't wanted to see that before. I wanted to imagine that the world was like a Walt Disney film. But after that switch moved and clicked, I saw it all. It all came to me in a flash. I saw the whole picture. I saw it clearer than I had ever seen anything in my life.

"I knew what it was all about. I knew what I was, what I should do, what I wanted to do. I owed nothing to no one. I had, you might say, a secret answer. I knew I had to have everything. To take everything I could get. It was all there waiting to be taken. I was going to get it. Everything! Why not? What else was there? What was there to stop me? Nothing. I could do anything and not worry about guilt. It was just a matter of being careful. Careful about the laws made by weak, frightened people. It was easy to be careful and I knew I wasn't afraid. What was there to be afraid of? People were afraid because of guilt. I wasn't afraid. I could do anything and not worry about it.

"I saw everything. I saw exactly who I was, what I was, the way things really were. I knew a person could rule the world with the understanding that I had. I knew what I was going to do." The words had come out in a gush and Kerner was now breathing hard.

Dr. Lehman looked down at him, showing no expression.

"So what do you think?" Kerner asked.

"I don't think anything, Mr. Kerner."

"No?"

"No."

"Aren't you surprised at my new outlook?"

"Thoughts are one thing, Kerner, deeds are another," Dr. Lehman replied.

Artie Kerner chuckled slyly. "Oh, I know that, but I'm not finished telling you my story. Let me fill you in on what happened next and how I translated my ideas into actions."

"Go ahead," Dr. Lehman said, gesturing with his hand.

"All these thoughts were flashing through my mind. I don't know exactly how long I sat there on my bed thinking. It was probably about an hour or two but it seemed much longer. In a way it was like both an eternity and an instant. Then I realized there was no way I was going to live on a kibbutz. There was no way I was going to give up anything. I was going to keep everything and get more. I was going to get whatever I wanted. The first thing I had to do was get my hands on some money. As I thought this, I realized I was staring at the red cylinder lying at the foot of the bed. Then it hit me that I had the solution to all my problems. It was right there in front of me. It was as though I had somehow known it all along.

"It was so simple, it was unbelievable! It all fell into place in an instant. I would replace the plan of Weisskopf and Mandelberg's land with the plan of my land. As I mentioned, my

262

property was in the same general area as theirs. In fact, it was about eight miles away.

"At seven-thirty in the morning I called up a draftsman I knew. I offered him a hundred dollars for an hour of his time. He was over at my place by eight-fifteen. By nine-thirty he had redrafted a large official-looking plan from my own small plan of my piece of land. I replaced Weisskopf's plan in the cylinder with my own.

"Now my piece of land was registered in the name of the farmer who still lived on the property. But, the same as Weisskopf and Mandelberg, I had a deed signed by the farmer testifying to the fact that he had sold the land to me. I took the cylinder to Lemay. It was in his hands by noon that day. Then I drove over to see the farmer on my land. I told him that he might soon be approached by someone who wanted to buy the property. I told him to ask eighty-five thousand for it and to carry on as though he owned it. I promised him five thousand if everything went well.

"Then I waited. Everything came off perfectly. Hankleman came to see Lemay. Lemay sold him my plan without ever knowing it. Hankleman's notary approached my farmer. My farmer told them what he wanted. They checked out the deed. They bought the land. I got the eighty-five thousand. I gave the farmer a hundred bucks."

"A hundred bucks?!"

"That's right," Kerner said, laughing. "You think I'd give him the five thousand just because I promised it to him?"

Dr. Lehman made no reply.

"I'd have to be crazy to do that. What's the point? What could he do – sue me? Oh, he raised shit when I gave him the hundred. He wasn't happy. But what could he do?" Kerner laughed. "I came away with a clear profit of fifty-eight thousand dollars. Then I had to do something about my business. I couldn't declare bankruptcy because when they investigated the company, they would find out I had been pulling funds out illegally; but there was no way I was going to pay off the debts I owed to those leeches. So I began to think. And I'll tell you, it's amazing how clearly a person can think when his mind isn't obstructed by guilt. You see a million ideas that you could never think of. It didn't take me long to come up with a good one.

"I found a guy who owned a big warehouse. I asked him how much he wanted to rent it for six months. He told me four hundred a month. I told him to make up a lease, setting the rent at a thousand dollars a month. I told him that the rent would be paid and that, out of the thousand, he could keep five hundred and he would give me back five hundred. I had him sign a document to that effect.

"Then I went out and invested a few hundred dollars in several thousand old burlap sacks. I had these filled with a combination of sawdust and shit from various renderers. I had these sacks stored in the warehouse. Then I contacted my creditors and told them I was broke but indicated I had various goods stored in this warehouse. There was a mad rush to the courts by all my creditors for first crack at my goods. While the courts were involved with deciding who gets what and when, they of course declared the goods in the warehouse frozen. No one could even step inside the warehouse. They were all convinced that there was a fortune of chemicals in those sacks.

"Of course, to have any legal claim to the goods, they had to keep paying the rent on the warehouse. When they checked the lease, they saw it was a thousand dollars a month. So they paid it. They've already paid it for two months now, which means I've gotten back a thousand dollars from the landlord so far. My creditors are so greedy to protect their own interests that they've each hired their own guard to make sure no one else takes off with those sacks! By the time the courts decide what to do with those sacks, it could be another six or eight months at five hundred a month for me and in another few months my creditors will have forgotten all about me. By the time they get to see what's inside those sacks, they won't even remember who they belonged to." Kerner began to laugh.

"I'm glad to see you can still laugh after two months in the hospital."

"Why not? It's funny. It's hilarious. I ripped them all off ... and you know something? ... I enjoyed it. I really enjoyed it. I made a bundle on my piece of land. I fucked my creditors good and I didn't pay back Hankleman a cent. ... Oh yes, and one other thing ... I also fucked Weisskopf's daughter and ... Mrs. Griff."

"It seems like you fucked everyone, Mr. Kerner," Dr. Lehman said.

"Yes, that's what I did," Kerner replied, grinning.

"And so what did it get you?"

"It got me a lot of money and a lot of satisfaction."

"You call being in the hospital for two months, satisfaction?"

"It'll be four months or five by the time I get out, but so what? When I get out, I'm really going to enjoy myself. Besides, it's a good rest. They take very good care of me here. I have everything. I even get blow jobs from one of the nurses whenever I want. They do everything for me."

"It's sort of like being a little baby again, eh, Kerner?"

"You can call it whatever you want but, believe me, it's not all that bad."

Dr. Lehman gave a whimsical shrug. "And how about your buying habit?"

"I've got it under control. It'll never rule me again but eventually I'll be able to buy anything I want. I figure in a year or two from now I'll be a millionaire. There's nothing that can stop me."

"No, I don't imagine there is," Dr. Lehman said softly. "Unless, of course, you run into someone like Hankleman again."

"Oh, don't worry, I'll be a lot more careful in the future. And, besides, it wasn't him who did this to me."

"No? Then who was it?"

"It was Weisskopf and his partner."

"How do you know that?"

"Before the two goons started working me over, they said, 'Here's a message from the Hawk and Big Moishie.' I guess when they saw that nothing was happening with their land, they must have put two and two together and figured out that I had screwed them somehow."

Dr. Lehman nodded slowly. "One last question before I leave, Mr. Kerner."

"Sure."

"Why did you call me down here?"

"Why? Because I wanted to show you how full of shit you are."

"Oh, really? Why? Because I had a bit of faith in you? Because I really believed there was a chance for you to be a mensch? I actually did, Kerner. I actually had faith in you."

Kerner began to laugh. "That's what I mean. I wanted to prove to you how full of shit you are. How futile your whole shrink bit is."

"By telling me what you did, by showing me what you are now, you don't prove anything to me at all. I have no illusions about my abilities as a psychiatrist. I do the best I know how. I can live with myself."

Kerner was still laughing. He was staring up at the ceiling and cackling.

"The only thing you've proved is that I was right in calling you what I did that first day when you ran out of my office. You're a shlepper, Kerner."

Dr. Lehman turned and walked away. He headed out the door and walked along the corridor. He could hear Kerner laughing in the room. The sound echoed along the hallway like a cry.

Chapter Forty-Nine

Solly the Hawk was seated at his desk. Big Moishie was standing next to him. The Hawk picked up the telephone receiver and began to dial.

"I'd like to speak to Mr. Marvin Saltpeter," the Hawk said.

Big Moishie dragged on his cigar.

"Hello, Marvin ... Yeah, it's Sol Weiss speaking ... Yeah ... Not too bad ... yerself? ... Good. Good. ... Lissen, Marvin, I finally got it set up wid dis guy from de Roads Department. ... Yeah, yeah, I know. It took a long time. But it's all set. ... Oh, you're ready to shmear. ... Good, good. Okay, lissen, here's what you gotta do ..."

Big Moishie puffed on his cigar while the Hawk kept talking.

Chapter Fifty

Morrie Hankleman was driving slowly along Westmount Boulevard. He felt good. Things were rolling along quite well. He had been wise to back the beaver gland formula idea. It was proving to be a real winner with only minimal advertising. Yes, things were looking up. The terms of his divorce would be finalized any day now after more than three months of hassling with his wife and her lawyer. She would keep the house and everything in it, but he had gotten away with a lot more than he'd expected as far as alimony was concerned. His lawyer had done all right for him. She would keep the kid, which was fine with him.

Yes, things hadn't turned out too badly. It was as though he was starting from scratch again but without having to worry about making it because he already had it made.

Hankleman smiled. He felt good. Things were all right. ... If only something would break with regard to the land he had snatched from under Weisskopf and Mandelberg's noses. It was almost three months since he had faked them out but he had yet to hear anything official about the new autoroute extension, let alone receive an offer for his land from the Quebec Roads Department. Well, he could wait. He'd probably hear from them soon.

He chuckled softly to himself. Even now he still derived immense satisfaction when he thought about how he had bugged their office and ripped them off. The great thing about it was that they had obviously thought Kerner had fed them a phony story. Why else would they have had him beaten up. They had really done a job on him, but if anyone deserved it, it was Artie Kerner. Kerner still hadn't repaid him the money. But he would get it back, all of it, with interest. The day Artie Kerner stepped out of the hospital, he, Morrie Hankleman, would be waiting for him; and if Kerner didn't pay up, he would end up in the hospital again. It was as simple as that.

Morrie Hankleman slowed the car, turned his head and stared out the back window. The girl was still running about twenty feet or so behind the Mercedes. Hankleman checked his mileage. He had already kept her following for two-tenths of a mile. He shook his head. Incredible how people fool themselves, he thought. Maybe he could break his record with this girl. She wasn't even breathing hard. Hankleman waved her on.